The Beloveds

The Beloveds

MAUREEN LINDLEY

G

Gallery Books

New York   London   Toronto   Sydney   New Delhi

G

Gallery Books
An Imprint of Simon & Schuster, Inc.
1230 Avenue of the Americas
New York, NY 10020

First Gallery Books trade paperback edition April 2018

GALLERY BOOKS and colophon are registered trademarks of Simon & Schuster, Inc.

For information about special discounts for bulk purchases, please contact Simon & Schuster Special Sales at 1-866-506-1949 or business@simonandschuster.com.

The Simon & Schuster Speakers Bureau can bring authors to your live event. For more information or to book an event, contact the Simon & Schuster Speakers Bureau at 1-866-248-3049 or visit our website at www.simonspeakers.com.

Interior design by Davina Mock-Maniscalco

Manufactured in the United States of America

1   3   5   7   9   10   8   6   4   2

Library of Congress Cataloging-in-Publication Data
Names: Lindley, Maureen, author.
Title: The beloveds / Maureen Lindley.
Description: First Gallery Books trade paperback edition. | New York : Gallery Books, [2018] |
Identifiers: LCCN 2017022893 (print) | LCCN 2017026448 (ebook) | ISBN 9781501173301 (ebook) | ISBN 9781501173295 (trade paperback)
Subjects: | GSAFD: Gothic fiction.
Classification: LCC PR6112.I49 (ebook) | LCC PR6112.I49 B45 2018 (print) | DDC 823/.92—dc23
LC record available at https://lccn.loc.gov/2017022893

ISBN 978-1-5011-7329-5
ISBN 978-1-5011-7330-1 (ebook)

To Archie, Lollie, Sophie, and Danny, with my love

Acknowledgments

M Y HEARTFELT THANKS TO each and every one of those generous colleagues and friends who helped *The Beloveds* on its way to publication. I am truly grateful to them. They are: Heather Lazare, Jackie Cantor, Jill Marr, Patricia Callahan, Derek McFadden, Thao Le, Sara Quaranta, Jennifer Kim, Jamie McKenzie, Jenny Parrott, Clive Lindley, Julia Gregson, Jane Ridley-Griffiths, Stevie Lee, Trina Middlecote, Richard Gregson, Liberty McKenzie, Chris Murray, and Lisa Litwack and the talented art department at Gallery.

Prologue

M Y DEEP DISLIKE FOR my sister first struck me at the age of nine, when I shut her in the linen cupboard. We had been ordered by our mother to play hide-and-seek, and I told her to close her eyes and count to a hundred before coming to look for me, and then I quietly left the house. I wanted to go swimming alone in the man-made pool we call the water hole, in the field at the back of our house. I would be in trouble later, for swimming without permission, and for not taking her with me. Nothing I couldn't handle, though.

Gloria was only allowed to swim when I was in the water to care for her, to keep my eye on her and make sure that she stayed in the shallows. I knew that she would want to come, that in her company I would become her nursemaid and have no fun myself. She had been following me around all morning, whining that I was walking too fast, that I wouldn't play her stupid games.

"You be mummy, and I'll be your baby."

I was particularly annoyed with her that day, for trailing her jammy fingers along my bedroom walls, and for howling when she stumbled as I shoved her out my bedroom door, bringing our mother running. I must have told her a hundred times to stay out of my room.

"She's only six. Please be extra kind to her today," Mother pleaded. "Her kitten is missing; you know how she loves it."

In some secret part of me, I waited out the anger I felt at the look in my mother's eyes as she bent to comfort Gloria. Revulsion overtook me at the sight of their petting, at the tears, and the "there, there, don't cry." It is true, you know, that eyes light up when they focus on the one they love. Mother's did for my sister. For me, though, the light was at best occasional, and never as bright.

"Shut up," I hissed at baby face out of our mother's hearing. "Stay away from me, you little creep."

The water hole is bigger than it sounds. More like a small lake than a hole. It was scooped out by my grandfather, Arnold Stash, at the junction where a gushy stream suddenly dives underground. A mini army of ash and alder half circle the water, creating in their leafless season the illusion of a man-made ruin; there is a cloistered feel to the pool—some secret, delicious, hidden quality.

The day was cool. A sharp little breeze agitated the air and set the water lapping. I stood shivering on the creaking wooden jetty for a minute or so before diving in. A brief submerging, then surfacing with a whooping intake of breath, a complaint against the frigid water.

I swam to the middle, raised my arms above my head, and allowed myself to sink slowly to the pool's muddy bed. Spongy pondweed brushed against my body on the way down, causing a small panic. I hugged the panic to me. Then as now, I like the feeling I get when I do something daring, something with risk attached.

Such a silence down there in the deep, a strange sort of

hush that wraps itself around you, brings the relief of being completely alone. I have always wanted to be an only child, but I think that I could have borne a brother more easily than a sister. A boy who would have followed his own path, not bounced about on mine, a brother who would have looked out for me. Why, little sister, if you had to be at all, why could you not have been a boy?

It was early in the season to be swimming, but in the cool depths of the lake where nature has set pale plants that drift toward the light, my heartbeat slowed, I felt at peace. My breath was running out, but I didn't want to surface. Then as now I am at home in the shadows, those dusky places where Mother held the devil lurked. I have never been afraid of the dark.

When I broke the surface again, the weather had changed. A sulfurous yellow stained the sky, the clouds had clumped together, and lanky shadows stalked their way through the trees. And there, on the jetty in her little pink swimsuit, was the thorn that was my sister, waving and calling and jumping up and down, and I knew suddenly that it wasn't simply irritation I felt. The loathing I experienced at the sight of her pulsed in that part of me, somewhere middle chest, a dark liverish thing that's still there after all these years.

Her hair had escaped her plaits and was whipping about in the wind like corn in a storm; her narrow legs were white and straight, her fluttering arms those of a ballerina. She was nearly as tall as me already, not yet beautiful, but its promise loitered around her, waiting to settle. Even then I knew that her loveliness was unfair: the gift of her golden hair, her sunny nature, her popularity, accepted without a thought of what it might be like to be without those things. She had the angel's share, but I was the one who understood beauty, who valued it beyond the usual limitations of a child's senses. It came to me in a flash, a "lightbulb moment," as they say, that life was not fair, that it picked its favorites, soft-padded their lives; the rest of us are expected to make the best of being satellites to their stars. Not me.

In those days, people often remarked on the family likeness between us, yet I was not on my way to beauty, I was already made pretty, beauty's poor relation. If the resemblance was ever there, the grating years since have muddied it.

I closed my eyes and trod water. I hugged to myself the secret knowledge of where her cat had gone. Nasty little thing—peeing in all the wrong places, scratching the furniture, always yowling for food—untroubled in its watery grave now, the river a pleasant enough resting place.

I played dumb, pretended not to see her, pretended not to hear that trilling voice. I turned from her, pressed my hands together as though in prayer, and sank to the bottom of the pond.

———

I HAVE HEARD IT said that a woman is never completely free to be herself until after her mother dies, until the maternal strings are cut. We are supposed to rise, like the phoenix, from the ashes of our mothers' lives, stretch our wings, and fly alone for the first time. My freedom has not been so easily won. I have found nothing easily won.

I rarely think of my mother without memory dragging me to the remote scape of childhood, to those flashes of toddler recollections, the denied plea for ice cream, the outrage of that stinging first slap. More usually, though, I am taken back to my nine-year-old self, when, regardless of what others thought, I knew that I was already formed, sharp as a lemon, and the brightest in my family, yet the least appreciated. My intelligence has rarely been recognized; in childhood it was not to be spoken of, unless to warn me of the sin of pride.

"Pride angers the gods," Mother would caution. "Top of the class doesn't make you the best person."

Even then I knew Mother had chosen her favorite child; it was, and would always be my annoying little sister, Gloria. Pouty, shiny Gloria, a scene-grabbing enchantress of a child. Then as now I was alone in noticing her faults, the way she manipulates with sweetness. Others would enthuse on what a darling girl she was, a little sunbeam who paid back the smallest kindness with a smile and a hug.

I was forever in my mother's bad books for not sharing, for being too rough with Gloria. Despite that yesterday I pulled a single gray hair from my head, the first one to show itself, those memories still offend.

On my sister's behalf, Mother would step out of her placid nature to lecture irritably on sibling rivalry. I shouldn't resent her, she was younger, I should make allow-ances, her nature was more sensitive than mine. She accused me of being thoughtless, of holding grudges. She never, though, accused me of not loving my only sibling. The thought perhaps had not occurred to her. We were family, so it was a given that love for each other swam in the current of our blood, was set deep in our bones.

Mother was generally a bit of a Pollyanna, but she had her faults and could be ruthless. Kind to others, she was be-hind glass to me: don't touch, keep your distance. Perhaps she sensed that was how I wanted it, that I wasn't one for cuddles and hair stroking. I have never experienced those sentimental feelings that others lay claim to. Some would say there is something missing, I suppose, some melting, saccharine quality. Nothing is missing. It is simply that I have evolved more than most.

1

THE CASUAL GRABBING OF what should be mine, if only by first-child blood rights, has gone on long enough. It is time to act. I have borne the pleas of poverty dripped slyly into Mother's ears by my sister and brother-in-law, borne their tortuous presence until it can be borne no longer. Watch out, dear Gloria, darling Henry: I have cause and there will be consequence.

How I will go about it is just the tiniest shoot of an idea at the moment. I will cultivate it diligently, as you might a bonsai, shaping it with attention to detail, encouraging every little leaf.

My sister, Gloria, is standing at the Aga stove, wearing that childish apron of hers with the smiling duck on it, a smile she echoes as though full of good intention. She spears me carelessly with her know-it-all air.

"I don't think the doctors have it right," she says, speed-reading their report.

"Oh, you'd know, I suppose," I say mildly, without the malice I feel. "So what do they mean by *objectophile*?"

"Well, it's someone romantically in love with an object—a car, say, or a building. There is actually a woman who married the Eiffel Tower, one who is engaged to an oil rig, or so they believe. And you must have read about the artist, Tracey Emin?"

"No, what?"

"Married herself off to a rock."

"He won't be helping with the housework, then," I say.

Gloria gives one of her full-throated laughs.

"It's ridiculous, I know," she says. "But that's hardly you, now is it?"

"Hardly," I say.

I wish now that I hadn't told that puffed-up doctor about Pipits, our family home. *My* family home. He obviously made up bits of this and that and tagged a label on it. How they love labels. Truth is, all I gave him were fragments, small memories from my childhood that he asked about. I told him that Pipits was named in 1760, after the birds that lived in the meadows around the house. There were hundreds of them then, not so many now.

I did give him a description of the house, and I think that he fell a bit in love with it himself. It doesn't surprise me. Who could not delight in Pipits' beauty, its flowing contours, the spicy scent of logs burning in its fireplaces, and its dark wooden floors that are soft underfoot? I didn't tell him much of that, but I did confess that to be alone in Pipits is never to be lonely. I shouldn't have confided that, though. Easy to tell that he was not a free thinker; feelings must be raked over, run to earth, named. Ordinary people like him are blind to the intricate maze of feelings that binds me to Pipits, and it to me.

Not wanting to invite his closed-minded opinion, I didn't speak of the house again after that first time. I chose not to tell him of the day the house spoke to me, the day that saw the commonplace leave my world forever. The memory of it is too precious to be shared with people who play mind games, think they know more of me than I do myself.

Twenty-five years may have passed since that moment, but you don't forget something as seminal in your life as that. I remember the tiniest details of it, everything.

The day had begun as Saturdays did in our household, with Mother sleeping in, so that breakfast was served an hour later than on weekdays and leisurely eaten by her and Gloria in their pajamas. I had woken at the usual time and was dressed and in the garden when I saw Mother open her bedroom window. She gave me a little wave but didn't smile. I think it irritated her that I made my own way, didn't join in with hers. I knew that she would quiz me later about what I had been up to.

I was ten, almost eleven years old. It was a fine morning; the sun had returned after a long absence and was high in a pallid sky. The air was moist and warm, bees had arrived in the garden, and our fields gleamed brown-gold in the sunlight.

Mother and Gloria were going into Bath to shop. I didn't want to join them, to suffer feeling left out in their girlish company. They had an exclusivity about them, a shared silliness that bored me.

At first Mother denied my request to be left at home.

"What will you do all day by yourself?" she fussed.

"I'll read," I said. "Sit in the garden, in the sunshine."

"You'll go to the river; I know you'll go to the river."

"I won't, I promise."

She thought that it might be against the law to leave a

child of my age alone. In the end, though, my stubbornness held firm against her better judgment, and she caved in.

"Mr. Beard is coming to mow the lawns," she said. "I'll ask him to keep an eye on you. Go to him if you are worried about anything."

I said that I would, knew that I wouldn't. Mr. Beard was old, and deaf, and could hardly have been of any help to me. All he wanted to do was to sit on our mower, to follow the lines of his last cut, and smoke his disgusting old pipe, which was crusted with spit.

Why it happened on that day in particular I am not sure. Perhaps it was because I was alone, relishing the silence. My mother and sister's intrusion into my life has never been welcome. Their incessant chatter frequently had me running to my secret place by the river to get away from the sound of them and from their sickly displays of affection. Mother knew it, I think; I often caught her looking at me as though I were an impostor, a changeling smuggled under the cover of darkness into her true baby's cot.

I had dozed off in the sitting room while reading, and came to in that dreamy state that often follows sleep. I was aware of the distant sound of the mower cutting the rides through our woods, and saw that the light had changed, so that everything—tables and chairs, vases and lamps—was surrounded by a shimmering halo. At first, I thought it was the spring sun in my eyes causing an illusion, but then other things began to happen; sounds and colors seemed more intense than ever before, the floor appeared to swell under my feet, inducing a touch of vertigo that was not unpleasant. I fancied that I wasn't alone. And then Pipits' familiar shape expanded; the room I was sitting in seemed bigger, the ceilings higher. A rush of warmth ran through me, and I suddenly felt lighter, freer, as though by some strange chance I had stumbled into ecstasy. Minutes passed, during which I felt exquisitely alive, and then a high whine, like that of a mosquito, vibrated through the house, vibrated through me.

I shut my eyes and attempted to understand this novel, wordless language, one of chants, and rhythms, nature's voice, quick and exciting as a spark of silver. Slowly some secret, unexplored part of me opened, and then as though I had always known it, I recognized the sweet drumroll of Pipits' voice calling me.

Elizabeth, Elizabeth.

For hours after I was dizzy with the ecstatic feeling of being adored, of being chosen. It was as though lightning had struck and changed the shape of things forever. Straw to gold. Let Mother and Gloria have each other. I had my beautiful house.

I was so excited that when Mother returned, I gushed out the news that the house could speak, that it loved me.

"Oh, silly girl," she said, laughing. "It's an old house. The boiler rumbles, floors creak. It's just an old house. What an odd child you are."

Her response instilled forever in me the need to hold my secrets close.

It draws blood to have your confidences dismissed as nonsense, to be laughed at as though you are a fool. I was angry at Mother and told her that if Pipits had wanted her to know that it could speak, it would have spoken to her, chosen her instead. When I accused her of being the silly one, I was sent to my room to think about my rudeness. I went with my head held high, visiting her bedroom on my way, to blow my nose on her favorite dress.

Since that lovely shimmering day, I have never been truly happy away from Pipits. Life, marriage, and work have intruded, stilled that inner voice that tells me I should have stayed, stood guard.

I question now whether the half-hearted choices I made in life have been worth anything; marriage is too dull a thing to stir my blood; work interests me, but does not enthrall.

Now, when we are not together, I prefer to think of Pipits' rooms empty without me. The house should be mine alone; instead, there is Gloria and her husband Henry's life impinging itself. Henry in the shed at his potter's wheel is bad enough, but Gloria's dispiriting patients traipsing through the halls are an outrage. It's a disgrace that Mother allowed her to work from the house. Who knows what kinds of strangers we are letting in?

I've marked my territory, though, hidden something of myself in every room; a lavender pouch, a lock of my hair, ribbons and childhood toys. They nest behind the furniture and under the floorboards, little favors, gifts of devotion.

When I was young, I had a secret hiding place outside, too: an abandoned badger set screened by a thick laurel hedge. Brambles and stinging nettles barred the way to fraidy-cats like my sister. I kept a tin box there with things filched from Gloria and Mother. Gloria cried for hours over her money box shaped like a pig with two pounds fifty in its stomach, while Mother searched for and fretted about her missing silver christening spoon. There was pleasure to be had in the satisfaction of having sway over their moods.

"Loki's about," Mother would say, referring to the little

god of mischief featured in the stories she read to us. "We'll catch him at it one of these days."

Now Gloria finishes stirring something in a pan and moves away from the Aga. She makes a space amid her mess and places the clinic's report on the kitchen table. I'd like to sweep her mess away, sweep her away, claim what should be mine. Be gone, unloved sister.

For the moment, though, I must play the waiting game. She touches her hand elegantly to her temple. She has that helpful look on her face, a combination of optimism and sympathy common to her profession. How do they manage that? She's trained to be something called a psychodynamic psychotherapist. Such names!

She is like those clinic doctors, wanting to label, to tick a box, but because I am her big sister, have always been brighter than her, and know her weaknesses, she can't.

If you ask me, no one is truly like anyone else. People hide their true natures, fearing to expose their shadowy side and be found unlovable. Originality, though, lies in those shadows, the traits that make us who we are, the deep-set ones that people choose not to recognize. Gloria may think otherwise, but I believe that there is a spider in all of us weaving a selfish web; it is simply a question of survival. Ego takes precedence. No matter how my sister and her kind show off their sweetness, their so-called goodness, they are made of more than honey; we are all only half-known.

I guess Gloria secretly agrees with the report, that she's noted enough of the indicators listed there to confirm the diagnosis. It's a long list, and apart from the "possible objectophile" reference, it includes "intentionally misunderstands things," "feels put-upon and left out," "gives compliments with a sting in the tail," "is secretive"—I could go on.

I'm amused that the doctor who wrote all of this down was able to summon such nonsense with what little I gave him to work with. That morning when he turned up with his clipboard, biting on the end of his cheap ballpoint pen, I wasn't in the mood to engage. Nor did I care to fill his long silences with anything other than polite platitudes. I watched as he scribbled down his thoughts, noted the nervous blinking of his beetle eyes, saw the satisfaction in the stretch of his thin smile.

Maybe I showed Gloria the report to distress her, to see her smooth forehead crease in concern. I wish now that I hadn't. It should have been for my eyes only. Well, if the medics had their way, not even for my eyes, really. I took the report from the drawer my interrogator put it in when he left the room for a moment to mumble something to his office girl. It was careless of him, very unprofessional.

I'm sure that he thought me the big sister screwup. Not that he said as much, but references were made in the document to sibling rivalry, to something he refers to as the "narcissistic wound."

"I can't imagine how they got to this," Gloria says. "So hurtful that you have read such things about yourself. They've got it all wrong, though. Most probably because you're unique, a one-off."

It's as though she's been reading my mind.

"Isn't everyone?"

"Well, yes, but you're particularly special."

I want to slap her, to wipe the sympathetic smile off her beautiful face. Instead, I raise my eyebrows and give a shrug, as though the report doesn't matter. I never let the hurt show. Well, mostly never. I hid it well enough when they forcibly sectioned me for a week—such a ridiculous thing to do and quite unnecessary.

I wasn't mad, just anxious. Who wouldn't be, locked up in Ward Eight of Parade House? Why they don't call it what it is, a mental asylum, just makes you think they are ashamed of the place. Parade House sounds like somewhere Jane Austen might be staying while she takes the waters.

I decided while there to take the waters myself, not to let my anger show, to act as though I were a guest at their dreary watering hole. It mostly worked, they didn't patronize me, but they have a way of pushing you with their questions until something of yourself leaks out. You can't help but give away little bits of information that they string together to fabricate a story that satisfies their need to diagnose.

So, that's why I am here at Pipits now with Gloria and her husband, Henry, occupying my treasured childhood bedroom, communing with the dear house. Time off work, time off marriage, time to heal under my sister's caring eye.

"You must stay as long as you want," Gloria says, as though it is up to her. "We love having you, and you mustn't rush things."

Gloria thinks that she knows me. She does not. Because she loves the world, loves me, she thinks that I love her. I do not. She thinks that I loved Mother. I did not. She thinks that I love my husband, Bert. I do not. As sisters go, we are a poor match, cobbled together.

Gloria doesn't get it that it is not her I need, but the house. It is only when I am with Pipits that the tightness in my chest relaxes, that I breathe easily.

People think me slow to anger. It has been said, under the guise of a compliment, that I am always in control, so being gathered up by do-gooders as I swayed on the edge of Beachy Head that day, then breaking down at the doctor's, kicking her desk and swearing, was, as far as they were concerned, out of character.

It's true that I have learned how to appear calm when I am angry. But that doesn't mean I don't feel things. To have my way, I practice charm, keep my true nature hidden. People find it hard to deal with a person who doesn't emote in the way they expect. They want you to empathize with their trivial problems. They shy away from superior intellects, so I find it easier to act the part of loving sister, forgiving sister-in-law, accepting friend. I'm a good actress.

Don't ask me why things didn't hold together that day, why they leached out on that gusty cliff top. A sudden kink in the mind, maybe. I have been suffering episodes like that one lately, times when I've needed to give vent to my emotions. If it weren't for Gloria and Henry squatting at Pipits, changing things, upsetting me, I could have run to its embrace, taken comfort and gathered myself.

On that chilly morning a couple of weeks ago, as I stood at the cliff's edge with the wind pushing at me, my fury rose to a boil, so hot that I could hardly bear it, so extreme that I hardly knew myself.

It was not my intention to jump off that cliff; of course I wasn't going to jump. I wanted merely to hover on the edge, to feel something different than what I suffered every day. A psychiatrist at the clinic, a woman not unlike my sister, suggested that I had been teasing death. She thought it the equivalent to being a "cutter." It was just a different sort of bloodletting, apparently.

"No, I don't believe that you are mad," she had answered when I suggested that she was hinting at it. "I would like to know, though, what has brought about this heightened emotional state."

"Nothing I can think of," I said.

But I did wonder the same thing myself. There's been a hold up in the reading of Mother's will, something to do with tax, and her overseas assets, but I don't think it was that. The least you could say of Mother was that she was dutiful, and a proper little traditionalist to boot. She always favored Gloria, of course, but in this most important thing, I know she will have done her duty. I am the eldest, and Pipits is mine by right. Mother knows that.

I had received a photograph on my phone from Gloria the day before the Beachy Head incident. She wanted me to see the "brilliant space" they had created by knocking down the wall between the kitchen and the sitting room in our family home. Apparently Mother had agreed to it before her death.

What a pity she won't see how well it has worked out, Gloria texted.

What had once been our delightful country kitchen, and separately Mother's cozy dayroom, was now, without my consent, merged into a huge arena-like space. I was heartbroken at the destruction. Gloria's text, accompanied by the nasty image of gaping hole and rubble, ruined my day. She signed off with her usual smiley face. I find those smiley faces vulgar, like the circles in place of dots that were all the rage in handwriting a few years ago. Minds with little heft find such things amusing.

Our wonderful new kitchen. Can't wait for you to see it.

I hate the way Mother allowed Henry and Gloria a free hand to change things at Pipits. Under her weak rule they have demolished walls, painted rooms in the childish, rainbow colors of their natures. They must color and primp and smooth. They like things smooth.

Gloria had no right to go ahead with knocking the wall down. Whatever Mother had agreed to in life, it counted for little after her death. When Pipits is mine, I will stop their surgery, see them off. I will let the walls crumble, hear only the echo of my footfall on its floors. I will give up everything: husband, the London life I share with him, the art gallery we jointly own, everything. House and I will shut out the world, grow old together.

Our wonderful new kitchen.

I remember throwing the phone down when I read that, listening to it thud on the rug, remember the hot rage that leapt in me and the poisonous taste in my mouth.

I felt the pain of Pipits' wounds in my own limbs, a horrible nervy sort of ache. In that moment I could have killed Gloria, with a bit of torture thrown in. I wasn't going to tell that to the shrink at the clinic, of course. She would have fabricated some half-baked story about Gloria and me. No doubt she would have had me down as the one feeling like the cuckoo in the nest. That's the easy sort of judgment these people make. It's not me who is the cuckoo.

"No, nothing I can think of," I repeated to the psychiatrist, squirming at her little mews of encouragement. She had zero to offer me. I imagined her a middle-class housewife, suffering from empty-nest syndrome, with an urge to mother, but no one available in her own household to satisfy the need. I told her what she wanted to hear and watched her puff up with the thought that she had brought about some magical change in me.

"I'm feeling so much better," I assured her. "One week here and I already feel back to my old self. Of course I will take the pills religiously, I can promise you that. You've really helped me. How can I ever thank you?"

Gloria's attempt to soften the fatuous report on my state of mind hasn't worked. She likes to comfort, to be the one to make things right; white lies are one of her rare sins. Niceness waters her blood; it's a worthless coin, in my opinion.

In order that I won't feel crazy, she confides to me about her clients. The pitch of her voice lowers, takes on that caring social worker's drone. She refers to them as client A or B, to protect their identities. Does she imagine I care to know who they are, or that I will ever give them another thought? She powders her descriptions of them with allusions as to what's broken in them; they are obsessive, or infantilized. My own little episode is nothing in comparison. Back in charge of myself, I smile at her as though she is being helpful. She rushes over and hugs me.

Oh, the power of a smile.

After the anger on the cliff that day, when the lava in my blood had cooled, something had moved in me, created a fissure capable of spillage. I sensed it at my core, a sort of loose stitching. It's an unpleasant feeling to have been caught out of control, no matter that the episode had lasted for barely an afternoon.

As far back as my memory goes, I have felt the unfairness

of being in Gloria's shadow. She has supped the juice out of each and every one of my successes. Neither marriage nor financial success has helped. Mother once said I should have married for love, but as I hadn't, I couldn't really expect to feel like someone in love.

Easy for her to say; her brief marriage was the romantic legend that our family promoted. *Romeo and Juliet*, complete with the tragedy.

There's nothing to prove the great love now, though, so I haven't swallowed the story whole. People like legends better than the truth, anyway. They indulge the idea of everlasting love, the fairy-tale made flesh and blood. Who is to say that if my father had lived, my parents' union, like so many others, wouldn't have slid into the mundane?

"Coffee?" Gloria offers.

"Mmm," I say, "I'll put my own milk in."

I hear Henry's step on the path outside the kitchen door, and the familiar twinge returns, as though I have scraped the surface of old scar tissue and must now press down hard to stop it bleeding.

It is taxing for me to even look at him, especially now as he enters the room with the light behind him, his body a silhouette of lean strength.

"Oh good, biscuits," he says, scooping up a handful of Oreos. Henry's voice, the familiar ring of it, stirs an ache.

"Careful, you'll get fat," I say, meanly.

"More to love eh, Glory?" he says, encircling Gloria's waist as she pours him a coffee.

I feel disgust at their display of affection. It's so childish. *Look at us.* I know that others find it charming, even sweet. But not me. Never me.

Seeing them together reminds me that I am not one of the Beloveds. You know those people with a star above their heads: loved and admired, lucky in love, lucky in everything. Beloveds are the planet's dirty secret, the secret that keeps the hopeful battling on, swallowing whole that hoary old chestnut that hard work and perseverance bring success. Hope is luck's cunning agent; it sugars the medicine, masks its true flavor.

Henry, in a hurry, gulps down his coffee and blows Gloria a kiss. I try not to look at his hands: such strong hands, the nails, despite his work, always clean. The drawing qualities of the clay, perhaps.

"Back to work," he says. "Those bowls won't fire themselves, and the kiln is playing up again."

Henry was a teacher at the Slade art college when I first met him, but he always wanted to be a potter. He jumped at the chance when Mother offered him the shed to install a wheel and kiln. When it comes to taking over things he has no right to, Henry is as bad as Gloria.

I watch him leave, duck his head as he goes through the door on his way to the shed that he now refers to as the pottery. Henry Bygone, the man who had once thrilled me, whose net I had confidently swum into, happy to be his catch. Foolish fish. I should have been wary, known that I might get eaten up.

Henry was the only person I have ever met who I thought Pipits would accept as it had me. Once we were sure of each other, I would teach him to listen to its voice, to live there with House and me and be part of its magic. I put my trust in Henry, until he chose to break it on that sunlit weekend when I took him home to meet the family.

I wanted to show him off, wanted Mother to see me as the chosen one for once. Before I knew it, though, I had been relegated to the audience in what became the Henry and Gloria show.

In that first brief glance between them, I became the other, watching them play out their attraction as we played croquet. I took pleasure in beating them at the game that day, but Gloria won out in the end. Graceful in her flowery dress, serenely beautiful, she cast her spell. And they say there is no such thing as magic.

Henry, his shyness dismissed, openly flirting with her, surrendered himself. I watched him slide away from me without a backward glance.

My sister was apologetic in a helpless sort of way.

"It just overtook us," she said. "You didn't want him for keeps, did you? We haven't hurt you, have we?" Her words left bite marks on my heart.

Henry says now that we never really dated in the true sense of the word, that from our first meeting we were destined instead to be really good friends.

"And good friends we are, aren't we?" he says with slithering eyes.

I guess that makes him feel better about dumping me. He forgets the way we spied each other across the room at my friend Alice's party all those years ago, the way right from the first it was as if we had always known each other.

It came to me then that there must be something in Gloria's kind of beauty that has the clout to wipe men's memories, to make them rush toward it, not caring who gets trampled under their big feet.

I was late getting to Alice's party that night. I didn't have high hopes for it, but there he was, standing a golden head above the rest, empty glass in hand. The moment I saw him I knew he was my chance to put Gloria in her place. I knew it in the way that all of us do, sometimes, when the future beckons. On handsome Henry Bygone's arm, no one would pity me, the less beautiful, less popular sister. I would be the envied one.

Henry seemed out of place in the small crowded room, a man made for open spaces, big horizons. It was obvious that he was shy, so I made the first approach. I sensed he was relieved that I had done so. He gave me a hapless smile and ran his hands through the mop of his hair.

"Let me get you a drink," he offered. "I need a refill myself."

Henry's shyness made him a bit panicky about relationships, so I knew it would have to be me who made the first move. I sensed him to be the sort of man who likes to take his time, so I didn't push too hard. At my invitation, an exhibition at the Tate, followed by his one to dinner, to thank me for mine, as he put it. Although, apart from a peck on the cheek, we had not yet kissed, Henry was beginning to thaw. That is, until Gloria carelessly snared him, and he went into free fall.

My once best friend Alice is Gloria's now, too. They imagine that I'm happy about that: the three of us as one, not to mention Gloria's making off with Henry. It was mean of Gloria, shallow of Alice, who despite that we were friends first has been serving in Gloria's court for years. Damn them all for it.

I first met Alice at the Sunday school that Mother insisted we girls attend. She was a year or so younger than me, babyish, not very popular. I tolerated her following me around, taking on my style, even mimicking the way I spoke. It was a flattery I didn't let go to my head. How could I feel flattered by plain, rabbit-toothed, easily led Alice? There were times when she had her uses, though, when she was a convenient scapegoat: an excuse for being late, or for not including Gloria in our play, or for swimming in the river when I had been explicitly told not to.

"Sorry, Mother. Alice was slow as a tortoise today."

"Sorry, Mother, Alice didn't want to play with Gloria."

"Sorry, Mother, Alice pushed me in, what could I do?"

When Alice was fourteen, her mother was run down by a tourist coach outside Saint Dubricius, our ancient village church, where she had been arranging the flowers for a local pensioner's funeral. The gossip was that she had been flattened, roller-pinned thin as pastry by the heavy vehicle. I remember thinking that someone else would need to arrange the flowers for Alice's mother's funeral now.

In his grief, Alice's father hardly remembered that he had a daughter. She was left to her own devices and latched on to our family with a determination that surprised me. Her grip was firm. She joined us for meals, for the hour of television we were allowed each day, hanging around Mother, her pale eyes begging affection. It was more than annoying.

Despite my being the elder sister, she ran to Gloria for comfort when I told her I had thought her mother a bit of a whiner, that she would do well enough without her. Gloria, the banner carrier for kindness, and ever the little mother, went to war on Alice's behalf. She was angry with me at the time, a rare and most enjoyable thing.

"You were cruel to say it," she said.

"Oh, who cares, Miss Goody Two–shoes," I dismissed her.

Ever since that day, Alice has taken shelter under Gloria's wing. She is as eager as a puppy to be included in Mr. and Mrs. Bygone's starry life. She will drive Gloria to the station, shop for her, house-sit when asked. As if Pipits needed house-sitting, needed someone like Alice in charge.

These days I live a couple of hours away from Cold-Upton, in London, and it's convenient for Gloria to have Alice to call on. But I never stay away from my true home for long. I am a child of my enchanting village, and I know every lane, every tree, every shortcut to everywhere in it. I know where the snow bones lie in the fields in winter, I am familiar with every hedge and soft-stone wall. When I think of Pipits, I think of Cold-Upton, bound to it with the tightest of knots. Cold-Upton means more to me than to either my sister or my faithless former friend. How dare they make me feel like an interloper.

Alice is our local librarian. She drives the mobile library van around the villages like ours that circle Bath, dispensing books and advice. People think her kind, and no doubt she is, but she's a busybody, too, and a bit of a gossip; she seems to know everything about everybody. She calls it being involved with the community.

Being plain, she has always attracted the sort of men who are looking for an easy lay, men with no intention of making a commitment. She is overeager, greedy for affection, too quick to let them bed her. I long ago stopped listening to her sob stories.

"Why do they never stay?" she would weep.

These days, though, she doesn't expect them to stay.

"I like sex," she says. "No point in depriving myself."

She is not, nor will she ever be forgiven for abandoning me, for so easily changing sides. The same goes for Henry. What is to be said for the pair of them other than that they are both fickle, vain people, who have cynically attached themselves to a Beloved. Well, they will pay for it. When the time comes, I will cut deep, straight through the soft tissue, and into the bone.

"Alice is coming to dinner," Gloria says, moving heavily around the kitchen. "She's looking forward to catching up with you."

Gloria isn't showing yet, but she likes to huff and puff just to remind you of her fertility. It's obvious she is going to be one of those women who enjoy pregnancy.

"Oh, really," I say. "That's a pity. I was thinking of giving dinner a miss. I'm not feeling up to company just yet."

"Alice is hardly company, Betty. She's family, and she loves you. She won't judge."

I wonder. Does Alice love me? I think it's more that I come with the package that is Gloria and Henry. And of course, however Gloria thinks of her, she isn't family. There's not a drop of Stash blood in her.

"I'm not hungry," I say. "A cup of tea and a biscuit in my room will be fine."

"Sometimes, Betty," Gloria simpers, and I know what is coming, "you remind me of Mother. So self-sufficient, so independent." I take it as the put-down she so clearly intends. Gloria can be snarky at times.

I wish she wouldn't compare me to Mother. My character is nothing like hers. Gloria understood Mother about as much as she understands me, which is to say hardly at all.

The only thing I truly shared with Mother was my love of Pipits. Her love for it, though, was a shallow thing compared to mine.

The mention of Mother has stirred me up somewhat. Gloria says the pain of our loss is halved because we share it. I cannot agree. Her tears have been copious, mine not so. I am happy to allow her the grief. She makes the most of it, after all.

"Maybe just something light, then, a salad?" she persists.

She runs her hand through her thick hair with its perfect wave. Now that she is in her thirties, Gloria has reached her luscious peak. Her eyes, her best feature, are pools of the loveliest green, her skin tans evenly to honey. Her mouth is a little too big, her nose, too, but taken as a whole she is what they call a stunner. Everyone says she takes after our father, and the photographs we have of him lend truth to that. He was certainly striking. Since his unreliable heart gave out when I was six and Gloria three, he remains, through legend and photographs, the model of young manhood. I guess I saw a look of him in Henry. Perhaps Gloria did, too. They say girls marry their fathers, don't they?

"I'm going up now," I say with a sigh. I couldn't be more bored with her. "No salad, and don't bother with the tea, I've changed my mind."

At the turn of the stairs on the first-floor landing, the house ticks softly:

Can you hear me?

"I hear you," I say.

I am flooded with warmth, with pride.

I spy a photograph of Mother on the bookshelves, a gaudy shot of a full-breasted young woman wearing a kaftan and smiling toward the camera. I have her nose, her straight dark hair. It doesn't please me to look like her.

"You better have done the right thing," I say to her image.

In my room, I lie on my bed and think of Mother. I hadn't seen her in the months before her death. Work, and the thought of Henry and Gloria snuggled up so happily in my family home, kept me away. So I wasn't there when it happened, even though it was a weekend and I had thought of visiting. Gloria was there, of course. The Beloveds are always in the right place; their timing is impeccable.

2

WHEN I RETURNED TO Pipits after Mother's death, I was mortified by Gloria's almost hysterical grief, her breaking down at every offered sympathy. She has so little dignity and no concept of how a member of the Stash family should behave.

I experienced a mild sort of surprise at Mother's absence, and the irritating niggle that, however I succeeded now, she would never come to know that she had favored the wrong daughter. At the very least, I wanted her to know that.

The secret joy I had that Pipits would soon be mine was marred only by the presence of Gloria and Henry playing the hosts in my old home.

The day before Mother's funeral, as I drove to Cold-Upton from London, I nursed my resentment. For the past five years, my sister and her husband had kept up the pretext that they were saving for a house of their own. Mother went along with their story, but I think she knew the truth and was pleased that they had little if any intention of moving out. It was obvious that she loved their company. I will not make so soft a landlord.

The air-conditioning in my car had broken down, and it was Hades hot. The sky was a field of Titian blue with dollops of cream clouds seeded about. I had pulled off the road onto the hard shoulder alongside an acre of fallow meadow to gather myself for what I knew would be days of dreary reminisces. I took a nip of gin from my flask and saw in my peripheral vision a Meadow Pipit, a dusty olive-colored creature walking jerkily on the ground.

I practiced my "good to see you" face in the rear mirror. It came out as a grimace. I took another longer gulp of gin; it swabbed my mouth, hit my throat, purred its way down to my chest, and oiled the dry place inside me.

Never mind that there is the funeral to be withstood. It is always tough being around Gloria and Henry. They are so obviously in love that it's an embarrassment. They cannot pass each other without touching; the slightest brush of their hands as they cook together, a waltz-like hug as if they hear music when they meet in the hall.

Not so for Bert Walker and me. Ours is one of those so-called nurse and purse marriages. I'm wife number two, half his age, and the one who is meant to look after him when he's really old. In return I am to inherit everything: the apartment, whatever monies are left in the pot and the art gallery where I work, and have my name now alongside Bert's above the door. Walker and Stash. I like the balance of it. It sounds grassroots and fancy at one and the same time, as classy as Fortnum and Mason. We are just around the corner from that gilded grocery, in a street full of galleries, where one is in need of a trust fund just to shop for dinner, much less a piece of fine art.

At almost seventy, Bert seems to be thriving, despite the pleasure he takes in eating, in good wine, despite his only exercise being the walk to nearby restaurants for lunch, so things may not work out if the long run is going to be just that, the long run.

I've known for some time that Bert and I are not compatible. Not really. He would never admit it, of course. With one failed marriage behind him, he is keen to make this one a success. He speaks of being fond of me, of how much we like each other; neither of us speak of love. The truth is, though, that my affection for Bert has always been conditional at best. I like that he's smart, and that he wears his intelligence lightly (I couldn't bear to live with someone who had too fine a conceit of themselves). I like that he has created such a prestigious gallery, that he is admired by those in his field. But love? No.

I keep a running balance in my mind of the pros and cons of Bert. He has wit, to be sure. And an inability to lie without coloring up, which I've always found a welcome attribute in a man. It's not easy to make me laugh, but he sometimes manages it, and because he can't lie, I don't need to worry about him having secrets. And there's the fact, minor perhaps, that he calls me Lizzie. I was christened Elizabeth, a name that suits me, I think. But my sister, knowing how to inflict pain even when a baby, lisped *Etty* from her cot, and in that moment to my family I became Betty.

"You'll always be our lovely Betty," Gloria says now. "Too late to change."

As to Bert's cons, well, it's mostly all those old-man things: snoring, lethargy, the fear of technology, and the mess that even making a cup of tea entails. And there is the fact that he must always know where I am.

"Oh, where are you off to?" he will ask. Or, "How long will you be?"

That's the thing about marriage, you have to report to each other endlessly, nothing is private. Yes, the ties that bind definitely heads the list in the con column.

I've never known anyone as popular as Bert, not even Gloria. People love him, and he loves the world back. Everyone gets a share of his time. I suspect that's what made his first wife run. She wanted more of him, a husband to herself, and the kind of togetherness that Gloria and Henry display.

Bert and I work well together. We drink together, too, not so much that it is a problem, we keep our eye on it. I'm discreet when I wander, which is hardly ever these days. There are rules to cheating, which I stick to. No need to trouble my husband. And, unlike Gloria and Henry, we don't plan on having children. I'm still in the running, just—but Bert's not up for it. He says it wouldn't be fair on a child to have such an elderly father. I let him apologize to me, although I don't want children, either.

As well as a good memory, I have an eye for a good painting, and the gallery does well. Whatever that thing is that hits nine times out of ten, I have an instinct for it. It is what attracted Bert to me when I first worked for him, that and my skinniness. He likes the Lowry look in women. I like Lowry's linear figures, too, although I think his painting somewhat overrated.

Mother died at the start of a big week for Walker and Stash. We had two Lichtensteins up for sale, large brash canvases that gave the gallery the garish look of a newsagent's stand. I wonder about Lichtenstein's work, although I haven't entirely taken against it. I don't like the idea of being taken for a fool, but there is definitely something there that is hard to quantify, something that goes beyond the cartoon.

I advanced the deal, which was quite a coup, so it should have been me taking the credit, but timing as usual barged in. We had just that week lost our one member of staff, and so, with no time to replace him with anyone reliable, Bert had to forgo my mother's funeral. One of us had to be in the gallery.

"Everything comes at once," Bert said regretfully. "I will be thinking of you all." And he will of course, be thinking of us. It's not just the words with Bert; his sentiments are heart-felt. Obvious to say that he is as fond of Henry and Gloria as I am not.

People say that time is their enemy, don't they? But they just mean that they are busy. When I say it, however, I mean it. Bert would host the gallery show now, bask in the glory, thrill to the sale of the Lichtensteins. No matter what, though, you can't miss your mother's funeral.

Gloria had assured me that "Mummy didn't suffer." A massive stroke while she slept in her armchair in front of the fire; so massive, there was no waking from it. She had been baking for one of her charity coffee mornings, and needed a sit-down. She hadn't complained of feeling ill, only of a sud-den wave of tiredness. Mother wasn't one for complaining; she was more the pull-yourself-together type.

I pictured her dozing in her chintz-covered chair, a small smile set on a fallen mouth, fronds of her wispy hair damp from her baking fizzing around her face.

Henry had to phone with the news, Gloria couldn't speak through her sobs. Tears come easily to my little sister, and they leave in the same way. She is embraced, held up by her happy past, her expectation of a fortunate future.

Sitting in my hot car, I imagined her sobbing into Henry's

shoulder while he comforted her. His precious Gloria. I took a big glug of gin from my flask, and then another, and another. Friends will come and hug her; she will hug back. She will be Queen Bee holding court.

I pictured the mourners' sympathetic faces, the syrup in their voices. "Darling Gloria. Such a loving daughter, so full of goodness."

I didn't doubt her sorrow would be genuine; she loved Mother. But hers would be a short season of grief, and she would be through the worst of it in no time. That is part of the nature of the Beloveds, the will to be joyful, no matter what befalls them. They are childlike. In the knowledge that there will always be good things to come, they let go of bad things with an optimistic heart.

I ached to be in my room at Pipits, but I was not topped up enough to bear their grating company. So I sat in my stuffy car, sipping more gin and waiting for the anger to drain, waiting until I could gather myself and become their Betty. And slowly, as I drew the thought of the house into me, the calm came. My Pipits, my gem of soft rose bricks, wisteria-fringed sills, perfectly proportioned windows, began to work its magic. I conjured up the land that surrounds the house: two wild meadows at the back margined by woods, six thousand trees, all native species planted out by my grandfather. As I pictured its lawns spotted with daisies and buttercups, and the turkey oak almost as old as the house that sits to one side of the front door, and the huge copper beech that spreads itself luxuriously on the other, I was ready. I started the engine and put the car into gear.

HENRY AND GLORIA GREETED me at the door with red-rimmed eyes, their arms around each other.

"We're in shock," they said in unison.

"Me too," I said.

I *was* shocked, it's true. Mother's death had been unexpected, after all, and the timing of it was damned inconvenient. But, there was no point in lying to myself, it would move things on, give me what I have always wanted, long before I thought there would be a chance of it.

"She was fine that morning," Henry said. "No indication of anything wrong."

"Yes, she was," Gloria whimpered, nuzzling her head into Henry's neck. "She was in the kitchen in her blue gingham apron, humming to herself. She had just baked a big batch of fairy cakes, and the whole house smelled of them. That sweet eggy scent. Remember?"

Of course I remembered. I nodded. My sister makes everything sound like a story from Beatrix Potter: gingham aprons, fairy cakes. She paints such pretty little pictures.

Gloria described how they came for Mother. An old man in a dark suit, and a younger woman dressed like a bank clerk in a black jacket and white shirt.

"It was the hardest thing to see her go," she sobbed.

She handed me the card they had left on the hall table. It was a horrid plasticky object with a slippery surface. Looked like a visa. "Looton's Funeral Home," printed in black on a blue background. "Home!" Such cringing terminology. Home for the dead, the quietest of guests, and no meals required.

Henry put his hand on my shoulder and squeezed. He must go to his studio, he told me, to finish the pot he was making for Mother's ashes.

"A tribute to her," he said.

"So sweet," Gloria said.

"We want to bury her ashes in the garden," Henry called from the path. "Do you agree, Betty dear?"

"Is that legal?" I asked.

"Probably not," Gloria said. "But we'll do it anyway. We'll do it as soon as we can after the funeral service. It will be just us. Who's to know?"

"Where in the garden?"

"We thought under the buddleia tree by the summer-house. She loved to sit there and watch the butterflies."

I thought of Mother's geraniums that flowered in the summerhouse so generously, of the apricots that never fruited for her no matter how much she tended them. They would fruit for me, though. Did I mention I have a way with plants, a gift, you might say?

There was something hyped-up about Gloria, and I didn't think it was about Mother. She was shifting her weight from foot to foot, in the habit she has had since childhood when she's bursting to tell you something. She's hopeless at secrets.

"I know it's terrible timing, but I just have to tell you, Betty. I just have to."

"Tell me what?"

A pause while she bit her lower lip as though to smother a smile. "I'm pregnant!"

Oh God, of course she was. Despite her grief, she had that glow; there was a nascent sort of expectancy about her. No doubt her guardian angel, always on duty, thought it a good idea to replace Mummy with a baby. New life for old. Move on, Beloved.

"I never told Mummy," she sniffed. "I wanted to be sure. Isn't that the most wretched thing? It would have made her so happy."

So now it was all about her. She must be protected, cared for, not allowed to grieve too much. I felt the fissure inside me widening. I couldn't bring myself to congratulate her; I more wanted to slap her. I was put in mind of my tenth birthday, the treat of the film *Annie* and then supper at the Priory Hotel. There was my yellow silk dress, the promise of a chocolate cake, ten candles to guarantee a wish, ice cream. Not to be, though. Gloria's near-to-bursting appendix put an end to that.

"Can we concentrate on the funeral for now?" I said.

"Of course. Yes, Oh God . . . of course, Betty. Poor you."

She hugged me to her, and I smelled the figgy fragrance of her scent. I hugged her back forcefully, hoping more to hurt than comfort.

"Henry is being sweet," she said. "But there's nothing like a sister at a time like this."

––––––––––

THE FUNERAL SERVICE WAS well attended. Mother's friends from the Women's Institute came, soberly dressed; there were members of the local Conservative Party that she dutifully leafleted for, plenty of our neighbors, as well as our postman, and an assortment of people who were strangers to me but who Henry and Gloria greeted like old friends.

Alice sat with us in the front pew, weeping quietly. Henry did a reading with glistening eyes and a shaky voice. Then Alice was called to the lectern. She spoke of how my mother had treated her as a third daughter since her own mother had died young, how she would never forget her kindness. She talked of Mother's joy in her children, the wonder of her garden, which gave her such pleasure. When Alice returned to her pew, Gloria put her arm around her, and Alice lightly touched her head to Gloria's shoulder. There's a bit of the cuckoo in Alice, copycatting herself doggedly into our nest. It felt to me as though *I* were the third daughter, the one who hardly had a role to play.

And then the tea, spongy little sandwiches, cakes with butter icing, and wine for those who wanted it at four o'clock in the afternoon.

I took Gloria aside.

"It is just us tomorrow with the ashes?" I said.

"Yes, just us, and I thought Alice, too, of course."

"It should be just us," I insisted. "Just Mother's real family."

———

WE STOOD AROUND THE buddleia while Henry dug the hole. Gloria was holding the pot. It was round like her belly would be soon: brown earthenware with a white butterfly fired on its fat waist. It hadn't quite worked, the lid was a little too chunky, not a good fit, and the butterfly wings had powdered in the firing. Little pins of paint were scattered on the pot like sprinklings of icing sugar.

"A couple of tiny faults," Henry said. "But almost better that way, don't you think? Perfection can detract."

"Oh, poor Henry," I whispered to Gloria. "He does try so, doesn't he?" I savored the frown that my words stamped on her forehead.

I do think that Henry should have stuck to teaching; he

is an average potter at best. If it weren't for Gloria's patients and Mother's hand-outs, they'd be as poor as church mice.

I know plenty of men like Henry Bygone. They come to the gallery, calling themselves artists, incapable of making anything you would care to have in your home. They present their work, which is always a metaphor for something or other. They begin the story of the piece, and, believe me, every piece requires a story to explain it. They say "fundamentally" to add gravitas. They love the word *sexy*.

"It's subtly sexy, don't you think?" they say, in the hope that it will set up dollar signs in your eyes.

They confuse art with conception. I have given up explaining to them that conception is flower arranging, selecting wallpaper, hanging a painting where you think it will look good. Conception is the stuff of everyday life. Some are better at it than others, but it is not art. Art is bigger than conception alone. Conception is only the beginning. Art is actually painting the picture. It is something thrilling and wonderful that transmutes the conception through the artist's hand, and only the artist's hand, into something shattering. It is Nietzsche's "inner anarchy." It is not a toilet bowl bought at a bathroom outlet and exhibited as "Society's Sewer."

It speaks to the daft side of art that these incompetents find collectors to buy their trifling conceits. I once turned down a wire coat hanger with a torn shirt hanging on it, titled *My Father*. Not for Walker and Stash, but three thousand paid for it by an ego-driven collector. It is festering away in a warehouse now. Best place for it.

Bert is more open to the scam than me. He likes to go to

the art college's final shows each year, and he'll talk to any young person about their work as though they are already famous. I tell him that the junk we are looking at is the monosodium glutamate of art, a gloopy thing that makes the piece seem tasty in the moment but will make you queasy later.

"Oh, some of it shows promise," Bert says. "And the young are lovely, aren't they? So full of enthusiasm, so vital. In any case, it keeps my eye in."

Into what, I wonder. Bert is kind about Henry's work, too. He says Henry has a light touch, that he is talented enough to leave things to the imagination. He says Henry will surprise us all one day.

When Henry finished digging his hole, he lined it with leaves and sprays of buddleia. He placed the pot in it tenderly and tumbled the dug-up earth carefully over it with his big hands. Then he stood, brushed his hands off on his trousers, and put his arms around his swaying wife. He gave a dry little cough and started to read the poem that Gloria had chosen but was too weepy to read herself.

> "*I have desired to go*
> *Where springs not fail,*
> *To fields where flies no sharp and sided hail,*
> *And a few lilies blow.*
> *And I have asked to be*
> *Where no storms come,*
> *Where the green swell is in the havens dumb,*
> *And out of the swing of the sea.*"

"Manley Hopkins," Gloria said, swallowing hard. "Wonderful, isn't it."

Henry bent to pull up some weeds at the base of the buddleia.

"Leave them," I blurted out. "Mother wasn't afraid of a few weeds."

It was nothing to do with Mother, though. I did not like Henry's hands messing around in Pipits' dear dark earth. I would come back later and dig the weeds out myself.

3

O UT OF THE BLUE, and hardly a fortnight or so into my get-better stay at Pipits, Mother's will has been probated and is finally ready. At last. I can hardly stop my smile from surfacing.

We agree to meet up in the hall on the day of the lawyer's appointment.

"Make sure Henry's not late," I say to Gloria. "You know what a poor timekeeper he is."

I am there first, of course, out of good manners as much as eagerness.

"Ready?" Gloria says briskly, as though she is the one who has readied herself in time and is waiting patiently in the hall for me.

"More than," I say.

I hear their bedroom door close, and Henry appears on the stairs. He wears a suit well.

"Don't you wish he always looked like that?" I say.

Gloria winces, but she doesn't answer. The pair of them look relaxed as Henry helps Gloria on with her jacket. I imagine they think the roof above their head is safe with me.

"I'll drive," Henry says. "We'll pick up Alice on the way."

"Alice is in the will?" I question.

"So the lawyer tells us," Henry says. "I thought I mentioned it."

"You didn't," I say.

"Well, it's hardly a surprise. Mother loved Alice."

Did Mother love Alice? Or was her care for her born out of duty toward a motherless child? It irritates me that Alice is mentioned in the will, even if she is only bequeathed a token of Mother's affections, some sentimental little offering. Why should she have anything?

In the lawyer's office, we sit all in a row facing his desk, Henry, Gloria, me—and Alice, a little apart from the three of us, as though she knows that her true place is not at our side.

The words fall into an attentive silence. Ugly words that will change everything for all of us. It is Gloria and Henry who are to have the house. They are to have the house. Mother says, and here the lawyer's voice takes on a kindly note, that what with the baby coming, they need it more than me.

"Oh, she knew." Gloria beams. "She knew, Henry."

Only in the event of Henry's and Gloria's death will the house come to me. Mother says she would like it to stay in the family.

It takes all of my willpower to stop myself from wailing, from opening my mouth wide and howling like a wolf. I feel sick. A salty broth swirls around my tongue, and my throat has hardened as though it is closing up, as though soon I won't be able to swallow and the broth will pour out of me in foamy waves of misery.

I don't want the money she has left me, or her rope of pearls, or the painting that looks like a Miró but isn't; shiny things given to assuage her guilt at ditching her firstborn. How could she not know that the house by all rights belongs with me? It is a terrible injustice.

She should have left the money to Henry and Gloria. With it they could have bought a cottage, a barn, somewhere more suited to them than Pipits. What difference is it to them where they live? Wherever it is, they will set about smashing it up until it resembles something completely different from what it was in the first place.

Third daughter, Alice, has been left five thousand pounds and a gold bracelet that she had always admired, along with a first edition of the original Harry Potter novel that Mother bought as an investment. Clever Alice, weaving her life so intricately into the fabric of ours.

The lawyer stands first. The reading is over, done and dusted. We follow him down the stairs. Henry and Gloria shake his hand; Alice murmurs a thank-you. I give him the briefest of nods. He half bows and opens the door to usher us out onto the street, where we stand around as though we have lost our bearings.

A rush of flirty schoolgirls plows through us, leaving the dewberry scent of cheap perfume and peppermint gum in their wake. They flutter by like a flock of startled birds: tweeting voices, short skirts, kohl-rimmed eyes, glossy pink-daubed lips. Bosky with sex and fertility, they lend heat to the pavement. I wish that I were one of them, pretty and posing, the world before me, waiting.

I rock a little on my heels after they have passed. I can feel my blood seeping like slush through my veins, my heartbeat thumps out of rhythm, my saliva has dried up, turning my tongue to sandpaper. If there were ever a chance that

Gloria and I would grow to be closer, more loving sisters, it has gone. Mother's will has divided us forever.

Gloria links her arm through mine.

"Such a lot of money, Betty. Mother was quite the dark horse."

"A very dark horse," I manage.

"You will look lovely in the pearls," she says. "And you will always be welcome at Pipits."

Oh God, save me from the mercy of my sister.

4

BACK AT PIPITS AFTER the reading of the will, I endure lunch with Henry and Gloria and Alice. The food tastes like dust.

"Congratulations," Henry says, handing me a glass of wine. "Who knew Mother was so rich?"

"All from her side of the family," Gloria says. "It was wonderful of her to give us the house. Lovely we can keep it in the family," she says to me.

"Yes, lovely," I repeat.

I am barely in control, and with the excuse of a headache I take to my room. It is a good room, probably the best bedroom in the house. It was my grandfather's in his last years, the one where he lay on his deathbed. I don't mind that. Seeing as how I am the only one who ever mentions him, the only one to give him credit for all he achieved here, it is fitting that it should be mine now.

I surrender myself to grief, to a pain like nothing I have ever felt before. I am without a shell, no carapace to absorb Mother's final blow. Pipits' walls are damp with tears; it has lost its voice.

I lie on my bed and pull to my chin the patchwork quilt that Mother made for my thirteenth birthday. She thought it odd that I wanted one sewn from the clothes I had grown out of. But they would only have been handed down to Gloria, and she had plenty of her own. I wasn't about to let her take anything else from me if I could help it. I have a permanent reminder of those clothes now; my mauve cotton blouse, the pajamas with little cherries bouncing over the brushed cotton fabric, my primrose yellow party dress that Gloria once had hopes for.

My window is open, a trace of smoke from someone's bonfire drifts through it, laced with the tart scent of brambles. I can hear a dog in the village barking in a loop, two brief yelps and a little howl, then the repeat. Dusk comes and the crows are flying, then the dark, and the bats and owls. Before my eyelids get heavy I hear Alice arrive, the sound of laughter and music and more laughter.

When I wake next morning my first thought is that I have lost House, and the second is of Mother's betrayal. Rage seizes me. I cool it down in the bath, dress slowly, and tell my reflection in the mirror to give away nothing of how I feel.

Downstairs it is quiet, and there is a note on the kitchen table from Gloria. The long sleep will have done me good, she writes. She hopes my headache has gone.

She reminds me that Henry has gone into Bath to a committee meeting of his potter's group. They are planning a Christmas fair in May Park. I picture home-knit sweaters, sandals, badly cut hair. Gloria is with a patient in the dining room, no doubt talking her usual psycho-jargon. I think about the word *therapist* in my head and split it into two: *the rapist*. I wonder if Gloria has ever thought of that.

I smell traces of bleach, and some horrible air freshener mimicking the scent of freesia. I'd forgotten that it's one of

Mrs. Lemmon's days; she's the cleaning lady Gloria feels the house needs. Only a couple months on the job, and already devoted to her employer.

She will have zapped the poor little silverfish, seen off the spiders. Despite her meddling, her sweeping and squirting, I feel the complex soul of the house, sense the arteries that run behind the skin of its walls, and hear the soft hushing sound of its lifeblood flowing. I smell the drydown lingering scent, of the lives that Pipits has known, damp tweed, notes of mothball, tobacco, and wax polish, and the gamey mold that rises from the cellar. It is all as one to me. Love is love, after all.

It comes to me that I must save House. Who else but me? Whatever it takes, I will have Pipits. I will overturn Mother's legacy; she will not have her way. The dead will not be allowed to direct my future.

Just five months to go before there will be a baby wailing. I can't bear to think of a child here. Sticky hands that pull at things, stair gates, plastic toys, a baby-carriage parked in the hall. A disturbing picture comes to me of a swollen-with-pride Gloria. Mother earth dripping milk. The vision is intolerable.

I CANNOT SEEM TO tear myself away from Pipits. I am in stasis.

Bert is concerned for me. He drives down from London every Saturday, arriving in time for lunch. Gloria and Henry look forward to him coming, as does Alice, our chirpy little cuckoo. They laugh at his jokes, think him the sweetest man.

"What a delight he is," Henry says. "Lucky Betty."

"Yes, lucky Betty," Alice echoes.

Bert leaves after lunch on Sundays, and it is a relief to me to see him go. He is a city chap, too urban for the country. Admittedly, some call our village "the weekend Notting Hill." And it is true that there are a handful of sophisticated weekenders, but the planning laws in Cold-Upton are strict, building applications are always objected to and rarely approved, and there's no destination restaurant in the village to draw the crowds. It is not yet a theme park of a village, more old-fashioned and solid and, if I'm honest, what with the council houses, a bit rough around the edges. We don't take kindly to strangers here. Most of the families are at least third generation, and even the young are set in Cold-Upton's ways.

I tell Bert that there is no need to come every weekend, but he doesn't listen.

"We're there for each other," he says. "That's the deal. But you could come home, Lizzie, and let me look after you. I miss you, and I'd make a good nurse, don't you think?"

I always thought it would be Bert who needed looking after. I don't like him feeling responsible for me.

"Soon," I say. "I miss you, too, and the gallery, of course."

Business at Walker and Stash seems to be picking up. The money from the Lichtensteins, sold to a Belgian collector, has allowed us to take a gamble or two on the lesser-knowns, which has paid off. We, or should I say Bert, have a show coming up for Tony Ward, an artist in the Bacon style, big canvases, meaty colors; it is hard to tell whether his twisted forms are human or animal. There's a dark sort of power in them: rusty blood, the suggestion of demons, and sallow streaks as though he has mixed sulphur into the paint. They induce a hollow feeling in me.

I remember turning Ward away when he first turned up with a huge canvas that he had somehow managed to carry on his bicycle through the West End traffic. Too derivative, with a tinge of street art about it, I thought. Bert agreed with me then, although obviously, he thinks differently now. He says that the more you look at Ward's work, the more you see how original he is, how fresh and complex.

"We were lucky to get him," he insists as we sit at Pipits' kitchen table eating Gloria's version of Sunday lunch, an overdone beef and lentil stew. "Soon, he'll be able to take his pick of galleries to represent his work."

I can tell Bert feels slighted that I don't just pick up and return to London with him. He is a little off with me, so to appease him, I move to top up his glass with the indifferent wine of Henry's choosing. He waves the bottle away.

"I'm cutting down," he says. "You have my share."

I decide that I will, and fill my glass, wishing that it was gin. If I must drink wine, I would prefer it to be a good one. I think of the flask nestling in my bag and experience a sudden longing for the clean juniper taste that so perfectly comforts me. In order to stomach this lunch with a show of good humor, the bag and I will need a visit to the bathroom soon.

There is something different about Bert. I can't quite place what. It isn't just the cold eye he occasionally turns toward me. It's more that the language of his body seems somehow to have subtly altered; there's the slightest positioning of it away from me as though his attention is elsewhere. He moves with a lighter step now, and there's an unfamiliar firmness to his voice.

"Never known you to turn down wine," I say. "What's brought this on?"

"Oh, Helen's getting to me," he says with a cracked sort of laugh. I can tell that he is embarrassed "She's a bit of a health freak. Even got me walking to work."

"Really?" I don't manage to keep the sarcasm out of my voice.

"Yes, I feel a lot better for it, too."

Helen is my temporary replacement at the gallery. Bert met her at a dinner for a sculptress whose pieces we have shown in the past. They talked art, apparently, and she ended up offering to help out in my absence.

I taste bile in my mouth; my stomach dives. It is not Helen's place to be talking Bert into anything. I tell myself not to worry. I remember meeting her at an opening last year. She was introduced to me as a lover of art. Ha!

I judged her to be a phony, all dressed up in some odd bohemian getup, rings on every finger, and smelling of something green, Ma Griffe perhaps. Not Bert's type at all. And she is older than me, besides, by a good ten years I'd say, and plump verging on fat, the squishy sort, the type that Bert calls motherly. It is hard to imagine her walking anywhere without a good deal of huffing and puffing. I can count on Bert, can't I?

"It's time I came back," I say now, a bit uneasily. "Back to work. Back home."

"Well, I don't want to force you," he says, changing his tune. "Come when you're ready. We're managing well enough."

5

Bert has always been susceptible to a woman's flattery, so when it became a rare email from him that didn't mention Helen, I decided it was time to return to my London life. I wasn't giving up on Pipits, just biding my time. I couldn't believe Helen was a real threat, or any kind of competition, but I wasn't about to let her muscle into my territory.

Gloria waved me away with kisses and hugs.

"See you soon," she said. "You know you're always welcome, and our lovely Bert, of course."

One of the first things I had planned to do on my return was to interview for a new gallery assistant, a young man perhaps. You know the type: Eton boy or aping it, a touch precious. We'd employed that sort before, and they suited well enough. I wanted someone I would be happy to leave as helpmeet to Bert while I worked on getting Pipits back. It would mean letting Helen go, of course, but I didn't see that as a problem. She had only been a temporary solution, after all. Bert wouldn't hear of it, though.

"People like her," he insisted. "She's warm, and there is a rather lovely openness about her."

"Is that what we need, do you think?"

"I do, Lizzie. New money is a bit intimidated by all the trimmings. Someone like Helen puts them at their ease."

Someone like Helen? Someone with a fine conceit of herself, someone with that lark-like voice that yanks at my nerves. How is it that a woman so odd, so strangely dressed puts people at their ease?

But with my head full of Pipits, I don't feel like taking on Bert at the moment. I must work out how to get House back from Gloria. How to ensure that it isn't ruined by their desire for change, by their horrible renovations. I am still reeling from the blow of losing it. I decide to let the question of Helen go for now. Just for now, though.

Since I have been back I have noticed that Bert is less obliging than usual, more determined to have his way. He shows interest in my opinion, but it seems feigned to me, part of the good manners that never let him down. It is as though he is paying me back for my desertion, for not trusting him to take care of me. As part of this payback he sleeps now in the guest room.

"I know my snoring bothers you," he says. "We both need our sleep."

Well, he is right about that. His snoring does bother me. I confess that I enjoy having our big bedroom to myself, the plush comfort of the king-size bed. And lately, since suffering the reading of Mother's witchy will, I wake at odd hours through the night and need to pace. It niggles a bit, though, that it was Bert who suggested the sleeping apart.

I cannot say I am happy being back in London. Pipits is always bleeping on my radar. My first thought when I wake is how to find a way to have it to myself.

The time I have spent away from Bert has changed me, too, so that I question whether I even need him in my life. Nothing about him charms much anymore. I am irritated by his slowness, the way he wastes his time on trivia, the fact that he is late for everything, his forgetfulness.

Maybe he is questioning our relationship, too. He doesn't take my hand as we cross the road anymore, or put his arm behind my chair in restaurants in the old familiar way. He has a shifty, concealed look about him; there are unspoken boundaries between us now, which I somehow know not to cross. He seems to have a different agenda these days, one he doesn't care to share with me.

In my absence, he has turned the apartment upside down: clothes left lying around, damp towels in a huddle on the bathroom floor, newspapers on every surface. Left to his own devices, he would live in chaos. He has become someone I hardly know, someone whose behavior I can no longer predict. It is unsettling. And to add to my discomfort, I have become suspicious that he is up to something that is not in my interest.

I can't imagine why Bert thinks Helen has a warm personality. A vague one, perhaps, but warm? No. One might excuse that in the young, but she is, Bert tells me, fifty-seven years old. I question sometimes whether the problem with Helen is actually vagueness or just plain insolence. She overlooks the instructions I leave her. She never apologizes when I mention her tardiness, never apologizes for anything. Her friends are always calling into the gallery; wealthy bohemians who treat me like an assistant rather than the owner. Apparently, Helen is rich, the granddaughter of some Spanish wine magnate. A trust-fund kid, still behaving like one, as she heads toward sixty. I wonder why she bothers to work at all.

I had a falling-out with her the other day about having her friends visit her at work. They are a bizarre lot, most of them around her age, fluttering about in inappropriate clothes just like her, commenting on what they consider to be our conventional choice of paintings, suggesting new artists that I haven't heard of. I recognize a couple of them, one a television art historian, thin as a rack, and smarmy with a syrupy voice, another a sculptress who is known for creating giant wings out of glass she has somehow managed to make look like gold. It's obvious to me they think themselves the pinnacle of the art world hierarchy. Bert says that they are.

"Ha," I say. "More like self-professed."

"Aren't we all," he sighs.

The other day five of them came in, hardly acknowledging me. Helen opened wine, gave them free catalogs, and Bert enthused with them about the paintings we have coming up. It was as though we were having an opening.

"It's absurd," I told her after they left. "This is a gallery, not a wine bar."

Bert called me aside and said objecting to Helen's visitors was bad judgment on my part. According to him, they encourage business, liven up the place. Besides, he pointed out, what was wrong with looking like we were having an opening?

"God knows," he says. "Things are quiet enough at this time of year."

"Except that we are not having an opening," I tell him. "And, if we were, invitations would have gone out to the right people."

"They are the right people, Lizzie."

Well, clearly, we don't agree on that. He finds Helen's friends quite charming, and of course they love him to bits.

I cannot get through to him. He listens to me with his

head on one side, eyes widening, nodding a little, as though he agrees with me, then he goes his own way.

Helen knows that Bert is on her side. She has that look on her face as though she is hugging a secret to herself. It is quite ridiculous that suddenly I am the one who feels like the outsider. If Bert won't sack her, then I will.

"If you insist, if you really can't get on with her, then I'll have a word," he says when I tell him. "It will be better coming from me."

"You'll ask her to leave?"

"Yes. I don't think that we will find anyone as good, but my loyalty is to you, Lizzie. And if that's what you want . . ."

He suggests we take a break before he talks to Helen. Go somewhere nice, somewhere warm. Spend some time together, reconnect.

"Are we disconnected, then, Bert?"

"I think that we are, Lizzie."

Now that Bert has caved in, I am suddenly torn. Despite the fact that I could change things, get rid of Helen, return us to something like the way we were, is that really what I want? Never mind Bert, never mind Helen. I wouldn't be here at all if Pipits were mine. It's all I long for, it is my priority, it is everything.

Something is wrong with my stomach. It hurts all the time, a strange sort of pain as though I am bruised inside. The thought of food stirs a tannic saliva in my mouth.

Against my will, Bert books me an appointment with the doctor. He knows how much I hate seeing doctors, hate being probed and questioned, so he drives me there to make sure that I go.

"And your appetite?" the doctor asks.

"Okay, I suppose. I've never had a big appetite."

He takes my blood pressure, presses his clammy hands on my stomach, weighs me, murmurs a little as he makes notes.

"Well, nothing obvious is wrong that I can see," he says. "Your weight leads me to suspect possible malnutrition. Not something that I see much of these days, but you are much too thin. You must eat more, drink less. Take a break, perhaps. Stop work for a bit, if you can manage it, and go somewhere relaxing. I would suggest you are suffering from stress. Sunshine, heat, and food is what you need."

Stop work for a bit, he'd said. And so I will. Bert will understand that I am not well, that I left Pipits too soon, that I must continue my convalescence where I am at home in every sense of the word. I have no wish to go abroad to fester under the sun and pretend to be enjoying myself. I won't say that to Bert, though, I want to keep him sweet, keep things running smoothly until I decide how to move forward.

"You can't be serious," he says. "Surely somewhere warm with me would be better."

"I don't feel well enough to travel far," I say. "Perhaps later."

"It's always later with you, Lizzie. Do what you want. You will anyway, no matter what I say."

I've never heard him speak so bitterly.

"We can go away another time," I say. "It's not the end of the world."

"Far from it," he says, and something in his tone unsettles me. "You go. I'll look after things here."

"I need your support," I wheedle. "I don't feel well

enough to travel abroad at the moment." This time, though, he doesn't smile, doesn't gobble up the bait.

I email Gloria and tell her I am coming home.

GLORIA WELCOMES ME BACK with a hug, but I notice a reserve in Henry's greeting. His jaw tightens a little, his smile is a touch too bright.

Alice is sitting at the kitchen table eating a bowl of soup. Is she never at work?

"Good heavens, Alice," I say. "Here again. Who's dishing out the books while you visit us?"

"There's been a mouse infestation in the library van," she tells me. "Two nests found behind the shelves. Pages nibbled from Hemingway and Wordsworth, and my chocolate bar tattooed with teeth marks. Ugh!"

"Highbrow mice," Gloria laughs. "And only the best dark chocolate for them."

"The van's being decontaminated," Alice says. "So I have the day off. It's lovely to see you."

"Mm," I murmur. "You too."

What I want to say is, Why don't you spend your day off in your own house, stop imposing yourself in mine. Manners must be observed, though. I bite my tongue.

The house greets me with a quiet hum, but I can tell it is restless, the signs are all around me: plugs spark, pipes gossip, dust motes fly madly in the halls and stairwells.

"Soon," I whisper to my fretting Pipits. "Don't fuss."

I unpack, settle into my room, and the house begins to echo my own questions. Where to from here? How will I make it mine?

Every morning I hear Gloria retching into the toilet bowl. She is saintly about the sickness, of course. No complaints that it seems to be going on throughout the pregnancy. Her stomach is a globe now, no discernible sign of her waist. Fingers crossed she won't get it back.

In my absence, they have named the embryo the Apple.

Henry rolls his hand around her stomach possessively. "Our little apple," his voice is pure sugar.

Mother's bedroom is to become the nursery. They have stripped off her chinoiserie wallpaper, taken apart her four-poster bed and stored it in the woodshed. They plan a circus scene on the walls, white floor paint, mobiles dangling. A commercial artist will do the mural; Gloria has already given her a plan, a clown with a halo of red hair, gigantic shoes, and the big top with a monkey hanging from its guy rope. Everything about the scene is a visual cliché. I'm finding it hard to breathe.

I've noticed a tiny patch of loose carpet at the top of the stairs. I was going to mention it, but I fear it will encourage them to rip up the whole thing, discard the lovely old wool, and replace it with something new, some eco-friendly thing made of grass, no doubt.

If I don't do something soon, I will be standing among the ruins of Pipits. I will have lost it to Henry and Gloria's mutation. It will have become entirely theirs. Is it any wonder I feel betrayed?

I must find a way to right the wrong that I have been dealt.

I asked them the other day if they would sell Pipits to me.

"But why?" Henry said. "You stay whenever you want to. We love it, too, you know."

He didn't say I *was* welcome to stay whenever I wanted to, just that I did. I couldn't fail to notice the drop of venom in his words. And, really, Henry, if you love it, why have you so viciously set about changing it? Go find yourself another house to tear apart. You have each other. The pair of you could be happy anywhere.

What I actually said, in my sweetest voice, was "Thank you, Henry, how kind."

Mother let this happen. She stupidly allowed them to work on her with their charm, their neediness. The one thing I thought I could rely on her for, and she let me down.

I've loosened the carpet a tiny bit more, just under the nose of the top stair where you can hardly notice it, where it could easily catch the heel of a shoe. The stairs murmured their approval.

ALONG WITH THE HOUSE martins, summer has left. I wake to the sight of soft frosts icing the lawns and to the honking cry of the departing Canada geese repeating harshly on the air. Good riddance.

Foolishly, this year under Gloria's new rule, the geese have been encouraged, because she thinks them beautiful, and says it is cruel to unsettle them.

She doesn't seem to mind that they defecate like dogs, foul the swimming hole, and will increase year after year until hardly a blade of grass will be left to us.

"One season of them is not enough to see the worst of it," I warn.

In the past, even though Gloria pleaded for them, Mother discouraged them from laying by driving her car straight at them, banging saucepan lids, running toward them whooping like some mad person. If they persisted, as is their way, she would get one of the local farmers to shoot over their heads and scare them off.

"They must not be allowed to lay," she would insist. "Once they lay, it's all over."

Gloria was probably too young to remember, but I recall Father complaining as he reached for his gun, "Those damned Canadians are back." He knew how to manage the land and would shoot them without a thought. It is probably illegal now, although if I had a gun, I wouldn't bother with merely scaring them off; I'd do the same as Father. Horrible, messy, uneatable things.

The meadows are full of mushrooms. Henry loves them. He's out each morning gathering them up, laying them tenderly on the paper towel that lines his basket. He takes his illustrated mushroom book with him and meticulously inspects each cap, each little pleat of their velvet underbellies.

"Can't be too careful," he says. "*Amanita virosa* lurks among the delicious *Agaricus macrosporus*."

"Really?" He has my attention now.

"Both white and firm to the touch," he says. "Deceivingly similar, only the *virosa* is deadly. It's referred to as 'the destroying angel.'"

Gloria shudders when he speaks of mushrooms.

"I can't bear the slimy things," she says, screwing up her face. "They remind me of slugs, horrible slimy slugs."

"They're not slimy," Henry insists. "It's just the morning dew on them."

Gloria can't even bear to touch them, so Henry must

cook his own, which he is happy to do, fried in butter, dotted into a creamy pasta, folded into a risotto, his favorite. He thinks himself a bit of a chef.

I contemplate adding a couple of those noxious ones into his bowl. I may do it, just to slow down their nest building for a bit.

When I think about it, Pipits' garden is laden with venomous plants, a veritable pharmacy; there's daphne, and the rhododendron gone wild by the water hole, a clump of wolfsbane in the shade of the trees at the margin where meadow meets wood, the queen of poisons, they say. There's laburnum and the shiny red berries of the bryony, and there's yellow toadflax alongside the hedge. Mother used to boil its flowers in milk as a poison for flies, until a neighbor's dog on the loose lapped it up and was found on our terrace, stiff and grimacing. Dogs are unlucky creatures, no nine lives for them.

October is a dangerous month, fungi and the black veined nightshade catch the eye. The yew sprouts its little jelly tots, each one housing a single toxic seed. They would go unnoticed in a summer pudding.

Measured amounts are a fine art when considering such things. You might say much of life is about the right dosage. Mother love springs to mind, fairness, too, and luck, of course, especially luck. If we all got the right dosage of these things, what need for shrinks, what need for the fight.

If all I want is to hold up the works, to buy some time, then not too much, or too little, is the way to go. If all I want is to buy some time.

THE GIRL WHO HAS been hired to paint the mural has stumbled on the loose stair carpet and cracked her wrist on the banister as she grabbed it to save herself. She won't be able to continue her destruction in Mother's bedroom until the bone has healed. Six weeks should do it, she apologizes. A small victory for me, but still a victory. I'm inspired to take things further.

Henry has hammered in tacks to flatten the carpet and make it safe. They can't afford a new one, he says. At least not until after the show at May Park. He's convinced he is going to sell out of his quirky mugs and sure that his fat-necked flower vases will delight. No chance with the mugs, but the vases have a naive, unvarnished sort of charm, so who knows.

THE RAIN HASN'T STOPPED for three days. It has churned up the mud in the river and spun the water into a ribbon of chocolate. There is a drowned rat drifting on the surface of the swimming hole. It annoys me to see it out-of-bounds there. Rats are usually good swimmers.

The downpour has found the split in the roof and dripped into the attic where we have had to put buckets to catch it. I don't mind the drumming soundtrack. The split can be repaired, and a bit of damp is hardly something to stress about. I'm amused, however, by Henry's distress at the leak.

"Houses like this cost money to keep up," I remind him.

"Feel free to help out with that if you like," he says without humor.

I won't, though. Why should I make it easier for them?

As far as Henry is concerned, I have outstayed my welcome. I'm sure he would tell me so if it weren't for upsetting Gloria. They lived happily enough with Mother, so why not with me? It's my family home after all, not Henry's.

I'm amused at the relief on his face when I go to London to visit Bert. I know he hopes that Bert and I will resume our marriage and live happy ever after, far away from Pipits. Dream on, Henry.

It's a journey I make less and less often, not because I like to annoy Henry with my presence, but because things are no easier with Bert, and I have not yet made up my mind where to go with the marriage. There are financial things to consider, and if I leave Bert, I want to know that I am choosing something better.

Odd, isn't it, how things go along in the same way day after day, and then suddenly when you least expect it, everything changes. Along with the rain, news is streaming in from everywhere. Gloria and Henry have had some sort of spat. They are skirting silently around each other. I get the feeling the spat was about me. I can't be sure, of course, but neither of them will look me in the eye. They will make up soon, as is their way, and when they do, they will be more lovey-dovey than ever. For the moment, though, I am enjoying the peaceful distance between them.

And now an email from Bert. He needs a break, and as luck would have it, we have been invited to Helen's mother's house in Spain. It's just for a long weekend, and he thinks the sea air would do me good. October is a gentle month in that part of the world, he writes. He would like us to accept. What reason not to?

I get the feeling that he is pushing me to say yes or no to

our marriage, rather than to a weekend away. I decline the invitation, tell him I'm not up to the travel. I have no desire to stay with some old lady in Spain who is probably as odd as her daughter.

And then, suddenly, without warning, without the tiniest sign to prepare us, comes news that obliterates the lovebirds' argument and Bert's little holiday, news that puts Alice in shock and leaves her struggling to summon her courage. Feeling fine one day, she woke up yellow the next. Jaundice, she thought. But no, she has been diagnosed with pancreatic cancer. It has prospered under the guise of no symptoms, and in the wake of its devastation they say she has only weeks, months at the most left to live.

I came across Gloria in the kitchen sobbing at the news of it. Henry had his arms around her; he was kissing her hair, making little soothing noises. He looked quite distraught himself. Well, that sort of news is bound to be a shock. I'm shocked myself, although no one seems to have noticed.

Now Gloria is insisting that Alice must leave her house in the village and come and live with us. She wants to be the one to nurse her, to care for her dearest friend. Her dearest friend. Once again, my saintly sister is to be the fulcrum, the linchpin in one of life's dramas.

"I'd like her to live to see the baby," she snivels.

"Unlikely, my darling," Henry says.

"Well, Christmas, at least, then."

"We'll make it a wonderful one if she does. We'll treasure her for as long as we can."

Henry is against Gloria nursing Alice. There must be a better solution, he says. I hear them talking it over in what they take to be the privacy of their bedroom. Henry's tone is firm for him; Gloria's, pleading. Guess I know who will win that one. When does my sister's obliging husband not give in to her demands? They are so sweetly insisted upon.

No surprise then that Henry has caved in and Gloria is to have her way. He is concerned, though, and has confided in me.

"It is so typically generous of her," he says. "Kind but impractical. How can she care for a dying woman when she is carrying our child?"

He worries the pregnancy should be a time of celebration, that the sadness of caring for her failing friend will harm Gloria and the baby.

"Of course, we must care for Alice," he says. "She really needs us now. Such bad timing. What's to be done?"

He delicately implies that I could move in with Alice, nurse her. I won't, of course. I can't leave Pipits to them, and besides, I will not allow Henry to put the burden on me. Alice might as well start packing. She will be here before we know it.

Bert, back from Spain with a light tan and a guilty conscience, is going to New York. There's a chance of a Hopper through a colleague who owes him, and he can't hang about. It's one of the few Hoppers in private ownership, and would be just the boost the gallery needs. The Lichtenstein did well for us, but the Tony Ward show was a bit of a flop, and business has slowed, worryingly so. A Hopper would certainly pep things up.

I think about going with him, but I feel rooted here, waiting. He hasn't asked me, but I tell Bert anyway that my energy is low and that he should go on his own. I wish him

luck with the Hopper. He says that he understands. Is it res-
ignation or relief I hear in his voice?

I am drinking too much, I know. It is my comfort, but it
has to stop. Those extra tipples make my head feel mushy,
mess up my thinking. I wake so late sometimes that the
house is already in full swing when I come downstairs: the
kettle whistling, the self-satisfied tones of that woman on
Radio 4 who imagines herself in charge of the news, repeating one pointless question over and over. She presses for the
answer, yes or no, as though there are no intricacies to be
considered, no subtle shades. She's desperate to force an answer worthy of a sound bite that will be repeated on every
news program throughout the day. Is that what we pay our
license fee for?

I would prefer to be the first up, to watch the light sneak
through the curtains, to hear my dear home waking. Those
extra shots of gin soothe, but they must stop. I need a clear
head, a plan to see off the Bygones, and I need action. From
now on, I resolve not to take a drink before six in the evening.

———

MY ROOM IS ROSY with the russet light reflected through the
leaves of the copper beech tree that spreads its branches outside my window. They tap on the glass in the wind, comforting chatty little taps. I have always loved the sound and
delighted in the swaying branches that throw flying silhou-
ettes around my room. Henry says the tree doesn't look well
to him, that the leaves are dead.

"They are holding on, won't let go," he says. "A sign that
something is wrong, surely."

"They are always the last to leaf, the last to let go," I tell him. "Haven't you noticed?"

It's true that their fall is later than usual, but I'm not worried, things in nature change their habit from one year to the next. The leaves will be blown away on the wind soon enough.

"The roots of it are dangerously close to the house," Henry drones on. "Part of the trunk is hollow. I think it's on its last legs. We should consider chopping it down before it does some damage. Horrible, I know, such a magnificent thing."

I'm too shocked to answer. I love that tree. Mother loved that tree. See, Mother, see the outcome of your foolish bequest. Henry is not the benign creature you thought him.

My sister and her husband are endlessly annoying. Their presence in what should be my home eats into my peace of mind, scratches around my insides until every organ throbs. Henry with his absurd adoration of his wife, his determination to cut down and smash through; and Gloria so nauseatingly saccharine in her pregnancy. Henry would love me to be gone; Gloria, too, most probably, but she would never ask me to leave; I am the eldest, and she feels guilty being the chosen one, being willed our family home, which she knows means so much to me.

Each morning now when I look in the mirror, I see a different face from the one I am expecting. Is that me? Surely my eyes were never that dark, my skin never that sallow. I get thinner as Gloria gets fatter. It feels like I'm matching her pound for pound, but in the opposite direction.

6

I HAVE NINE YEW BERRIES in a plastic bag hidden in my underwear drawer. I'm not sure if nine will be overdoing it, or if cooking them will lessen their kick. It's a problem.

There was a hard frost on the ground this morning, and a wintry light, hardly the season for summer pudding, but I have been dropping hints that I fancy one.

"No law that says it must be summer," Gloria says obligingly. "I fancy one myself, and it might even tempt Alice."

Alice, who, in the space of the last fortnight, has left her job, shut her house up, and moved into one of our guest rooms on the first floor, is having a sleep.

"Summer pudding and a thick crème fraîche," I encourage Gloria pointlessly. I know she's up for it. She hardly needs coaxing with food these days. Her appetite is huge.

"Eating for two," she says, as though that is an original excuse.

"There are some raspberries and black currants in the freezer from the garden, and the last of Mother's strawberries," she says with a wobble in her voice. "They'll do, Betty, won't they?"

I start the cooking, while Gloria sits at the table cutting crusts off the thick white bread. When the fruit begins to bubble, I strain off some of the juice to marble through the bread later. I'm still not sure that I will do it. I have Mother's gingham apron on, the yew berries snuggled now in the pocket.

Gloria is in and out of the kitchen. She has to pee a lot these days. She weeps a lot, too, the slightest thing and she's blubbering like a child.

"Happy tears for the Apple," she says. "Sad ones for Alice. I hardly know how to be anymore."

"It's probably just hormones," I say.

With my back to Gloria, I stir the berries around in the remaining juice, and then as though it has a mind of its own my hand reaches into the apron's pocket and before I know it the yew berries have become as one with the simmering fruits.

Gloria is humming along to a tune on the radio. It is the first time that I have heard her hum since the news of Alice's illness. It's the long-dead Ella Fitzgerald singing about love and loss, sad lyrics accompanied by trembling trumpet notes. Gloria says she is a fan of Ella's. I have never understood the nature of a fan, never been prepared to hero-worship anyone myself.

I take the saucepan of fruit to the table, and Gloria starts building the pudding. Bread and fruit, a glug of cassis, added to the juice for a treat, she says. The pudding shines garnet red through the cut glass bowl. I watch her layering, fascinated. I have no idea if what looks like the most delicious pudding is in fact a deadly one.

"There, all done," she says. "Put it in the fridge would you, Betty."

I take up the bowl, heavy with the bread and the glistening summer fruits, and we both admire its beauty.

"Gorgeous, a dish of jewels," Gloria says.

"Rubies," I agree.

But then as I turn from her a sudden vision of Henry and Gloria, tongues out, lips black, dead on the kitchen floor, and Alice expired on the sofa, puts me in a panic. There may be carnage. Everyone likes summer pudding, after all. Have I thought it out well enough for myself to be in the clear?

I hesitate by the fridge. I should have planned it better; it's a lesson I will learn for next time. I let the bowl slip through my fingers to the floor. It shatters, and glass splinters mix with the pudding as the juice seeps across the kitchen flagstones like a run of blood.

"Oh no," Gloria cries. "And it looked so yummy."

"Pity about the bowl," I say.

"A wedding present from Alice," she says. "Don't let's tell her."

A shadow shifts at the corner of my vision. I feel a puff of warm air on my cheek. Heat from the Aga or the wafting of angel wings? Lucky, lucky, Gloria.

I feel regret, a coward. If I am not prepared to save Pipits from my sister's meddling, then why do I stay? I had thought myself ready for the battle, but had hesitated, held back, let myself down.

In the gloom of disappointment, I catch the train to London the next day for an overnight with Bert, who has returned from New York. He sent an email to say he is too busy to visit me at present, no other news except that he will leave it to me to come when I want to. Well, I would like to see the Hopper.

"Just overnight," I say to Gloria.

"Well, as you like, but perhaps you should stay longer," she says without guile. "Bert will be thrilled to see you."

I can tell that Henry is delighted at the sight of my suit-case.

"It's time you went home," he ventures boldly. "I mean, Bert must be missing you."

Gloria throws him a frown, and he says he is off to the studio.

"It's only an overnight stay," I tell him.

"Well, have a good time," he says. "Love to Bert."

THE GALLERY LOOKS DIFFERENT, wrong somehow. I notice it the minute I enter. A vase of mixed anemones droops on the reception desk where there should be orchids. They are purple and puce with some drained pink ones scattered among them. How irritating. We always have white orchids, always. They are elegant. They enhance rather than clash with the art.

The desk, an elongated white curve, designed especially for us, designed with clean lines to impress, to give the look of style and order, is cluttered with the debris of what I take to be Helen's mess. There's a box of tissues by the phone, a bowl of jelly beans, and a tub of assorted pens. The place has taken on the look of one of those gift shops selling a mess of itsy-bitsy little things that you can't imagine ever needing. What is going on with Bert, letting things slip like this?

Helen has put down the book she was reading when I first came in.

"Oh, hello," she says. "I wasn't expecting you. Bert's out to lunch, but he'll be back soon, I expect."

I don't answer. I remove the tissues and jelly beans and the tub of pencils and put them in a drawer.

"What has happened to the orchids?" I ask, offering Helen the anemones and indicating with a nod for her to take them to the kitchen.

"Bert and I thought some color would make a change," she says.

Bert and I! Bert and I!

"We saw something similar in New York. Color against the white. We just loved it."

Shock scurries through my body. A pulse beats painfully in my head. I feel as though I have been punched in the gut. Helen went to New York with Bert!

I make an effort to calm myself and act as though her trip with Bert is no surprise. I'll have it out with Bert, not her.

There's an unapologetic edge to her voice. She doesn't take the flowers from me, offers coffee instead as though she is some kind of hostess. I look at her pudgy face, her watery blue eyes, her dark-painted lips; I take in the strange velvet dress she is wearing, which drags around her ankles. It's hideous, a tabby-cat mottled hodgepodge of a dress. She looks like a mad bag lady. I see my enemy. Could this woman, this messy creature with lines on her face and iron-gray hair, also be my rival? And, if she is, do I care? Would I even bother to fight for Bert?

Knowing him as I do, the thought of the two of them making a pair seems ridiculous, but then the truth so often is. I may not be sure that I want Bert, but I've had enough of people taking what's mine.

When Bert comes back, he is on edge, not at ease with me. It is the surprise of me just turning up without warning,

I suppose. He is wearing his salmon and cucumber bow tie, so I guess he lunched at the Garrick. He bustles around showing me the new pieces, which include, I can't imagine why, a canvas covered in hundreds of pieces of what look like Post-it notes but are in fact little squares cut from the assorted flags of Europe.

"More a designer piece," he says, shooting an anxious look at Helen. "But sort of engaging, don't you think?"

"It either is or it isn't engaging, Bert. We don't go in for 'sort of,' do we?"

He's forgotten how I dislike those wishy-washy words, "sort of," and "kind of," and, especially, "if you like." It either is or it isn't. You either like or you don't, there's no "if" about it. Why water everything down?

"Where is the Hopper?" I ask.

"Sadly, that didn't come off," he sighs. "They didn't want it leaving America. In any case, we couldn't have come up with the money. You wouldn't believe the asking price. They had found a homegrown buyer before we even got there."

"And you didn't think to tell me?"

"You look well," he says, baldly changing the subject, blushing a little.

It isn't the truth. I know I don't look good. I'm thinner than ever, I have the start of a cold sore, and I'm having a bad hair day. Not to mention that it's a "flag day," as Gloria likes to call the monthly bleed.

"Tea at Fortnum's?" he offers.

In the store, heading toward its splendid Diamond Jubilee Tea Salon, we push our way through the crowds, who are gawping at the groceries, as though they are looking at things magical, as though they have never before seen melons, strawberries, or confectionary. There's a display of choc-olate teddy bears guarding a mountain of sugary truffles, one of huge seashells awash with silvered almonds. There are gold-themed tables, boxes of candied peaches, gilded dragées, and glistening jars of honey that catch the light. You have to hand it to whoever arranges the tables. Each one looks like a still from the film *Babette's Feast*.

Bert stops in front of a stand where every kind of short-bread is displayed. He fingers a tartan tin. "We need to fat-ten you up," he says, taking it to the till.

The sight of all this food quite sickens me. I am put in mind of the seven deadly sins. All this excess, this licking of lips, eyes alight with . . . what? Is it lust or gluttony? I need a drink.

"I hate shortbread," I say to Bert.

"Oh, never mind, then, we'll eat them at work."

The tea is good, hot and sweet. I can't face the sand-wiches, but I nibble at a cheese straw, the best I've ever tasted. When Bert goes to the men's room, I pour a shot of gin from my flask into my tea and outstare the uptight woman sitting at a table nearby who looks across at me with disgust on her face. Silly bitch.

When Bert returns to the table, I pour him a cup of tea and get to the Helen thing.

"So you took Helen to New York, Bert?"

"Well, I . . . you know." He colors up.

"I know what?" I say.

"You didn't want to come, and I didn't fancy doing it on my own. It was a last-minute thing. Spur of the moment, you know."

"Spur of the moment?"

"Yes. She wanted to see friends there, and she paid for herself."

"Good," I say. It's hardly up to us to pay for her to see her friends, is it?

Back at the apartment, Bert takes to his bed for a sleep before dinner. He has booked the Wolseley, where he is a favorite. He can have his special table. No need for him to obey the two-hour time slot they've allotted to other diners, either. I have never cared to stand in the light of my husband's popularity; it would be demeaning to do so, like hanging on to the coattails of a celebrity in order to feel important oneself. I wonder, though, how it must feel to be so celebrated.

His bedroom door is ajar. I watch him through the open gap for a minute or two. Crumpled into the duvet, his soft body appears like some life-size rag doll. His mouth is open, and every so often he gives a little whistling snore. He has taken his shoes off, left his turquoise-and-yellow-striped socks on. Colorful socks are Bert's idea of what a gallery owner should wear, those and the bow ties he collects. He may not be an artist, but he doesn't want to appear like a conventional businessman, either.

He looks vulnerable lying there with his slack mouth gaping. He looks sad and old, older in sleep than when I picture him in my head. Being married to this old man has made me feel old myself. I am repulsed, and it's in this moment that I withdraw from him totally, know for certain that I don't want to pin my colors to his mast anymore. I want to be free, to do what I want without having to answer to anyone. Bert has become a burden.

I am done with marriage, but that doesn't mean I will

give Helen a free run. I will choose when to unshackle my-self from it. And, when I am ready, we will talk, talk things out, agree on how to share our spoils. But not now. Not on this fading day when all I can think of is getting back to Pipits.

I go to my room, pick up my case, and call a taxi from the phone in the hall to take me to the station. We were meant to have a lovely evening together, I was meant to stay, but I can't.

I leave him a note on the hall console.

Sorry, my dear. I'm not feeling too well at the moment, and I didn't want to bore you with having to look after me. Speak soon. Lizzie.

7

WE ARE ALL WAITING: Bert to hear when I plan to return, Gloria and Henry for the baby, and Alice, poor Alice, to die. I'm waiting, too, attempting to find a way to get Gloria and Henry out of the picture. I need a plan, some wonderful plan to rid me of the Bygones once and for all. Pipits hangs in there with me, cheering me on, breathing evenly while it waits.

With Christmas less than a month away, I suspect Alice may just make it. She has fixated on celebrating the yuletide, and it appears to be keeping her going. I have heard before that it's not unknown to keep death at the door while you complete the one last thing you have set your mind on doing. In Alice's case, it is Christmas Day.

She is a puny clone of her former self, yellow tinged, her voice fading along with her body. It is shocking how quickly things have gone downhill. She is quiet in her illness, bearing up without complaint. Sometimes I enter a room and it can be minutes before I know that she is in it. She will be sleeping in a chair, or pushed into a corner of the sofa, nodding over a book with her legs curled under her, so that she appears, in her bright knits, like another of Gloria's scatter cushions. She takes little rests throughout the day, and I wonder how soon it will be before she has to take to her bed full-time.

I heard a strange conversation between her and Henry yesterday afternoon as I passed the sitting room.

"It is too generous of you, Alice," Henry said. "Is there no one else who deserves it more?"

"Not really. Only you and Gloria, and it's for the two of you I'm doing it, really."

"She won't be grateful, you know. She's never grateful."

"Oh, I don't think that's true, Henry. In any case, I shan't be around to care about grateful, will I?"

"Oh, Alice," Henry said, before they fell silent.

It was obvious they were talking about me. I can't think of anyone else Henry would be so mean about. But then again, although Alice may look benign, she is not above meddling in other people's business. She involves herself so much in village affairs that it could have been anyone. I'll find out eventually, though. Henry will tell Gloria, and Gloria will spill to me.

Now that Alice is not so active, I find that I don't mind her presence in the house as much as I thought I would. I dare say it is something to do with her air of acceptance, and the fact that Gloria has cut down her client list so that she can spend more time with her. So, fewer sorry-for-themselves housewives trailing through the hall, fewer telephone calls from people requiring Gloria's urgent help.

It's Alice's visitors who come to Pipits now, not as annoying as Gloria's patients and not on the hour, of course, but still there they are, muddy feet and dripping umbrellas, haw-haw voices. With their roles reversed, they bring books to the librarian now and keep her current with the gossip. Who knew that milky Alice had so many friends? The house is full of their gifts: books and potted plants, endless jars of crab-apple jelly. Honestly, how many potted plants are we expected to water, and what is the point of crab-apple jelly? It is neither sweet nor sour, merely bland, somewhat like Alice.

The paraphernalia of Alice's illness litters the house: extra blankets on the sitting room sofa to keep her from the cold, foils of pills left lying around, half-empty glasses of water placed about here and there. Her bedside table hosts a forest of drugs, a thermometer, a blood-pressure machine, medicated wipes, and balls of cotton wool; and in the middle of this muddle a black-and-white photograph of her parents looking quizzically at the camera. Alice's father, stooped forward, mild-looking except for the rebellious jutting of his jaw, her mother mousy pretty, everything small, eyes, nose, mouth, tiny white teeth. Alice takes after her father, a gangly man, all angles.

I console myself with the fact that these trappings are transient things. Alice has set up a temporary camp, that is all. It occurs to me that Pipits hosted my father and grandfather on their way out; Mother, too. They left a stronger impression in its heart than Alice will, I'm sure.

Her oncologist, against his will but at her insistence, has given her a guesstimate of how long she has left.

"Weeks," he ventures. "But it is not an exact science. People are always surprising me."

How strange. Alice will be here and then not. I remember her in our young friendship, how she admired me, how easily led she was. We were not a good match as friends, I was too adventurous for her, she too timid for me. That doesn't excuse her jumping ship, though.

I take to walking the garden with her. She is slower than

I would have imagined possible, taking pleasure in every living thing.

"I never noticed before how exquisite bare branches are," she says with wonder. "How the laurel looks so perfectly polished."

"Oh, I have always noticed such things," I say. "Ever since childhood, beauty has affected me."

Gloria, huge now with her baby due in January, can't do enough for Alice. Henry is worried about how often she climbs the stairs to minister to her.

"It will wear you out, my darling," he says. "Just when you should be resting."

He often looks at me when he says it, as though it is my fault Gloria is putting herself to the effort. I suppose he thinks that I should be the one doing the nursing. It wouldn't help Alice if I did. I don't have the right attitude to cheer the dying. For one thing, I am disgusted by the stench that emanates from Alice's sickbed, a suspicion of ammonia, and the faint trace of bile; and, for another, I'm not good at the touching thing. Gloria is. I often catch her sitting hand in hand with Alice. She brushes Alice's hair, bathes her, helps her in the lavatory. I can't help thinking that this is what I signed up for with Bert. What was I thinking?

Things between Bert and me have changed. We hardly speak now, and although he says that he will come at Christmas, he has stopped visiting at weekends. His telephone calls have dried up, and his texts are so brief as to be abrupt. He prefers to keep in touch by email, and never asks when I will be coming home anymore. A stranger reading those emails would never guess that we are husband and wife.

They inform me of what is going on in the gallery; they offer details of who bought what and describe the latest pieces we have on show. He tells me not to rush my convalescence; for all her free and easy attitude, Helen has turned out to be brilliant at the bookkeeping side of the job, so no need for me to worry that my absence is hurting business. Hmm!

And now, Fiona, the mural painter—I can't bring myself to call her an artist—is back. She is mapping out her dreadful picture for Mother's wall, which has been skimmed with new plaster to make it smooth for her efforts.

"Not quite ready yet," she says. "A day or so more drying time should do it. It must be bone-dry, or my paints will flake."

So, for the time being she spends the waiting hours sketching outlines on a big pad while sitting on Mother's floor, sipping sweet tea from the cup of her thermos-flask. I often catch her just staring at the wall as though in a trance.

"I won't offer you any," she says, indicating the flask. "It's too sweet for most people. I'm hooked on sugar. Can't seem to do without it."

I wonder what else she might be hooked on. She offers me a piece of nougat from a pink candy-striped paper bag. She pronounces it "nugget," as though it is a chunk of gold. I can tell the nougat is the cheap kind from the covered market. I refuse politely.

"I have the addict's nature," she laughs. "Gave up cigarettes and took up sugar. Ah, well."

I notice the sugar has camped out on her thighs, which are somewhat lumpy. She actually wears dungarees and a patterned scarf around her hair, which makes her look like a

1980s member of the sisterhood. She is remarkably unaffected by the curse of her minor talent. One can only feel pity.

Two days now since the plaster dried out, but our little cartoonist has retired for the moment, suffering, she thinks, from a stomach bug. Not so. Not a bug, but the laxative I put in her flask of tea while she chatted to Alice as they shared a bag of marshmallows in the kitchen: syrup of figs with a hefty dose of sugar. Sweet enough for the aftertaste of the emetic to go unnoticed, I hoped. And that seems to have been the case.

Because of the risk to Alice, Gloria has asked her to stay away until she is completely back to normal. I hear my little sister speaking to her on the phone. "Better safe than sorry," she says in her best Mother Teresa voice.

I must admit to getting a thrill from the success of my experiment. It's exciting somehow to be the cause of the effect. It perked me up to no end, and gave me the idea to lace Henry's morning coffee with four of the Temazepam I get on prescription since the Beachy Head incident.

After breaking a couple of his pots, Henry took to his bed and slept for ten hours. Gloria thought he must have caught Fiona's bug, which set her to panicking about our ill houseguest.

"We must protect Alice," she said. "At the slightest sign of anything, Betty, don't go near her. We can't risk it."

It is fun, this taking a hand in things, but it's not enough. Slowing down their changes does not stop them. No matter what it takes, be it tears, or blood, or the crushing of bones, I must do it. My inevitable takeover of Pipits will happen. I lie in my bed at night and think of how to accomplish my ends.

The house is listening, I know, waiting to hear how I plan to save us from its intolerable owners.

Yesterday, dreading the crowds, I went to Bath to do a bit of Christmas shopping. I needed to get away from my sister, away from Alice's fading, from Henry fussing about having enough stock of his pottery for the May Park fair. House whooshed me out of the front door as though it knew I needed the break.

I broke my own rule about not drinking before six and had a double gin at the pub opposite the open marketplace. I needed it to keep going. I ate a packet of peanuts and felt a bit better. I can never stomach breakfast, and I couldn't remember when I had eaten last.

I bought Gloria some of her fig fragrance in a glass decanter, a so-called limited edition for Christmas. I balk at the thought of giving her a gift at all, but gifts are expected, so if I must, I want to outshine hers to me. Fig is her scent, and it occurred to me that even without the perfume, she would still smell sweet. I sometimes think her body is only part animal, there seems to be plant, too, musk and blossom. Another gift of the gods to their beloved. Hate for her prickles under my skin.

I used to love figs. And I would wait impatiently for the little black variety that grows in Pipits' garden to ripen. Now their fragrance brings Gloria to mind, and I cannot stomach them anymore. I will rip out the bushes in the spring, when I intend to take over the garden. I will say an infestation of root nematodes has split their roots, or that they caught fig rust.

For Henry I chose one of those chunky knitted snoods from a men's clothing shop. It looks a bit girly to me. Still I suspect it is his sort of thing. I couldn't help wondering if it was worth getting Alice a present. Despite her determination to see out Christmas, the way things are going, she may not. I decided to wait and see if willpower triumphs over mortality.

I must have had a premonition because later when I pulled into Pipits' drive, an ambulance was there loading up Alice.

"She's had a terrible day," Gloria said as our GP came bustling out of the house, bag in hand. "Ferocious nausea."

"Don't worry, they will get your pain relief sorted, Alice," he said, squeezing her hand. "It shouldn't take long. I'll inform your specialist. He will want to get you home for Christmas, I'm sure."

"I'll get back when I can," Gloria said, stepping into the ambulance to accompany Alice to the hospital.

I poked my head around the ambulance door. "Poor you," I said to Alice. "Take care." She managed a weak smile.

Henry came running out of the house with Gloria's coat on his arm.

"Here, my darling," he said. "I'll wait to hear."

———————

IT IS TWO DAYS now since Alice was taken in. She is due to come "home," as Gloria puts it, tomorrow. They have hydrated her, sorted her pain relief, found the drug that works on her nausea. I called in at the hospital with Gloria for a visit this morning. Alice, if not exactly perky, rose to the occasion: a smile, a thank-you for the grapes I brought her. The effort of it tired her, however, and we crept away when she fell asleep midsentence.

In anticipation of her homecoming, a cleaning frenzy is taking place at Pipits.

"So much illness around," Gloria fusses.

She lives in fear now of Alice catching something, of being responsible for fast-forwarding the end. She is obsessed with Alice lasting long enough to enjoy one last Christmas.

Everyone is at it like wasps to fruit. Mrs. Lemmon has been charged with giving the bathrooms a thorough going-over. Henry has taken on the vacuuming of every bit of soft furnishing, and Gloria is wearing herself out in the kitchen. They are all banned from my room.

"We'll leave it to you, Betty," Henry says. "Wouldn't want to intrude."

The whole house smells of bleach and of the vegetable broth that Gloria is making to tempt Alice, whose appetite is nonexistent. My sister's endless optimism is wearing.

They are playing their allotted parts to perfection: Gloria the warmhearted nurse, Henry the ever-patient husband, and Alice the needy, grateful friend. I don't want to be judged uncaring, so I join their tribe by helping out here and there.

Everything is out of kilter these days. We never know how Alice will be. It's either the drama of her being carted off to the hospital or long quiet periods of decline. I suspect that it's the sickly vibe in the house that has affected my own health. My insomnia, always with me to some degree, has worsened lately, so that I've taken to walking the house at night in what Mother used to call the wolf hours.

It's not all bad, though; I get to see the way the moonlight washes the halls, the way even on the darkest night, my eyes adjust to the gloom. I sense the mystery in the shadows, smell the cindery scent of the fire's embers. Falling into a reverie of the senses, I trail my hand along the sweet curve of the walls, plant a chaste kiss on the oak paneling in the hall, and shiver with the love of it. For an hour or two Pipits is mine alone.

In the soft dark that drifts toward dawn, I stand in front of the painting of the French priest that hangs in the hall, above a small Jacobean chest. My father told Mother that the chest is the oldest piece of furniture in the house, most of the others being Georgian. Like me, he had a talent for spotting the special. I wait for the light to illuminate the priest's pale face, and the mole-dark bowl of his hat. He has sad eyes, as though he has had enough of life, as though it has disappointed him. I trace my finger across his thin lips and feel his outrage.

"It's only me," I assure him in a whisper.

This morning, sleeping late after such a night, I came down to a scattering of boxes strewn around the hall.

"Your mother's things," Henry said sheepishly. "Thought we would save you the pain. And it is time, don't you think?"

No, I don't think. I start opening the boxes, ignoring Henry's heavy sighs. It is all there, carelessly jumbled together, Mother's books, her ornaments, even her perfumes and toiletries. And, around Mrs. Lemmon's neck, the trailing garland of Mother's favorite silk scarf, its soft green background spotted with white hydrangeas in full flower. Mrs. Lemmon notes my stare and slips it from her neck and hands it to me. I can smell Mother, the powdery scent of her. I've never cared for that old-lady smell, but damn Henry. Damn them all.

"We thought to give it all to charity," Henry says. "In time for Christmas, you know."

I ignore him and order Mrs. Lemmon to help me carry the boxes up to my room, while Henry flutters around uselessly.

When Pipits is mine, Mother's things will be returned to their proper place in her room. I will paint over the horrible mural, replace the wallpaper, and rehang her clothes in her wardrobe. I must resist their changes. Not for Mother's sake—I wonder these days if I will ever be able to forgive her for her last stab at me—but to keep things as they were, as they must always remain.

"I'm so sorry, Betty," Henry says, sounding impatient rather than sorry. "I had no idea it would upset you so much."

No, he has no idea. I wish they would all shut up, evaporate, blow away on the wind like the leaves of the copper beech tree he wants to cut down. I won't allow it, though. Not on my watch, Henry.

Later, Gloria knocks on my bedroom door.

"Can I come in?" she wheedles.

"If you must."

"We never meant to hurt you," she says. "We thought it was for the best. Mother wouldn't want us to make a shrine of her room, of her possessions. And we need the space for the baby's things." She laughs in an effort to lighten the mood. "There's so much of it, you wouldn't believe."

I see through everything Gloria does, know how she thinks it's her place to placate. My sister the peacemaker.

I don't laugh with her, don't even smile. I can see she is uncomfortable, but I stay silent.

"Perhaps it is too soon," she says. "You tell us when you're ready to let her things go."

I stifle the urges that threaten to overwhelm me. I could kill her, strangle her, stab her, stamp the breath out of her. How dare she tell me what Mother would want. It's not about what Mother would want. It's about Pipits being looted. Left to my thoughtless sister and her doting husband, there will be nothing left of the Stashes'. Every last bit of us will be swept away.

"It's a difficult time for us all," Gloria says. "I do understand, you know?"

She is too foolish to recognize that I'll never be ready to let go of anything that belongs to Pipits. I am not like my sister. I never let go. But I have already given more of my agenda away than I intended, so I just shrug as though it doesn't matter.

"Dinner at seven," she says with the biggest smile. The smile that implies we are back to normal, back to our happy selves.

"Henry has gone to pick up Alice from the hospital," she chirrups. "I'll heat up the broth; you never know, Betty. She might be tempted."

———

EIGHT DAYS TO GO until Christmas. Alice was returned to us looking rather better than I expected for someone who is about to withdraw from the world for good. She has a stack of presents to give out, bought and wrapped for her by Gloria. And just in case she should go before she gets the chance to bestow them herself, it is arranged that my sister will do it for her.

There are envelopes with money in them for the postman and the milkman, accompanied by thank-you notes for
their service to her over the years. You have to hand it to her,
she has found a well of courage from somewhere, and I don't
sense the slightest bit of self-pity.

"Heroes come in all forms," Henry says. "What a wonderful girl."

Alice has confided in me that she is giving Gloria the
Harry Potter book that Mother left her.

"To pass on to the baby," she says.

And, for me, there is a tiny thing wrapped in silver paper
with a dark maroon bow, my name written in glitter on the
gift tag. It is hanging high up on the fake Christmas tree.

A fake tree at Pipits! Hideous! Hideous!

Henry says it's the eco-friendly way to go. I miss the
scent of pine, the sweeping branches of a Norwegian spruce.

I will have to go into town soon to buy Alice something,
soap, perhaps, or cologne, nothing meant to last.

Henry is doing well at the May Park fair. People seem to
like his vases, and he sold out of the mugs on the first day.
Life is full of surprises.

"It's wonderful," he says. "Makes all the hard work
worthwhile."

The owner of Nest, the new design shop in town, has
put in a sizable order to be ready by Easter, and an online
catalog is going to offer his mugs to their customers. They
are coming to photograph them after Christmas.

Flushed with success, Henry says he'll be able to get a
loan now that he can put together a proper business plan.
He wants to use the money to fit out the shed as a more pro-
fessional pottery studio.

"Extend it, say, or knock it down and build a better one," he says.

He will replace his unreliable secondhand kiln, buy a sturdier painting table. It will mean workmen coming and going, noise and dust, and change, always change. He has already started hacking away at the wisteria that blankets the shed. It gobbles the light, he says.

Are they never going to stop?

———————

BERT ARRIVES ON CHRISTMAS morning with gifts for everyone.

"You're our Father Christmas," Gloria says, and hugs him. I give him a peck on the cheek, the thinnest of smiles. He hardly responds.

We open our family presents before the lunch guests arrive, Gloria's waifs and strays.

Bert has remembered Alice with a rose-pink pashmina from N. Peal's in Burlington Arcade. Alice is thrilled with it. She makes little noises of appreciation as she wraps it around her shoulders, stroking and touching it to her cheeks, which are rouged to a similar color. Gloria has helped her with her makeup: blush, a touch of eye shadow, soft pink on her lips. The colors float on her face, giving her the appearance of one of those funfair "Aunt Sally" dolls, doing little to disguise her alarming pallor.

No surprise that Bert's gifts have hit the spot with everyone. An exquisite fur hat evoking Pasternak's *Lara*, for Gloria; a Nespresso machine in readiness for Henry's new studio, and for me an indigo-blue velvet jacket lined with ivory silk. Bert has always loved giving presents, not to put you in his debt, but just for the joy of it.

Everything is wrapped in chic black-and-white-striped paper, all tied up with scarlet ribbons. There is no doubting his eye, or his generosity. Not for Bert, a tinsel-and-fake-tree Christmas; it is high style all the way for him.

He takes me aside to say we need to talk before he returns to London. He is cool with me, as though to let me know things are not repaired between us. I judge that's to be our path now, not side by side anymore, the distance between us lengthening until we lose sight of each other. I am not sad about this state of affairs. It is no surprise, after all.

"Things are on the move," he says mysteriously.

"Things?"

"Not now, Lizzie. We'll talk tomorrow. Let's enjoy today as best we can."

I watch Bert work his charm on my sister and brother-in-law and my former best friend. He helps lay the table, brings a glass of sparkling elderflower to Alice, who cannot face alcohol anymore. He sits next to her on the sofa and takes her hand.

"Here we are," he says to her. "All together."

I feel like the animal at the edge of the herd. They would hardly notice if I was picked off by some predator.

I don't know how to react to Alice's present to me. It is the most extraordinary, the most unexpected gift I have ever received. It is the key to her house.

"I'm giving it to you now," she murmurs. "I want you to have somewhere of your own near Pipits."

Everyone falls silent, waiting for my reaction as I look at the key, dumbfounded. I understand what she is saying. Get out of Pipits and leave it to Gloria and Henry to enjoy. Move over, get out of the way.

I recall the conversation between Henry and Alice that I'd overheard weeks earlier. So it was about me, after all. I am to have Alice's house so that her dear friends can be rid of me. I am the one who Henry says is never grateful. My absence will add to their happiness. It is Alice's bequest to them.

"Alice, I can't accept this," I say. "It is too much."

"Not really," she says practically. "I have to leave it to someone, and I know that you won't want to be in the way when the baby comes. Anyway, you can't refuse, it's in my will, all arranged."

I manage a smile. "It is too much," I repeat. "You really shouldn't have."

Gloria says she is thrilled for me. How wonderful of Alice, how typically generous. Henry doesn't catch my eye. Ashamed, I suppose, that he knew about it, that he conspired with Alice to see me off.

Bert hugs Alice. What a generous girl you are, he says to her. He pats me lightly on the shoulder, as though I am something broken, something with sharp edges that will cut him. "Somewhere of your own, in the village you love," he says.

Willed to her by her father, Alice's house is a poor thing. It was built in the 1950s when the planning restrictions were less rigid, a typically unambitious structure, with low ceilings, three square bedrooms, and an undistinguished sitting room. A scrubby patch of garden lies at the back of the house sporting a yellowing lawn and a small pond lined with blue plastic, the fish long gone. These days, though, with our village being so near to Bath, I suppose it would sell for a good enough sum.

They all seem so pleased for me, as though I have been given the keys to a palace. Well, it is a generous present, to be sure, but all the same, some primal part of me burns. Have they no understanding? Are they so oblivious to what House means to me, how meager Alice's gift seems in comparison? It is all just bricks and mortar to them.

We are nine for Christmas lunch. Among the guests is Fiona, the mural girl, who has just emerged from a two-year relationship and would otherwise have been alone. She arrives with a selection of market sweets in a green plastic bag spotted with fat snowmen wearing red scarves.

"How delicious," Gloria says appreciatively.

Behind mural girl, clutching a bottle of champagne, stands the octogenarian retired member of Parliament from the Old Rectory. He beams at my sister and nods to me, the thin end of his radiant smile fading fast. Long ago he shared the rectory with his wife before he bored her into bolting. I was just a girl then, but I remember the scandal, the village gossip.

He hands the bottle to Henry and kisses Gloria on the cheek.

"Angel girl," he says. "Where would we be without you?"

Twenty minutes later, a "him and him" couple rings the bell, friends of Henry's, both potters, wearing matching red Christmas hats with white bobbles. They have brought their dog, Truman, with them, a dalmatian sporting a sparkly bow on his collar. Handsome as dogs go.

"We just love Christmas," the taller one says. The shorter one nods in agreement.

We drink champagne, and there are little pastries stuffed with soft cheese that Gloria bought ready-made from Waitrose. Everyone agrees that they are delicious. Maybe they are. I don't indulge.

The turkey is huge, and has produced so much fat, it spills over the top of the pan when they take it out of the oven. Henry rushes to mop the floor with paper towel. It will take a year of washing to remove the greasy ring it has left on the flagstones. There is still a pinkish stain from the dropped summer pudding on the floor nearby. I think of yew berries, of failure.

Halfway through the meal, a deathly pale Alice has to retire to bed. She'll be fine after a rest of an hour or so, she says. She has had a lovely time, the perfect Christmas. She blows a kiss to the table, an actress acknowledging her audience. As Gloria stands to help her, she puts her arm around Alice, touches the pink pashmina to her own cheek, and says, "Mmm."

"I know," Alice says. "It's gorgeous, isn't it?"

BOXING DAY BRINGS A bitter snap. First a shower of hailstones, big as marbles, and then a bleed of snowflakes that scurry around for a minute or two before disappearing. The threatened snowfall has changed its mind, but toward the east a brouhaha threatens, black clouds spreading a sullen darkness over the village. The storm will be on us before lunch.

All I want to do is snuggle up in my room, drink a little gin, be alone, but Bert, who was up before I woke, wants a walk before he leaves. He seems nervy, on edge about something, a bit detached. I agree to the walk and get my coat. I'm interested in hearing what he meant by "things are on the move."

"Bring the key to Alice's house," he says. "I'd like to see it."

I slip it into my pocket, although I'd rather not.

He looks out of place walking in our village. His navy cashmere coat is cut too neatly for the country, his red-and-blue-print Liberty scarf, knotted just so, is too bright, too perfect. We favor the colors of the land here: browns and greens, the occasional pop of plaid.

"The thing is," he begins, and I can tell that he is anxious. There's a silence, which I break.

"Yes," I say. "The thing is?"

"Look, this is hard to say, so I'm just going to come out with it. I'm sorry not to have told you before, but I'm letting the gallery go."

"You're what?"

"Needs must, Lizzie. I've had to rethink the whole business. Things are changing fast, and we've been going downhill for some time now. Now, I know that you—"

"What the hell is going on, Bert? How has it come to this without discussing it with me?"

"Well, you haven't been around lately to see what's been happening, have you? I was going to discuss it with you at dinner on the night that you bolted. The fact is that we haven't an option. If we don't keep up, we'll go under."

"All the emails you've sent, and you didn't think to mention things were going badly? You've mentioned what we have sold, how well Helen is doing. Nothing about selling the business."

"You're not the easiest person to give bad news to," he says flatly. "In any case, it isn't about selling up as such, more like a change of direction. And I wanted to talk about it with you face-to-face."

"And here we are talking, but you seem to have made your mind up already."

"I should have spoken to you before, I know. I'm sorry. I'm speaking to you now, though."

"Oh, that makes it all right, I suppose. So come on, then, what things are changing?"

"Well, the single most important thing is that the gallery business is struggling. You can see it happening all over. It's all about art fairs now."

"Really? Art fairs? You can't be serious."

"I'm serious all right, Lizzie. Did you know that Bill Hartley went into receivership last week? Fifty years in the business, and nothing to show for it. I had lunch with him before I went to New York, he told me his story, and it rang bells. The slow decline, you know. He advised me to act fast, to get our bookings into the international fairs, change our way of doing business before we end up like him."

"Why should we end up like him?"

"Because the signs are there. Fewer sales, more borrowing, gallery costs rising year after year."

Whatever Bert says, I find it hard to believe that art fairs are the way forward. We went to one in a London park a few years ago. It was big and brash, more to do with finance than art, I thought. Now others just like it have spawned around the world. They attract new money, big money, Russian and Chinese mostly; new money that doesn't trust itself, but trails around in the wake of so-called experts who spout words like *realism* and *abstraction* and send out invoices that are works of artifice in themselves. God, the things people are talked into buying.

"That's the way you want us to go, Bert? We might as well take our wares to flea markets."

"Oh, come on, Lizzie, we will still be dealing in the art we like, and we saw some wonderful pieces in that London fair, didn't we?"

"I don't recall any wonderful pieces at that fair."

"Yes, some great paintings, and remember that pure white canvas you fell in love with."

"No."

"Remember, you said it was quite wonderful, that it would look good in the gallery behind the white desk? You were so taken with it that I would have bought it for you if it hadn't already sold. And we met some interesting people—it was exciting, wasn't it?"

"One piece I liked out of thousands, Bert. The rest was just the ugly sister."

I reminded him of the jumble sale piled high with "conceptual" bits of rag and recycled plastic that spread itself gracelessly in a bleak city of junk.

"Next you'll be suggesting we show a Magritte alongside one of Henry's mugs."

"Fat chance we'd ever get our hands on a Magritte these days."

"You know what I mean, Bert. I'm talking about quality."

"I know that you don't give art a chance," he snapped. "It's not all about names, you know. There's real undiscovered talent out there, Lizzie, open your eyes."

"And what if I disagree? Say no?"

"I'm sorry, but it's too late for that. I've sold what's left of the gallery lease to a jewelry designer. They're a big chain. We have to be out in a couple of months."

"You've what!"

I'm outraged at what's been going on behind my back. "How dare you," I stutter. "How dare you."

I see his mouth moving, but there's a thrashing sound in my head, and I can't hear his words. Then my own words pour out of me, and I see the shock on his face.

"You bastard. You bloody bastard."

I lash out at him with a fist, but he moves his head and my hand slaps the air. Will people never stop taking what is mine?

"Oh God, Lizzie, I'm sorry you are so upset," he says, visibly shaken. "I should have talked it over with you, I can see that now. But I had to move quickly. I got the offer for the remaining lease as soon as the word got out, and I couldn't turn it down. It really is for the best, you know."

"I only have your say-so for that, Bert."

"Look, I've just seen a great space in Vyner Street, one of those old warehouses in the East End. Mostly storage, but we could show there if need be. I was lucky to find it; they don't come up that often, everyone seems to be looking for spaces there. I'm going to take it."

"Oh, are you?" My voice is cold.

"I know how it must feel to you, everything moving so fast, but I see that as a good thing." His voice is soft, wheedling, as though he is talking to a child who is in the middle of a meltdown. "Come and see it. And look at this year's accounts, you'll understand why I panicked."

"No, Bert, I won't understand. Panic is never the answer."

"It could be fun, you know, traveling, being part of a new scene. A chance to start again, and not only for the business."

He is talking about us, of course, but I don't want to hear it.

"You had no right to go ahead without me."

"Right is debatable, Lizzie. You haven't been interested for a while now, and it's my business, after all. I am entitled to do what's best for it."

"I thought it was half mine, Bert."

"Not half, you own forty percent. That gives me the final say."

"I'd get half in a divorce." I want it to sound like a threat.

Bert sighs. He has a stubborn set to his lips. "Shall we go and look at Alice's house?" he says. "Talk about it out of the wind."

I turn away from him, leave him to find his own way back. I am angry and don't want to be in his company.

Fingering the key in my pocket, I head to Alice's house. My house, soon, like it or not. At least I can be alone there. It is only a few minutes from Pipits, in a grim little close, sitting alongside six other houses just like it. They are built low and square, and look out of place in our ancient village, similar to the council houses that squat at the bottom of the road that takes you out of Cold-Upton. Why things have to be built without beauty is beyond me. It would hardly add much to the cost to lengthen a window, widen a front door.

I let myself in. The hall is cold, the air a little fusty. I haven't put a foot inside the place since Alice's party all those years ago, the one where I met Henry. Gloria was meant to be there, but she was on her way back from Eurorailing with her university friends after finishing at York, and didn't make it on time. I can see now that my hopes for Henry back then were futile; her absence made no difference to the outcome, which was, if Henry is to be believed, set in his and Gloria's stars. Alice's dad was alive then, the house's interior pure seventies, an homage to brown.

Things have changed since then. Alice's love of color has transformed the place. Expecting a drab symphony of umber, I'm startled at her turquoise sofa, the soft terra-cotta pattern of the kilims. The space is Lilliputian, but there are books everywhere, shelves of them in the hall and in the sitting room, a neat pile on the floor next to an armchair. Alice has always been a reader; no surprise she chose to be a librarian.

I check the books out: a lot of classics, romantic novels of the literary kind, some self-help tomes, and a few biographies. One of Henry's failed pots works as a bookend for her collection of Virago titles, a long green line of them, Keane and Holtby and Taylor and the like. None of them first editions, none of them worth more than a few pence secondhand.

Everything is neat and tidy. Alice has finalized her affairs, left no mess to be cleared up after she is gone. She will leave no scandal, no problems, no trouble to remember her by.

I put the kettle on, drop a tea bag from a glass pot at the kettle's side into a blue and white mug, and settle myself at the small kitchen table.

I wonder if I could be happy here in this minor house. It might be made better simply by ripping out the nasty yellow pine of the kitchen cupboards, changing the cheap light fittings, and replacing the department store pictures of box-framed flower heads and passé seafront prints with actual paintings. One could hang curtains that sweep the floor rather than finish at the sill, replace the awful patterned carpet on the stairs. But, no, there is nothing to be done about the low ceilings, the meanness of the rooms; nothing to be done about the gait of the place. And prettying up this plain thing would feel like betrayal. I would be lonely here, lonely without Pipits.

By the time I get back, Alice is in the drawing room listening to music with Henry and Gloria. Not wanting it to look as though I have been checking out Alice's house, I don't tell them I have been there. They tell me that Bert has left.

"He seemed upset," Henry says. "Thinks he did something he shouldn't have."

"Good," I say. "He did."

There's a note on my bed. He is sorry I'm upset about the gallery, but the deed is done, he is going ahead with his plans. He wonders if I really care anymore. In any case, he is leaving it up to me to think about it and get in touch.

It doesn't sound like much of an apology to me.

8

ALICE DIED IN THE early hours of the morning, three days after Christmas. I had looked in on her on my way to bed the night before she went, just to say good night and to please Gloria, who had reminded me to do it, as she did every evening.

"No telling if she'll be awake half the night," she said. "It'll break up the boredom for her."

Gloria was huffing and puffing her way around the kitchen loading the dishwasher, clearing up from dinner. Her belly is big now, tight as a drum, she says.

"Refresh her water, would you, Betty? I'll be up soon."

My sister read to Alice every night, books of Alice's choosing, mostly novels, but lately those cringing celebrity "dish the dirt" scrawls.

"She's in the mood for something frivolous," Gloria says.

I often heard them laughing together, Gloria's girlish giggle, Alice's soft breathless roll. One wondered what these women, one with death in front of her, the other with birth, found to laugh about.

I knocked and entered without hearing an answer. I suppose Alice made the effort, but there was little volume left in her voice. I asked her how she was feeling and set about refreshing her water, closing her curtains, putting her slippers tidily under the bed. Gloria was in and out of Alice's room all day, yet the untidiness didn't impinge, or if it did, not enough for her to do anything about it.

"I feel sleepy," Alice replied. "But I can't seem to sleep."

She looked as she usually did, which is to say waxy and shrunken. She was propped on the pillow, her pink pashmina draped over her shoulders. I could see the little hills of her bones through it, bumping along her shoulder line. She was making an effort for Gloria, waiting with her hand resting on a book beside her on the bed. Waiting for the one she really wanted to see.

She patted the side of the bed for me to sit. I took the bedside chair instead. Her hands looked like those of an old woman's, bloodless, the veins raised, the nails faintly blue.

"You know, Betty, it makes me so happy that you will have my little house," she said breathlessly, as though continuing a conversation she'd been having in her head. "It's cozy, easy to run, and near to Gloria and Henry, lovely for all of you to be close but not on top of each other. Just perfect for weekends for you and Bert."

She didn't need to hammer the message home. I knew well enough why I had been given the house.

But really! Happy in her little house! You might as well say to someone who has just lost her alpha-male husband, "Look, here is a poorer, less interesting, less good-looking man, an inflictor of tedium, have him instead."

"Yes, you're right, it would make a good weekend place," I said eventually. "It was so kind of you, Alice."

"I guess you'll be going home to London soon," she persisted with that mulish streak so common in the meek.

I nodded but couldn't bring myself to answer right away.

If Alice hadn't been ill, I would have told her that where I lived was none of her business.

Out of kindness I let it go. I surprise myself, sometimes.

———————

GLORIA THINKS ALICE MUST have left us at around two in the morning. She had fallen asleep next to her on the bed and was woken by what she took to be a little cough.

"Her death rattle, I suppose," Henry whispers.

"Oh don't," Gloria cries.

The clock read a minute past two. Alice was not to be roused.

"At least she was not alone," Gloria says. "That comforts a little."

"We've lost our Alice," Henry says. "We'll miss that sweet girl."

The doctor has called; the undertaker is on his way to claim Alice. Pipits is good business for him. I wonder who will be next.

Alice has specified a quiet send-off, a short service, and then her burial in the churchyard alongside her mother and father. Of course, Gloria will invite the mourners back to Pipits for a funeral tea. She will revel in the rituals of death, accept the kisses and the sympathy, as though it is her loss alone. She will be thought the sweetest hostess ever. I can't wait for the sickly business of it to be over.

Gloria says she will be lonely without Alice.

"You have me," Henry says, and gathers her to him. "And soon you'll have our little Mango."

The apple has been promoted to a mango now. Gloria has burgeoned into something that looks like the human version of a mango herself; her skin is tinged olive with the ongoing sickness that lasted well beyond the first trimester; her breasts and stomach are swollen into one bloated mass.

It would be too humiliating to remind them that I am here, too.

"Oh, Alice," Gloria moans, and the tears, big opals of them, tremble on her eyelids, tip over, and stream down her cheeks.

Henry strokes her hair, hugs her tighter.

"It will be all right," he assures her. "We will never forget her. And you were the most wonderful friend to her."

Over Gloria's shoulder Henry catches my eye and gives me that pinched-up look that says *Poor darling, Gloria. We, the stronger ones, must look after her.*

I make sympathetic noises, but I know that Gloria will have forgotten Alice all too soon. She professes to miss Mother, but her shallow ditch of a memory rarely calls Mother to mind. Mother hardly gets a mention in this house these days, unless it is to complain about her so-called hoarding.

This from Gloria during the pre-Christmas cleanup.

"Believe it or not, I found a carton of cigarettes at the back of the cloakroom cupboard, and Mother gave up smoking a decade ago. Ten-year-old cigarettes. Just imagine!" She laughed.

Of course, Henry had to join in the conversation. "What with that and the moths eating every theater program and ticket for everything she ever saw, something has to be done."

"Honestly, this whole place needs a good clear-out." Gloria sighed.

Does it indeed, little sister. We'll see about that.

You have to wonder about death. Father, Mother, and now Alice gone, and the world rolling on, not giving a damn. I find myself thinking well of Alice, though. Her passage through Pipits has been calm, dignified. She will leave little of note, a trace of her energy perhaps, faint enough at the end to be absorbed without changing anything.

A LETTER HAS COME from Bert. The old-fashioned kind, through the post, on heavy white linen paper, his bold hand in black fountain-pen ink. He wants a divorce.

The missive is full of clichés. He has tried to make it work, but we haven't been on the same page for a long time now; we want different things, in business and in life; he cannot give me what I need, I deserve better than him. It hurts him to admit it, he writes, but he thinks our parting is for the best.

I rip his letter into four pieces, then Scotch-tape it back together. I am only momentarily angry, and not surprised, of course. I have sensed the break coming for some time, initiated it, really. I could have kept Bert if I had wanted to, but the truth is, I'm relieved. If it weren't for the Helen thing, I would be celebrating now. She set out to seduce Bert, swooped in to take what's mine. The very thought of the woman burns; she's nothing but a common thief.

I would like to have been the one to make the first move, to have allowed her my leftovers. I don't want to hold on to Bert, but I don't like being dictated to. And I won't stand for Helen having a say in how things progress from here. I must make sure that I get my fair share. And if it's about fairness, then I should get more than Bert. Without me, Walker and Stash would not have been a success.

I put more sweat into the gallery than Bert ever did. Truth is, he was always swanning off to lunch, wasting time with people who had no intention of buying art. And, of course, as well as the gallery, there is our apartment, with its fine furniture and paintings, no small thing. So, as long as the settlement is on my terms, as long as I don't lose out, my husband can have his divorce.

When the time comes, with Mother's money, and my share of Walker and Stash, not to mention the proceeds from our sale of the apartment, and Alice's house when it is sold, I could live in Pipits without a care.

I must get myself a good divorce lawyer. I will sort that out, go to London and see Bert, gauge whether things can be achieved with good manners and a cool eye. I won't be bullied, though, and I certainly won't allow Bert to make off with the bulk of the spoils from our marriage. I find myself excited at the thought of change.

Henry and Gloria claim to be concerned for me. But is it truly concern for me or concern for themselves? Concern that I might make my life in Cold-Upton now, concern that they will lose their lovely Bert.

"Thank goodness you have Alice's house," Henry says. "Bless her."

"Yes, bless her," I repeat, infusing my voice with kindness.

"But Bert is so lovely," Gloria says. "Are you sure that your marriage can't be repaired, Betty? I don't think divorce is what Bert really wants."

"It's for the best," I say. "At least now I won't have to

mash his food or change his soiled sheets when he's eighty." I put a lilt in my voice to make them believe that I am kidding.

"Oh, Betty, don't joke, it's Bert you're talking about."

"Yes, I know, wonderful Bert. I really don't want to discuss it, Gloria, it's between Bert and me."

"Okay, your business. I'll keep out of it, but I'm here if you want to talk."

No doubt on Gloria's advice, Henry decides that he shouldn't interfere, either, other than to say—more often than is necessary—what a good person he thinks Bert is. He is busy going over quotes for his new pottery studio and making the best mugs he can for the photo shoot. I can see now that they do have a naive sort of charm. The ones that don't work, that have tiny imperfections, hairline cracks, and color runs, end up in the house. They are mostly thick-rimmed and not that pleasant to drink from.

IF THE TRAIN FROM Bath to London didn't terminate at Paddington, it wouldn't be a disagreeable journey. The passing countryside is flat but not charmless, and first class secures a seat, at least. But Paddington station is not the best of places to arrive in the capital. I remember feeling differently as a child. There was beauty in the station then: the soaring iron-work ceiling, the fragrant flower stall, and the newsagent who knew about books. Mother would let us browse there while we waited for our train to arrive. Now, though, it is littered with sad little shops, and foul with the stink of hot dogs and kebabs. And it takes an age to get out of the place, since they have relocated the taxi stand away from the platforms and up escalators.

I am in no hurry, though. It won't do Bert any harm to wait for me. I walk outside the station to the pub I've spied on previous journeys and fortify myself with a couple of gins. It's cheap gin, you can always tell, but it does the job. In the taxi to the apartment I check on the list I've made of what I'll be looking for in the divorce settlement. Most likely Bert won't agree to it all, but that's an argument to be had between our lawyers, and I have engaged a pretty good one. It was wise, I think, to go for a woman, one with a good record in such things.

I give the taxi driver a three-pound tip for the twelve-pound journey. I've always been a good tipper. When I'm face-to-face with a stranger, I like to come off well.

I ignore the lift and take the stairs to the apartment. At the door, I struggle with the lock. For some reason, my key doesn't fit. I try a couple of times before resorting to the bell. Bert must have changed the locks. I am furious at the cheek of it.

It is Helen who opens the door. I can't say I am totally surprised, but what the hell is she doing here on the day she must know I am coming to discuss the divorce with Bert?

My first impression is that she is wearing a dressing gown, but then I realize it is a kimono of the like I have never seen before, red wool with white felt daisies sewn on its hem. Her crazy hair is piled on top of her head in a messy bun, and long earrings that look like tiny pieces of bone, mouse legs perhaps, swing from her earlobes. Her shoes have four-inch platforms of black rubber. I am put in mind of an eccentric fat geisha.

I don't show my surprise at her presence.

"Something's wrong with my key," I say.

"Oh, we've had a break-in. Had to change the locks."

There is no mistaking the way she emphasises the *we*. Adulteress, I think to myself. Such an archaic word, but satisfying somehow. By the looks of the flat, littered with her things, and the ease with which she lets me in, I can tell she has made herself at home here for quite a while. Probably before Bert's letter asking for a divorce landed in Pipits' mail. I take their haste personally, how else?

I suspected as much before I read his letter, of course, but still I find myself astonished. The attraction between this unlikely pair bewilders me. It is hard to believe Bert would give me up for Helen. Yet here she is, feet planted firmly on my expensive rug, at home in what, after all, is as much my apartment as Bert's.

I guess that I should have got the message a lot earlier than I did, what with the Spanish holiday, and the New York trip, and the way she always ignored me.

In those months when I was not around, when she thought me ill, she wheedled her way into soft old Bert's emotions. And now she stands before me, big and fat and in my sight line.

Without her on the scene, it would have taken Bert and me longer to get to where we are now; which of course is where I wanted us to be, but still, it's embarrassing that Bert chooses to replace me with her. She is so unlike his type, which I have always assumed was me, that it is hard to accept her presence, even now. I won't forgive Bert for allowing her to be here today. Perhaps he is scared to see me on his own. He has never been good with conflict.

"Really? A burglary?" I say. "What did they take?"

"Oh, obvious things. The iPad, some cash that Bert had in a drawer, and my jewelry. I expect the insurance will pay up."

"What was your jewelry doing here?"

She smiles, shrugs, says she stays over sometimes.

I don't believe there has been a burglary. She probably insisted Bert change the locks just so that I didn't catch them at it. I shudder at the thought of her and Bert in bed. There is something so utterly vulgar about her. I bet she gives wet open-mouthed kisses, keeps him warm with the heat coming off all that blubber. She'll help him out of his old-man's troubles, snore along with him, squeeze his spots, cut his toenails. Ugh. The thought is repellent.

"Where's Bert?"

"He'll be back any minute," she says. "He's just walking the dog."

"Whose dog?"

"Mine, actually." She sounds proud, as though she were speaking of a child. "I just got her. Little Molly, the sweetest thing, she's a cockapoo."

"A what?"

"A cockapoo. Half spaniel, half poodle."

"Oh," I say. "A mongrel."

Whatever the creature is, I don't like that it has the run of my apartment. Bert always wanted a dog, but he didn't push it with me. He knew I had contempt for them. Such needy creatures.

I do a quick look around for stains and chewed-up sofa covers and see a mark on the parquet floor by the window.

There's a thin smile playing around Helen's lips. She offers me a seat. In my home she offers a seat, tea, a drink.

"I'll get my own," I say.

She watches me pour a generous measure of gin, watches me take off my coat and throw it over a chair.

"Would you rather I left?" she says.

"To be honest," I say irritably, "I don't know why you are here at all."

"Well, we thought that it might be easier on all of us if we settled things together."

"But this has nothing to do with you."

"Well, in a way it does. You see, Bert is going to have to buy you out, isn't he? I'm going to put up the money for that, so we need to know what you want."

"And what do *you* want, Helen?"

"Well, I have Bert," she says impertinently, "so nothing more, really. I guess, though, that my money will make me a partner in Walker and Stash."

"Not if I won't sell my shares."

She puts her head on one side, raises her shoulders as though it hardly matters, as though I don't matter.

"Look, Lizzie, you will do whatever you will do. Bert and I, you can't break us now. The truth is that we are sorry to have hurt you, if indeed you are hurt. We tried to give each other up, even though we knew we were meant for each other. You know Bert, ever loyal. That was before he realized that you had already given up on him. Now, though, we're not going to let whatever you do spoil things for us."

"I suppose you know," I say threateningly, "I could make things impossible for you if I wanted to."

It wasn't an empty threat. I might keep my shares, turn up at their new storehouse whenever I felt like it. I could show the art I liked, generally be a nuisance to them. If I decided that was the way to go, there is nothing they could do about it.

"Why would you bother?" she asks with a sigh. "You don't care about Bert, do you? Your lack of insight into your marriage, into the kind of man Bert is, well, it's astounding. I love him, you know. You can't say the same, can you?"

She's standing, feet apart, one hand held questioningly in the air, the other on her hip, dressing me down like some third-rate teacher. I feel like I did that day on Beachy Head, anger racing through me, everything smoky red, as though I were seeing through bloodshot eyes. I want to spit venom at her, bite her, wound her. I rush toward her with a yell and find my hand fisted up, pounding into her face. My watch clunks into her skin, and I hear her gasp. She staggers a bit, her hand flying to her mouth. She has tears in her eyes, and a vibrant globule of blood trembling on her cheek.

"You bitch! You damn conniving bitch," I scream at her. "You can keep the pathetic old man. Only the dregs left, anyway." I raise my hand to hit her again, to smash into her smug face, but she turns, flies to the bathroom and locks herself in. Silly cow, silly drama-queen cow.

I grab my bag and am out the door and halfway down the stairs only to meet Bert halfway up them, leading a bundle of brown curls on a leash.

"Lizzie? You're leaving?"

I push past him. "Traitor," I hiss.

It is bloody awful how people let you down. I hit the pavement, the anger still fizzing in me. I rush on for a bit before it settles, before I notice how cold it is, so cold, I can feel it in my teeth. I've forgotten my coat, but I can't go back. I head to the train station.

I need to be back in Pipits' embrace.

9

H ENRY HAS A WORK team in, three noisy men with rolling West Country accents. Their radio thumps out a constant bass beat as they bang and drill and shout to each other over the din of it.

When they first arrived, Henry introduced them to me as though we were all about to become best friends.

"Terry, Dave, Bill," he said. "My sister-in-law, Betty."

"Elizabeth," I said.

Terry is the one in charge, a thin whippet of a man who chain-smokes cheap roll-ups and drops the butts wherever he happens to be standing.

I have asked him to pick them up, but he says they will clear the site when the building work has finished.

"Don't let it bother you, love." He smirks. "It'll get worse before it gets better."

Our old shed has been demolished. They have started digging foundations for the new pottery studio. Unless it is to be called something different now. Atelier? Henry rarely puts on airs, though, so I guess not atelier. He operates on a sort of reverse snobbery, likes to think of himself as the common man.

The air is full of dust. No sooner has one lot settled than they set about creating another. I can feel it sandpapering the back of my throat the moment I step outside the front door.

The wood from our dear old shed is piled high in the biggest of the three skips that crouch like coffins against the laurel hedge. Split and broken, the planks lie still as cut-down soldiers on the battlefield of Henry's ludicrous ambition. Before Henry barged in, it was the potting shed. In its musty interior, I learned how to pot up cuttings there, as a child, where the damp smell of compost once sweetened the air.

"Six weeks or so, and they've promised it will be finished," he crows. "If the weather holds, the foundations will go in next week. You won't know the old place."

It is to be brick built, have proper plumbing, electricity that is up to the job of running the kiln and the drying room.

"Bricks to match the house," Henry says.

I can't imagine that they will get that right. The thing will hunker down like some miserable squatter where the shed should be. I could weep.

Of course Gloria is in "lady bountiful" mode. She makes the men coffee every morning, which they drink in the kitchen, leaving behind their muddy footprints and the cold smell of cement. You wouldn't believe how much of Gloria's homemade shortbread they bolt down. It is obvious they think Gloria a star. Doesn't everyone?

With a series of little kindnesses and inquiries, she promotes the idea that she cares about them. She laughs at the builders' jokes as though she finds them hilarious, asks after their families, listens to their problems with her head on one side, like a bird feeding its young; that one's a real crowd-pleaser. Beauty and niceness. Well, not hard to be nice if you have everything you could desire, is it?

Gloria's always bleating on about how lovely people are: the workmen are lovely, the postman is lovely, her friends are lovely. She is blessed in her friends, she says. I wonder, though, does she understand friendship? She betrayed me with Henry and poached Alice, after all.

Now that Henry can't work for a bit because of the renovations to his studio, the two of them are entertaining more frequently. Henry does the cooking, not only because he enjoys it, but so as not to tire his pregnant wife, with her aching back and spreading feet.

"What do aching feet matter when I have these great boobs?" she says, pushing them up as though she is weighing them in the cups of her hands.

"Really great," Henry confirms.

Henry certainly treasures his wife. It occurs to me that people like Gloria have no idea what it feels like not to be treasured, never to get your heart's desire. There was a time when Bert treasured me, I suppose. But it doesn't count for much if it's the wrong person doing the treasuring.

The pair of them make little effort for their dinner guests. They think themselves enough of a treat for company, I expect. No silver or linen napkins, as has always been the tradition at Pipits, only Henry's hearty food, and plenty of cheap wine.

Their chatter goes on late into the evening, long after I have gone to bed. I can't sleep until the last of them has left, until the sound of the final engine has groaned its way up Cold-Upton Hill and faded into the night.

In return for their beanfeasts, Mr. and Mrs. Bygone get asked out frequently. I am rarely invited. Conventional minds don't like uneven numbers, I suppose. Not that I want to fraternize with their friends, who are mostly people I have little interest in: art teachers, other potters, a bookshop owner and his birdlike wife. People with airy-fairy beliefs, who never recovered from witnessing the tie-dye, crystal healing outbreak their mothers fell victim to.

That day when I watched Bert sleeping, when I knew that I didn't want to be with him, I realized that I didn't need anyone's friendship, either. I don't see what is to be got out of friendships. All people really want is for someone to stand by their side so that they are not alone. The thought of being alone terrifies them. I do not suffer from loneliness, however, and I rather despise people who do. It's childish to rely on other people to give your existence meaning. I will not kowtow to others, hoping for applause, or barter my independence for an ounce of popularity.

A new and annoying habit has sneaked up on me, literally sneaked up while I sleep. I am grinding my teeth. I wake each morning to the scouring sound of it. It is most disturbing. I have set my mind on stopping it. Habits are the indulgence of weak-minded people.

I blame Henry for it. His workmen crash about, banging and shouting, allowing their rubbish to blow onto the lawns and into the flower beds. I am forever picking up after them. It's so stressful, I'm surprised not to be pulling my hair out, too.

The mural is almost finished, and it's no surprise to me that it looks as ghastly as I predicted.

"Fi's so talented, isn't she," Gloria says.

Fi? Fi? I search around in my mind. Fiona, of course. I think of her as the mural girl, or Fiona, but I remember Gloria calling her Fi on Christmas Day.

"More turkey, Fi? We'll be eating it for days if you say no."

I cannot agree with Gloria that Fi is talented, so I just shrug my shoulders and raise my eyebrows. She knows I am not happy with what they have done to Mother's room.

Henry and Gloria coo over the mural, scary clown and all. They are in the throes of nesting, deciding on cots, and buggies, and car seats. It doesn't occur to them that things could go wrong. Not to them. Not to them and their little mango. They don't want to know the sex of the child; it will be mango until it's born.

"We want to be surprised," they say. "And we don't mind whether it's a boy or a girl."

Sweet, isn't it?

———————

SOMETIMES ON MY NIGHT wanders I stand in their so-called nursery and visualize how it was before Henry and Gloria started their meddling. I want to be sure when the time comes that everything will go back exactly as it was before. *Exactly* as it was before. The bed will be recovered from the outhouse, reassembled and dressed with its cream counterpane, which went so well with the soft blue curtains. I will find the same wallpaper, pink dog roses on an ivory background, have it copied if I must. I think there may be a spare roll or two in the attic. I shiver in pleasure at the idea of it, the peace I will feel when the circus nonsense has been seen off. And it won't stop there, because it is not about Mother; it is about House. I will put back everything, return everything to how it was before their changes. The walls they have smashed through will be rebuilt, their gaudy colors will be returned to the soft, time-honored ones they obliterated.

I haven't been able to think of the big plan yet. Little things, though, are going my way. Henry just can't understand why the spreadsheets he labored over with such diligence have disappeared from his computer. He is taking it in his stride, though, just as he is his broken spectacles, his missing car keys, his wallet that he is sure will turn up.

I want him to feel jinxed. But he doesn't, not yet anyway, and even if he did, it wouldn't be enough. These little things are just not enough. Not nearly enough.

"Ghosts about," I say.

"Never had you down as superstitious, Betty."

"Maybe this house is unlucky for you."

"You don't believe that, surely."

He has no idea what I believe, what I am capable of. It doesn't occur to Henry that I am a woman of passion, a woman that he will never get the better of. Henry is oblivious to the enemy he has in me.

———

MY SISTER AND HER husband have gone to Hampshire to visit Henry's widowed mother, who is crippled with arthritis and rarely travels far from home.

As soon as they left, I hugged the house to myself, running my hands lovingly along its banisters, going barefoot so that I could feel its floorboards move under my feet. I stood motionless in the still air of the hall and listened to the house murmuring. We breathed as one. I sang out loud, "They are gone, it is just us." The walls carolled the words back to me. *Just us. Just us.*

It was wonderful having Pipits to myself. I stayed up all night visiting every one of its rooms, reacquainting myself with every wall, every lovely curve, every odd little aberration, each bend and bump so familiar, so dear to me, that with every caress I felt flushed with a new optimism. I checked on my little hidey-holes, checked that my talismans were all in place. They had not been discovered, which pleased me. It just shows how little Gloria knows House. She only sees what is on the surface. Finding my charms intact cheered me up. I would save Pipits, whatever it took.

I spent a long time in the attic looking through a box of old family photographs, most of them creased and browning. My father is pictured in the early ones, sometimes holding the tufty-haired baby that is me. Mother is hardly recognizable: a trendy girl in a leather miniskirt, high boots, a long measure of dark hair tumbling over her shoulders. My parents made a fine-looking couple. Easy to see in those pictures where my sister sprang from.

In those careless three years before Gloria was born, I held center stage. Afterward, the camera sought her out, highlighted her no matter where in the family group she was placed. I was powerless to change things then. But not now, Gloria, not now.

Father's gun bag was there leaning against the attic wall, sans gun but filled with old tennis balls for some reason. I looked around for the gun but couldn't find it anywhere. Mother never liked having it in the house, so maybe she got rid of it when he died. Tsk!

His cricket gear was still in his broken sports bag. As I rummaged through it, the chalky smell of sweat wafted up, and for a moment I was again being held against the rough knit cable of his sweater. I remember Father favored me, his eldest. That would be natural, wouldn't it? I believe it was so, but memory is a ragged cloth full of holes, not to be trusted.

Dusty and neglected, the specimen cabinet that houses my grandfather's collection of bird eggs was wedged into a corner of the attic. It used to stand on the first-floor landing, where, when I successfully played sick to miss school, and didn't have Gloria to bother me, I would open its drawers and study its treasures.

My throat tightened at the sight of it. Years ago I could have reeled off the name of every egg without a pause, but now I needed the neatly typed descriptions underneath each specimen to remind me of its genesis: the clean ocean blue of the starling's, the ginger berries scattered like measles on the mistle thrush's, and, oddest of all, the red thumb-like prints, looking as though they'd been formed from blood, on the chaffinch's. There was the guillemot, the great tit, the collared dove, and the dunnock. It was a marvelous collection.

To my girlish eyes, they had shone like jewels. Dusted and placed in the right light, I am sure that they still would. I marked the cabinet in my mind. It, too, will be returned to its proper place. All in good time.

I looked around for spare rolls of the wallpaper from Mother's bedroom but saw only her mink coat buttoned over a stout tailor's dummy. It might as well have been her standing there in the flesh, plump and comfortable and holding herself a little away from me. I have always liked wearing fur, even though now people curl their lips if they catch sight of the tiniest little bit of it. I nuzzled my face into the musteline scent of the pelt before putting it on. It was surprisingly heavy. Mother never said, but it must have made her shoulders ache when she wore it.

I kept it on as I hauled the bag of Father's cricket gear and the box of photographs down the attic ladder to store in my room.

For those blessed hours, alone in Pipits, I could make believe that it was only me who inhabited the house; with Henry and Gloria out of the way, I could indulge myself in its endearing eccentricities. House was babbling with excitement, emitting its sweet sounds, filling my head with its thoughts. I put on all the downstairs lights and lit a fire in the drawing room so that we could comfortably commune there.

I suppose Mother, as she had done before, would have put Pipits' voice down to the gasps of the old boiler, or ghosts perhaps. What a dreary little woman she was. There may be ghosts wandering Pipits' halls, although I have never come across one. But if they do exist, they have no voice, and must walk different pathways than me.

I finally took to my bed just after dawn, only to be woken shortly after by the laborers arriving to set about their pillaging. I knew that I had to do something to stop them, to slow down their mutilation. With Henry and Gloria away, I had my chance.

I put out a whole packet of Maryland Cookies that I found in the pantry, and made them their midmorning coffee with a generous dose of Temazepam. I'm getting better at dispensing the right amount. Ten milligrams will calm, twenty makes you clumsy, thirty slows you down plenty. I could tell the brew didn't go down well, didn't compare favorably with Gloria's. They drank it out of politeness, and ate their way through the cookies.

To my joy, they downed their tools and left an hour or so before lunch.

"Some bug going around," Terry said with a slight slur. "Bill's cut his hand, can't concentrate, he says, and Dave feels so out of sorts, he needs to get his head down. Apologies to Henry, we'll be back soon as we can."

"Drive safe," I said.

It is dark by four o'clock now, which Henry finds draining but I find refreshing. Under shelter of the encroaching night, I set to the task of gathering up the workmen's tools, which have been hastily shoved under a tarpaulin. There are hammers and screwdrivers, plastering boards, and spades; there are screw guns and a couple of power drills. Three hard hats, one dented, lie on top of a pile of high-visibility jackets on the workbench, alongside a spirit level. It will give me a special pleasure to get rid of that.

Terry has left a tin of tobacco, cigarette papers, and the little machine that he uses to form his roll-ups in his jacket pocket. I've watched him making them, smoothing the paper, packing it with tobacco. Apart from him being a nicotine addict, I can tell that he enjoys the ritual. He always has a cigarette hanging from the corner of his mouth. Very unattractive.

All in all, I have a nice little haul. I double up some tough garden waste bags and divide the tools into them so that I can carry them without too much effort, then I back my car onto the site and stack them in the trunk. It is exhilarating work, and good to be doing something physical for once.

For the first time in a long time, I find myself hungry, so to accompany a revitalizing measure of gin and tonic, I eat a bowl of the cereal Gloria makes up with oats and raisins and the odd wrinkled prune. I pick out the prunes and throw the horrible things into the waste bin. I finish off the last inch of gin from the old bottle and fill my flask from a new one. Then I drive out to a reach of the river where a narrow bridge spans the waterway.

It is a magical place, near to home, somewhere we often used to picnic when I was a girl. Since as long as I can remember, the river has been a favorite haunt of mine. Alice and I used to walk there through the meadows when we were teenagers. We would meet up with boys from the surrounding villages who had fixed a rope swing from the branch of a huge elm tree that is dead now from the Dutch disease. I would hold on tight while Alice pushed me beyond the bank, and then hurl myself into the water. It was risky, dropping into the deepest part of the river where the tow was strongest, but I liked the thrill, and I couldn't let the boys see my fear.

Alice always held back, afraid of hurting herself. She wasn't afraid of kissing those boys, though, of letting them pull down the straps of her swimsuit as they pushed her up against a tree. I was ashamed of her and would swim around pretending not to see, congratulating myself that those low-born lads knew better than to try it on with me.

These days you never see children playing by the river. Something to do with health and safety I suppose, and the modern-day fear of child catchers.

It is a quiet spot, off the towpath, down a deep rutted lane that, at its end, knits itself up with nettles and balsam. I like that it is unchanging, that it remains as unkempt as I have always known it.

I sit in the car for a while, lights and engine off, waiting for my eyes to adjust to the dark and checking that no one is around. When I am sure I am alone, I take a deep breath and a good swallow of gin to gear me up.

I haul the bags to the center of the bridge and drop them one by one into the black water. They sink almost instantly. I am reminded of another time long ago, when I stood in the same place on this bridge. I think of the mewling squirming sack I carried here when I was nine, tiny claws ripping through it, the way it floated for a moment or two before sinking. It must still be down there, wedged in the silt somewhere. I've heard that bodies dumped in the river never make it out to sea.

How quickly Gloria recovered back then from the loss of her pet: a cuddle from Mother, an extra kiss at bedtime, and me being made to help her finish her puzzle, to take her mind off her kitty. I didn't object at the time. I was the secret winner of the day, after all, a payback to my sister for being the chosen one, for not being aware that she was the chosen one, for her creamy skin, her childish lisp, for bloody well everything about her.

People like Gloria think themselves guiltless, but they push you to do things that you wouldn't normally think of doing; they glide along in their careless way through their fairy-tale lives, gobbling up the best bits in life, the biggest portions of everything worth having. Gloria has guzzled the lot: my best friend, my lover, our mother. And Pipits. Damn her to hell.

With the bags safely dumped, I sit on the riverbank,

drinking my gin and watching the swollen river push downstream. The dark hushes the clamor in my head, releases the pressure that has been building in me ever since Henry's workmen set about their destruction.

A light breath of wind stirs the grasses at the water's edge. I feel it cool on my face, the gentlest of touches. I listen to the slurp of the river licking its banks, to the distant hoot of an owl, and feel satisfied with the day's work. Above me a single star pulses in the night sky, on, off, on, off. The dark deepens, and suddenly, as though the star has been blinking a warning, the rain arrives.

IT WILL BE AT least a week before they can replace the tools, they say. They ask me if I'm sure I didn't hear anything, and look bemused when I say, No, nothing, not the smallest sound.

Dave is the angriest. Apparently his tools were originally his father's; they are irreplaceable, he says. What rubbish, hammers and screwdrivers are hardly things to grow attached to. Who would have thought that an oaf like Dave had a sentimental streak?

"He's heartbroken," Terry informs me.

Terry says that since they left everything easily accessible, it is unlikely the insurance will pay up. They hadn't been themselves at all yesterday, they agree, shaking their heads, some bug had got them all.

"Down like ninepins," Terry moans. "A twelve-hour thing, I guess. We all slept like babies."

"Nothing like a good night's sleep to put things right," I say.

"We'll be more careful in future," he says. "The police say the thieves will leave it for a while, then most likely come back when they think we have forgotten about it. They won't get easy pickings next time."

"Ah well, easy to be wise after the event," I say with a sigh.

Terry narrows his eyes and gives me a quizzical look. "Yeah, I guess," he says.

I wasn't going to intrude on Henry's visit to his mother with the news, but Terry decided to do so. Apparently, Henry groaned at the thought of the delay. The interest on the bank loan is mounting.

"What kind of people would do such a thing?" he agonized to me over the phone later, as though he doesn't live in a world where things are being stolen all the time, as though in some way he is entitled to escape what everyone else has to put up with.

"These things happen," I say.

I can't summon any sympathy for Henry. I know what I'm doing is for the right reasons. He and Gloria must not be allowed to go on smashing, and smoothing, Pipits.

Gloria took the phone from Henry to check on me, make sure I was okay. "Thank goodness he—they—didn't come into the house," she said. "That would have been awful with you all alone."

"Yes, I would have been no match for the brutes," I said.

———————

THE HOUSE IS A bit down today. Its walls are clammy to the touch, its voice is sluggish, the air tearful. No doubt it has picked up on the gloomy mood that seems to have overtaken everyone. Gloria is not feeling well. Just a general malaise, she says.

"And Alice leaving us," she simpers. "It comes out of the blue and hits me sometimes."

"It is the same for me," I say.

Henry is worried about money. He has had to pay for new tools, the sum is to be taken off the final works invoice, but the studio build is running late due to the tool situation—and to the weather, which has turned bloody awful.

"You wouldn't believe what a week's delay costs," he groans.

Stirred by the theft, he has had an alarm fitted in the house. It had to be done, he says, but cost-wise, the timing is bad.

The rain has hardly stopped since it came on the night that I sat in my car by the river. The bottom of the village has flooded and turned the dip in the road into a lake. A couple of pioneer swans have claimed it.

Due to the flood, we are only able to leave and enter the village by the long way, up the hill and through the narrow road that winds through the woods. It puts five miles each way, on the journey in and out, for Terry and his boys.

He's moaning about the extra cost of petrol.

"Near enough sixty miles a week. I'll have to claim for it," he warns Henry.

And now, overnight, the rain, which turned first to sleet, has given way to a snowstorm that has muffled all of Cold-Upton. We woke to its fall, big downy flakes the size of a dog's paw. A dazzling white carpet morphs the roads and fields into one, so that, without the usual boundaries to guide, I am put a little off balance. It's tempting to wear sunglasses against the white glare. Two days now and still it comes.

"It's a whiteout," Henry complains.

"But rather lovely," Gloria says.

It is so cold that the floodwaters have frozen, and now the road looks silvery and quite beautiful. I saw children sliding over the rink of it this morning on their way to school. The swans have returned to the river.

Terry phoned to say the work will have to stop until the snow clears and things get back to normal. Impossible conditions to work in, he says. The news of the holdup has made me quite cheerful. It was worth throwing a wrench into their horrible works.

I helped Henry clear the snow from the drive this morning so that the postman and Mrs. Lemmon can get up to the house and he can get down to the road to take Gloria for her checkup. Henry is not afraid of work; it's one of his good points I suppose. We shoveled until our faces turned pink and our lungs began to burn. The exercise put us both in better spirits.

So far the pregnancy is going well; the hospital visit is just routine. Apparently, the baby is the right size, and Gloria is only marginally over her preferred weight at this late stage. She looks huge to me. Meanwhile, Henry says she is more beautiful than ever, and she gives him that *Oh you* smile.

Their New Year's resolution is to have more children after this one.

"Not right away, of course, but we want a clutch," Gloria simpers. Her pronouncement makes me feel quite desperate. I can't help thinking "heir and spare."

"We'll be all afternoon," Henry calls as I wave them away. "The hospital, first, and then flowers to Alice's grave, on the way back."

I often walk past Alice's grave myself. Not yet with a headstone, the earth needs time to settle, we are told. The sod on her patch is sparse, littered with never-ending gifts from her friends, of cut flowers lying in nasty cellophane wrap. They get shuffled by the wind, blown on to neighboring graves. I find the paraphernalia of death distasteful: those horrid garage flowers, and the little ornaments, and revolting tiny vases shaped like urns. The human blot of it brings on nausea. A simple carpet of grass should be enough.

10

I HAVE BEEN GOING THROUGH the family effects I found among the things of Mother's that Henry wanted to get rid of. There's a box secured with a blue ribbon, and in Mother's hand, *precious* written on the lid.

In it are bundled dozens of school reports, both mine and Gloria's; a velvet Alice headband Gloria loved so much that she wore it clamped in her hair for a year; a christening dress, white satin with pearl buttons, mine first, then Gloria's, the right way round for a change.

There are letters, too, mostly Father's to Mother, which he wrote to her in the early 1960s, when they were courting. In one of them, which he sent to her after he'd proposed, he addressed what clearly had been some concerns on her part. She was hesitating, if not exactly reluctant: they hadn't known each other long, she thought she would like to travel, she longed to see more of the world before marriage.

"We rarely regret the things we do," he'd written. *"Only the things we do not. Marry me, and we will see the world together."*

The words flashed at me as though lit by neon. It is as if Father is speaking directly to me. Otherwise, why did I open that letter first, the very one with just the advice I needed? I must stop hesitating, get on with the doing.

I am finally confronting the truth of it. Of course it is

Henry who must go. It is the only thing that makes sense. It cannot be both Gloria and Henry, because the child they would leave behind them might have a claim to Pipits. If it is just Henry who goes, it won't be hard to talk Gloria into selling Pipits to me.

I can't imagine why I didn't think of it before, instead of tinkering around with what could only be temporary setbacks. I can hardly wait. The thought of the Bygones finally seen off washes through me. Its wake is sweet.

No doubt this has been in my subconscious all along. The summer pudding episode was the germinating seed, and now it has sprung green shoots. It's a big thing to contemplate. Strangely, though, the thought has a surprisingly familiar feel. Haven't we all occasionally indulged the idea that the absence of someone will solve what seems insoluble?

With Henry out of the picture, Gloria's meager income won't allow her to keep the place going. With a baby to look after, selling will be the only practical option open to her. She could have Alice's house as part of the deal, so much more suitable for her than Pipits. I have no doubt that she would marry again. A decent pause for a widow's grief before the suitors come calling. Happiness, her default position, would be resumed before she knows it.

I need to think it out, take time to get it right. But it won't be an easy thing to achieve. It must look like an accident. Traceable poison would be foolish. And what poison that I could get my hands on wouldn't be traceable? The web informs me that aconite shows only asphyxia as a postmortem sign. Apparently, the emperor Claudius was dispatched by his wife Agrippina, who served the leaves to him in a bowl of mushrooms. Clever Agrippina. I like the idea of it—and I could easily get my hands on the purple shrouded aconite—but even one sign is too many in these enlightened times.

Whatever I choose must look accidental; there can be no disposing of the body, no need for an alibi. A method that doesn't require my presence is ideal. Henry's horrid building site comes to mind. All those glass panels lying around, the drills, the cement mixer. There must be something there, surely?

I wait impatiently for the right thought to take form. I study Henry carefully these days, note that he is a man of habit, breakfast at pretty much the same time each day, lunch, too. I see that he likes to finish one job before starting the next, that he is easily distracted. Once or twice he has caught me out in my inspection and given me a thin unsettling smile. Does he sense what I am about? Probably not; he has no idea how much I dislike him, and he is not particularly intuitive.

I cannot allow myself the smallest nod toward mercy. He is what stands between me and Pipits. I want him gone.

BERT, PROBABLY FOR SOME selfish reason, is suddenly in a hurry. He has requested a meeting between us and our lawyers. It seems he wants to be done with our marriage without a big legal battle.

My lawyer, Poppy Jordan, says she understands that he is prepared to be generous, to go beyond what a court is likely to decide.

I know Bert well enough to know he is rattled. He hates things hanging over his head, can't hack being anyone's enemy. I was prepared to wait it out, to work at getting what I want from the now dead marriage; but here we are, only late January, and he has caved.

Clearly he cannot bear the idea of court or of endless meetings where he knows I will not be easy to deal with. And why should I be? Neither Bert nor Helen has the right to expect an easy ride from me.

We meet up in Poppy Jordan's West End office. Bert has lost weight, lost that high color he had when his drinking kept up with mine. He looks quite healthy, in fact, as though he could last another decade at least.

Poppy's office is small, so we have the meeting in her firm's conference room. Bert sits in the chair opposite mine, a solid table between us. He is gazing over my shoulder through the window into the distance, as though what is going on in the room has nothing to do with him.

He has offered to buy me out of the business for five percent above the market value. On top of that, I can have the apartment, no strings attached. He will just walk away, move out as soon as I agree to the deal he's offered. I don't ask to where.

"It is most unusual not to split the value of the joint property," his lawyer says, frowning a little. "It is more than generous, and something I advised my client against doing."

I can have it all: the furniture, the paintings, everything. The only thing Bert wants is the small oil of a barrel of cranberries that sits on a little easel in his study. It has no signature and was the first piece of art that he bought for himself. He is sentimental about it. There is something that touches his heart about an artist with such talent who has gone unrecognized. It is a rather fine little piece, but without the right provenance, its worth most likely is only a couple hundred. I suppose he can have it; I can't be bothered to haggle.

The deal he is offering seems too good to be true. I am suspicious.

"What do you want from me?" I ask.

"Well," his lawyer begins.

"Not you," I say, turning to Bert. "You tell me what you want."

A short silence, as though he is thinking how to put it. Then, "Only that you agree, and that it is done quickly. I don't want a fight."

"What's the hurry?"

"Do you really want to drag this through the courts, Lizzie, and spend a fortune doing so, only to get less than I am offering now?"

I suspect a larger motive at work. "Mm, but still, what's the hurry? Why didn't you wait to see what I would have settled for?"

"The truth, Lizzie?"

"Of course the truth."

"I don't want to spend time fighting you. I want to marry Helen as soon as possible and be happy. You may not believe it, but I'd like you to be happy, too."

"Why should I believe anything you say? You were happy enough before your girlfriend came along. Don't deny it."

"You're wrong about that, Lizzie. It's love that makes for happiness. I was content to think that we had something near it, and perhaps we did at first. Not now, though, not for quite a while. There's hardly even affection left on your part."

"Or on yours."

"Well, perhaps when we are through this, it will come back."

He sounds stern, full of some new drive, distanced from me, letting me know I have lost my power over him. I hear the tone of Helen's voice in his usually gentler one. I guess he is still upset about my having slapped her. The smallest bit of a stew upsets Bert, and I bet that Helen made the most of it, instilled some outrage that's led him to this.

"No need to fight, Lizzie. You must have whatever you want," he says in a softer voice. "Let's be done with it."

I wonder if I am imagining that Bert is scared of me, scared of what I would do if he were to fight me for an equal share of our assets. Helen probably told him what I said about making things difficult for them.

I request a private chat with Poppy. Bert and his lawyer obligingly go to wait in the reception area of her office. I'm not impressed with Bert's lawyer; he is not pushing me on Bert's behalf, and he can't take his eyes off Poppy, who I realize suddenly is a very good-looking woman.

"It's more than a fair deal," Poppy says. "I strongly advise you take it, Mrs. Walker. I'm pretty sure you would get less if you took it to court."

"Mm."

I remind her that I prefer these days to be called Miss Stash. She smiles and apologizes.

She may be right about the court thing, but I think I could do better. I know Bert. I believe him when he says he wants things over and done with. He wants to avoid trouble, to write me off. He won't settle until everything is tidied up and behind him. Cash won't be a problem, not now that he is as one with Miss Moneybags. Whatever hole is left in his finances after his payout to me, she will pick up the slack. When you think about it, it's pretty insulting; any lengths to be rid of Betty Stash, worth it at any price.

I tell Poppy what I intend to ask for and she shrugs and gives me a doubting look. She buzzes her reception to call Bert and his lawyer back, and they return to the conference room carrying mugs of coffee.

"Great coffee," Bert's lawyer says to Poppy. "You must tell us what blend you use."

She smiles at him flirtatiously, puts her head to one side, and runs her hands through her hair. "Oh, it's nothing special," she says.

I'm impatient to get on with things. We seat ourselves in the same places again. Bert seems on alert now, shoulders forward, waiting to hear what I have decided.

"I accept the five percent over value offered," I say, and note the relief on his face. "But I want ten thousand on top of that, and all my legal expenses paid."

Bert's lawyer sucks his breath in noisily. He directs a grimace across the table to Poppy.

"Plus, until we sign and it's done with, I should have half of the profits from the business."

Bert blinks, but he doesn't look surprised. His lawyer's eyes, though, have widened, and his mouth has slackened in astonishment.

"I think that's unreasonable," he falters. "No court would give you anywhere near that percentage of the joint assets. Your husband has been more than—"

"It's a deal," Bert cuts in. He stretches his arm across the table and offers me his hand. "Shake on it?"

I do, but for reasons I don't like to think about, it doesn't feel good. Thoughts of old betrayals surface. The sour musk of them rises in my throat. I've had my way, but somehow once again in life I've been seen off.

"I'm glad it's settled," Bert says to me. "When you get to my age, you understand what it takes to make you happy. You can't hang around hoping it will happen. Whatever it costs, you have to go for it with everything you've got."

"I intend to," I say. "That's good advice."

"I wish you luck, Lizzie. No hard feelings?"

"None," I say, swallowing a gob of hot spit. "Oh, and one other thing."

"Yes."

"Call the business what you like, but please remove 'Stash' from its title."

"Consider it done."

Bert knew he was never going to get away with the biggest slice of our marriage cake, but notwithstanding the money I've cost him, I can tell that he and Helen will be celebrating later. I hadn't thought of it before, but suddenly I know that Bert's future is set fair. Despite Helen's ridiculous clothes, her layers of fat, despite her appalling taste in art, she is a Beloved. Bert will be marrying a Beloved!

11

HENRY HAS ASKED ME to move out. So much for: "It is your home as much as ours."

"Since Alice died," he says, "what with the sadness, and then the robbery, and the building work being held up, and now your troubles with Bert, well, we haven't been concentrating on the right things. We need some quiet time to ourselves to prepare for the coming of Mango."

He says it half-jokingly, making it sound as if they must prepare for the coming of a messiah.

"You understand, don't you?" he says. "Gloria has had a hard time of it. First her mother, then Alice."

"It's the same for me," I blurt out. "My mother, too, and don't forget that Alice was my friend first, and now the divorce."

He pats my shoulder, gives a little wince as though he's the one in pain. "Of course, of course," he says, his voice sticky with sympathy.

"But really, Betty, it's the best thing for us all," he insists. "Baby is almost here, and there will be upheaval, mess, noise; you won't like it."

Henry's insistence is a new thing. He's usually so accommodating. He needs to cosset Gloria, he says. And besides—and here his eyes slink from mine—they have rarely been alone in their marriage. They need some time to be together, just the two of them, before they become three.

I don't see how I am going to get out of agreeing to leave. Henry suggests that I move into Alice's house so that I can be nearby. Alice's house! A legacy to them, held in my name.

"We can keep an eye on you, and you on us. And you'll be near the baby when it comes. You'll like that, won't you?"

I don't answer at first. I'm finding it hard to breathe. However Henry puts it, they're chucking me out. He has elected himself master of the house, wife protector.

I have Alice's house and will soon have the London apartment, so no excuse that I'll need time to find somewhere to live. I am expected to pack a bag and go.

"So lovely that you'll be living in the village," Henry says. "And you'll be an aunt. We're making you an aunt." It sounds like a boast.

When Gloria appears, I can see that she is anxious. Her eyes dart about the room, she's doing her hopping thing, and her lips are swollen where she has been biting them.

"You don't mind, Betty, do you? I have to think of what Henry needs, too."

"Why should I mind, Gloria? It is your house, isn't it? Mother left it to you, after all."

"Oh, you do mind. I'm so sorry."

I shake my head and tell her not to give it a thought. Of course I understand. I drive a sword through my spoiled little sister's heart and twist and twist the blade. Such a pleasing image.

I return her nervous smile with a broad, untroubled one. I project composure, I tune my voice to calm, to obliging.

She accepts my words with relief. No checking beneath

the surface, no reassuring herself that I am actually okay with it. I sense one of my migraines on the way.

I tell myself I haven't lost the war, I am only retreating to regroup. I will suffer the temporary setback and stick to my plan. And now at least there is no need to feel pity for Henry. I'm reminded of how ruthless his true nature is.

I MOVE INTO ALICE'S house with no intention of changing anything. I will put up with her awful pictures, her polyester sheets, the cheap pine wardrobes that line her bedroom walls. I'll leave it to Gloria to knock through, rip up the floors, and paint dim-witted scenes on the walls. When Henry's gone, she will need a project. She can set about altering things with her usual passion.

Mrs. Lemmon has refused to clean for me here.

"What with Mrs. Bygone's work," she whines, "and Pipits being such a big house, I hardly have time for anything else."

I don't believe her. We get on well enough knowing our places, and I know she could do with the extra money. I don't dislike her, not at all. I hardly ever speak to her, so she can't hold much against me.

Her refusal comes about because she knows she can't fool me as she does Gloria. I've noticed how she moves picture frames, and ornaments on mantels, without really cleaning them. The old trick of placing things differently to suggest she has been there with her duster and polish. She has chosen her camp, and it is Gloria's. I don't intend to keep her on when I have Pipits. I am looking forward to taking care of House myself.

12

I'VE MADE MY DECISION. I am going for the simple option of following in Agrippina's footsteps. I've hurt my head thinking about more complicated scenarios: exploding kilns, cutting the brakes on Henry's car, even that plan from the movie *Strangers on a Train*. But I don't have the skill to fix the kiln, or to cut the brakes, and the train scheme is too complicated. One would need to find the right stranger with a similar problem, and then to trust her. Highly unlikely. Simple is best.

I dismissed the idea of poison at first because it could be detected, but what does that matter if it looks like Henry has accidentally poisoned himself?

Of course, I am not thinking of aconite, but of mushrooms of the mephitic variety. It is the perfect solution, particularly as Gloria hates fungi and won't be partaking. I rather fancy seeing her as the grieving widow; to observe her in defeat will be a rare and satisfying sight.

The only drawback is that it will mean waiting until autumn, when the spores poke through the dank run of earth where meadow meets wood. Until then I will have to suffer the frustration of dawdling through spring and summer. But I am used to waiting, biding my time.

Planning the details will be important. I will only get

one shot at it. Nobody ever poisons himself twice with mushrooms. Twice would look suspicious.

I have bought a book on fungi, beautiful illustrations and very clear. Reading it, I wonder how anyone can summon the courage to pick and eat them at all. Russian roulette comes to mind. I wonder how I ever trusted Henry to know good from bad when I ate the mushrooms he gathered. The difference between life and death can be as little as the depth of a cap, a pinkish tinge on the gills, hardly noticeable to the naked eye. A shade lighter or darker can mean the difference between the here and now or the hereafter.

When Henry cooks whatever he is going to cook with his first crop of mushrooms, usually his favorite risotto, he will, as far as anyone can tell, have poisoned himself. Whichever way you look at it, providing I proceed with caution, providing I get the amount right, it is rather a neat plan. No worries about leaving fingerprints, or traces of blood, no concerns that one has left a hair or a tiny thread of clothing at the scene, no question of motive or alibi; such seminal things in these days of DNA testing. It will simply be a tragic case of bad luck and ignorance.

I will study my subject, be an eager student. Meanwhile, I suppose things will progress as expected; the baby will arrive soon, and a great fuss will be made, no doubt. Henry will claim that it has the look of his grandfather, or uncle, or suchlike. Gloria will say she sees something of Mother in it. Parents seem to find pleasure in such things, as though they need proof that the child is really theirs and not some changeling, planted to make mischief.

When the time comes for Henry to leave us, I will take my proper place as Gloria's older sister. I will organize everything, make the decisions she will be too preoccupied with grief and baby to make herself. A simple call to Looton's Funeral Home should do it.

———

IT HAS BEEN A difficult time weather-wise; we've hardly seen the sun, and the storms keep coming. Gloria is due to give birth any day now. Henry is clucking around her like a mother hen; he cooks for her and makes her the ginger and lemon tea that helps with her nausea, which although ongoing, has lessened a little over the past few weeks. He would have the baby for her if he could.

Our turkey oak at Pipits, with its heavy mantle of leaves, stoically battles the unusually strong winds, but its neighbor the copper beech has lost two limbs, ripped from the trunk by a freakish storm. The wounds are deep, and I fear that the damage it has suffered will only reinforce Henry's view that the dear old tree must come down.

Meanwhile, his studio is finally finished. I was right about the bricks, which are the undistinguished red of all modern bricks. I knew Henry wasn't to be trusted, even though he said he understood when I pointed out that they should match the house, should be that soft rose color that suggests warmth and has a powdery depth.

"They are not too different," he insists. "Besides, they'll merge over time. The weather will do it for us." And he calls himself an artist.

Sometimes, when I cannot bear another day holed up in Alice's mean little house, where I am plagued by its low ceilings and the one narrow bathroom where there isn't even a windowsill to put a pot plant on, I take myself off to London, to the apartment that is mine alone, now that Bert, waiting for the divorce to go through, is cozied up somewhere in the city with Helen. Jack Sprat and wife licking the platter clean.

It's a comfortable apartment, a good-enough refuge. The rooms are spacious, the light not bad. I'm merely camping out, though, marking time. I cannot see myself wanting to leave Cold-Upton even for a day when House is mine. For all that I manage well enough in the city, I'm a country girl at heart, and long-distance relationships rarely work.

I bring bread and butter and cheese with me from Cold-Upton's shop and throw most of it away when I leave. My appetite is small, and I would not want to get fat like Bert's Helen. I do not approve of fat. It gives too much of one's character away, it highlights greed and a lack of control, not to mention self-esteem. Hard to keep your nature private when, like a penitent, you must carry your flaws around with you, in full view of the world.

There are no practical shops near my apartment in Mayfair. You cannot buy much in the way of food or get your shoes mended or your clothes cleaned. There is nowhere to buy a bottle of gin. It is mostly restaurants and designer clothes shops now. There are the bling jewelers, of course, the kind where the diamonds in the windows are so huge, so brilliant that you have to stop and look, the kind where you ring a bell and they decide whether to let you in or not. I've never put their bells to the test. I won't have some shopgirl denying me admission. In any case, if it were not for their worth, you might as well wear glass as diamonds. Give me the velvet depth of a ruby any day, the cool heart of a sapphire.

When I first met Bert, he told me that at one time Mayfair residents spoke of their postcode as the Village. That was before the conglomerates moved in, bought out the florists and the cigar shop, swept away the family-run café and the little outlets where you could have clothes altered and watches repaired.

The newly modernized neighborhood hardly affects me, though. I don't go out much, preferring to stay in the flat, reading or listening to the radio. Occasionally I'll visit a museum, the Natural History, or the V&A. I steer clear of the art galleries, unless one is showcasing an irresistible major exhibition. I don't want to think too much about that other life, which seemed so important to me in my gallery days. I am not good at things lost.

13

I T'S A BOY, BORN with the light at 6 a.m.

"Monday's Child," Gloria chants from the old poem.

"Fair of face," I finish the line for her.

He is to be called Noah. And his parents are beside themselves with pride. Henry, fizzing with excitement, brought his precious cargo of two home from the hospital, one swaddled in a white cot sheet, the other in her frayed-at-the-sleeves winter coat. And now the house is full of visitors come to praise the infant.

It seems that both birth and death attract spectators. There are flowers on every surface, congratulation cards illustrated with storks and cradles, and the words "It's a Boy," boldly printed as if to bring the fact to the parents' attention, as though they are unaware of their newborn's sex.

Henry has presented Gloria with a string of creamy pearls.

"For giving him Noah," Gloria told me, as though it had been an immaculate conception. I pictured her delight as she fingered the rope of them, the kiss that followed, and the two of them, arms around each other, gazing in awe at their tiny creation.

I have Mother's pearls; now Gloria has Henry's. My brother-in-law's Beloved must not be allowed to miss out on anything. I suspect she will get more pleasure out of hers than I do mine.

It is hard to know how to behave around babies. They are held out to you as though you will instantly see, and imitate, what mummy and daddy do, as though the squashed-up little package is the very essence of wonderment. You are expected to coo over the infant with love-light in your eyes. But I have to say that Noah came out looking smooth and angelic, not at all like the more usual gargoyle-type creature, and prettier than those solemn-faced Botticelli cherubs Bert gets all mawkish about.

I like it that Noah sleeps a lot during the day, and that Gloria and Henry are tired out because their nights are so fractured with his demands. Noah is on my side, no doubt: we already have an understanding of how things should be. He's a proper little Napoleon, determined to have his own way.

I walk to Pipits every afternoon on the pretext of visiting him. I am only ever at peace these days when I'm in the presence of House, even though I have to drool over Noah and agree with Gloria that he smells divine.

"Oh, that baby smell," she sighs, sniffing his head as though it is a drug she can't get enough of. "Better than honeysuckle, better than any perfume you could name."

In truth, Noah smells of sour milk and a sweet sort of urine. A primitive scent, hardly a perfumer's brew.

I always go to my bedroom on the pretense of needing to collect something I've left there. It annoys Henry. Mainly, I think, because it reminds him that I haven't completely moved out. I talk about my departure as a temporary thing. He can hardly say outright that it is for good, that they want

Pipits just for themselves. That wouldn't be nice, would it? He knows, too, that facing me down would upset Gloria. And she is so hormonal that she weeps at the slightest thing. He won't want to risk a meltdown on her part. Well, all the better for me.

Work in the house came to a standstill when Gloria went into labor. She was planning to have the landing bookcases taken out to make space for a sofa.

"It gets the sun there," she said. "It would be the perfect place to sit and feed baby. Unlikely that we'll ever read any of those dusty old books, anyway."

Now, though, she says she hasn't the energy to think about anything but Noah. Small mercies.

"Once we are in a routine with baby," she promises, "we'll forge ahead with our plans."

She doesn't say it, but I'm pretty sure that my bedroom is included in the plans for "forging ahead."

As I predicted, the baby has a big footfall. It is extraordinary how many things one tiny infant needs. There are nappies and bottles, and rubber nipples and bibs, and things that Gloria calls onesies that Noah spits up on so that they must be changed a dozen times a day. His clothes must be laundered with a special washing powder so that his skin won't be irritated. There are pots of Vaseline and a particularly off-putting thick grayish cream for the rash he gets from not being changed often enough. Despite its promises and much to Gloria's distress, Noah's little bottom is often red no matter how much of the stuff she slathers on.

Ugly bits of plastic equipment sit beside the sink now: a sterilizer to banish bugs from anything that goes into Noah's mouth and a tortuous-looking instrument that apparently pumps milk from my sister's bounteous breasts.

"So that I can feed him and bond," Henry says brightly.

"Oh, bond," I quip. "So that he knows that you are his father."

"Well, not so much that. More . . ." Henry begins, but I have tuned out.

A baby carriage they call a buggy is parked in the hall, its handle draped with the pashmina that Bert gave Alice for Christmas. Gloria often swaths Noah in it.

"Alice would have loved to see him all wrapped up so cozy," she says with a soft intake of breath. Her voice still shakes a little when she speaks of Alice.

"But it's pink," I say. "Pink for a girl."

"Yes, I know, but nothing to be done about that. Noah doesn't mind, do you, my darling?"

"Oh, well, if Noah doesn't mind."

I recall the last time that I saw Alice wearing that pashmina. It was the night of her death. I remember the pitiful way it fell on her shoulders, as if it might slip from the wasted peg of her and crumple onto the sheets. I thought the soft flush of rose against the white pillow rather striking. I miss Alice myself . . . sometimes. I can't imagine why, though, unless it is because she was so easy to impress, unless because if she were still here, I would not have to live in her house.

In these all-about-baby days, there is dirty laundry parked on every available surface, bottles bobbing about in a sterilizer, places around the house that Gloria and Henry refer to as "changing stations," piled high with assorted potions and wipes and baby powder. Noah lies on the floor on a brightly colored padded thing with an arch of mobiles over it. An audience of soft toys he is far too young to appreciate tumble around him. There is always music in the background to soothe him, something Gloria calls "baby Mozart." Honestly!

"He's aware of everything," Gloria says. "Quite the cleverest little boy, aren't you, Noah?"

TIME SEEMS TO HAVE stilled. Waiting is never easy. It is getting harder to keep my cool with Henry and Gloria. Their noisy, messy lives drain the true life out of Pipits.

Like a sick patient hoping for recovery, the house has gone into hushed mode. I have to listen hard to hear its voice these days. Mostly it is a low, ongoing grumble, a muted complaint that nicks at my nerves. Just wait, I say when I know no one is around. Be patient. I am finding it hard to be patient myself, though.

And then, suddenly, as though I haven't been watching, haven't been ticking the days off on my mental calendar, Noah is three months old, and summer is in full swing. Fly away, honeybee; fly away, summer.

I have taken over Mother's place in Pipits' garden. Gloria is fully engaged in the happy land of motherhood, and horticulture has never been Henry's thing. Time in the garden helps to keep my spirits up.

The Albertine roses are the stars of the show at the moment, quite spectacular, the best I have ever seen them. Their flowers scent the air as they trail over the arch that leads into the walled garden. There is little in my nature I believe I have inherited from Mother, except perhaps for her green thumb. Under my care everything is lush and flourishing.

Blue ceanothus spill down the steps to the summerhouse, contrasting so beautifully with the white buddleia, an elegant coupling that didn't happen by chance. Nature will have its way, but a good gardener leaves little to chance when planting out.

I am particularly fond of blue in the garden, iris and agapanthus, and those wonderful geraniums with their open cuplike flowers that are nothing like the pot-bound ones. Occasionally, a Holly Blue butterfly alights on them, fluttering its papery wings, blue on blue, a sight to sting the heart.

I sit on the old bench near to the hawthorn, which is in flower, and think about where I am in my life. Bert is gone; I have been exiled by my own family to Alice's wretched house, maddened by the slow burn of injustice that licks at me and the ever-widening hole somewhere in the region of my stomach where Pipits is missing. I can think of little else but filling it.

Not surprising, then, that I have to drug myself to sleep these days, two Temazepam along with increasing amounts of gin. I am at a simmer, waiting to come to the boil, waiting to be rid of Henry. My fingers itch to be picking fungi.

Sometimes at night, when I can't resist, I visit Pipits' garden. In the velvet dark, it's completely different than in daylight. Nicotiana overwhelms the senses with the soft mysterious aura of clove. It grows tall through the cracks of the summerhouse terrace, each flower head a small white light. I sit breathing in its scent, listening to the rustling nocturnal sounds, on duty while Pipits sleeps.

I listen for Henry to lock up. Returned from the pottery, he turns the big key in the front door and kills the lights. He locks his little family in, and me out. I picture him, keys in hand, all puffed up with being the man of the house.

Henry says it's wonderful to work with things that do what they should. The kiln in his new studio is practically trouble free, the painting table the perfect size, the stacking shelves stable. Bert's present to him of the Nespresso coffee maker is a treat that never fails to please.

He is experiencing a measure of success, particularly with his mugs. Nest, the design shop in town that he had high hopes for, closed down, but with his usual luck, Roses, the small, independently owned department store where Mother often shopped, took over the order, and according to Henry they cannot get enough of them. The catalog shoot went well, and sales, if not overwhelming, are regular at least.

I've rifled through his desk, seen the invoices he sends out, and it seems likely now that he could make a living of sorts with the pottery. Although unless he digs deep, ups his game, he is never going to make his fortune.

Gloria hasn't returned to work yet. She's debating with herself whether she ever will.

"Noah needs me," she says. "I can't bear the thought of not being with him all the time. Neither of us really wants to hand him over to a nanny. In any case, the wages for that would eat up what I could make, so it seems a bit pointless."

I must say her attitude about nannies suits me. A stranger at Pipits, living in the house, would interfere with my plans. And things are testing enough without having to cope with that.

With no challenges from either side, the divorce has been completed at a dizzying speed. The decree nisi came in weeks and was granted in under three minutes, and the marriage was officially dissolved six weeks later. No more Mrs. Walker, no more Lizzie.

Bert, in a similarly hasty vein, wasted no time at all in getting remarried. He and Helen did the legal bit at the Chelsea registry office, and the fun bit after, at the Arts Club. I know because although it is hard to believe, they sent an invitation to Gloria and Henry, which I came across when I was going through Gloria's desk.

The desk rightly belongs in the little dressing room off Mother's bedroom, but it has been moved to the dining room to be more convenient for Gloria. It is pathetic that she thinks she needs one. She is meant to be helping Henry out with the office side of things, but she is constantly losing paperwork, mixing up delivery dates and the like. If I were Henry, it would drive me mad. He just laughs at it, though. Gloria has never been well organized, but motherhood has made her even vaguer than usual.

She was out on a stroll with Noah at the time, which gave me an opportunity that for obvious reasons is not always available to me. It didn't take me long to spot the invitation. Its vulgar color drew my eye. Red! Helen's idea, I imagine. One can only shudder at the thought of what her choice of a bridal gown might have been. There was a note from Bert attached to the card.

> *I know it is unlikely that you will come. Your loyalties naturally lay elsewhere. But after all the wonderfully warm hospitality you have shown me in the past, I wanted to let you know, dear friends, that you would be welcome on what will be for me a very special day.*

Neither Henry nor Gloria mentioned anything about receiving the invitation. Well, they wouldn't, would they? Apart from the fact that they think it would wound me, I don't believe they are on my side anyway. They love Bert, have loved him from the moment they first met him. And they wouldn't want to join in any criticism of him. Whatever Gloria pretends to think, hiding the invitation just proves it is make-believe that we are a close family. Henry knows we are not. Gloria is my sister, so he cannot own up to his dislike of me. His body speaks for the words he swallows: a stiffening of the spine in my presence, thin smiles, a tightened jaw.

I am at the mercy of his resentment; he is after all the keeper of Pipits, at least for the moment. But his dislike of me is not his worst crime. His very existence is his worst crime.

I am, though, almost ready to turn that page and be done with him.

I still have my keys to Pipits, and sometimes I let myself in through the kitchen door when both Gloria and Henry have retired for the night. I know to duck beneath the alarm sensor in the hall before I get to the number pad to tap in the magic numerals. It is not a very original code, ten sixty-six, which every school child knows is the date of the Battle of Hastings. Bert used the same for all of his credit card pin numbers, such lazy thinking. Only four of us know the combination, Henry and Gloria, and me, of course, and for convenience's sake, Mrs. Lemmon.

I sit in the dark hall as Henry and Gloria and baby-makes-three sleep upstairs. Secret visits to sit and listen, to console the house. I will not allow them to dictate when I can come, when I must go. I will not be driven from Pipits as though we mean nothing to each other.

What I once saw in Henry, I see now was an illusion. I

remember the pain he put me through by choosing Gloria. And the time after, when I was expected to accept their engagement with a smile on my face. I still have a scar on my hand from punching it through a mirror when they made the announcement. I hardly knew how to contain my rage.

It seems quite ridiculous to me now that all that longing, all the sobs and sighs, should have been over Henry Bygone. Weak Henry, a man filled with unforgiving kindness, a passionless person.

The other day I heard him reading aloud to Gloria from the *Guardian* as they sat together at the kitchen table. He was shaking his head in disbelief at the story of a man who shot his wife because she had left him for a younger lover. The man dispatched her with a bullet, and then shot himself.

"Whatever that is, it's not love," Henry said.

As I said, passionless. It was obvious to me that the fellow couldn't let someone else have the person who was his by right, couldn't himself go on living without the wife who had vowed to be faithful, to be his alone.

But, to Henry, the story was beyond the realm of what he understood of human nature. He couldn't grasp that someone could feel so devotedly about the thing he loved, that he would kill to preserve that love. I can see now that Gloria's claim to Henry was a lucky escape for me.

14

THE MUSHROOMS ARE UP. One day there's no sign of them and the next there they are, strange hoary little aliens, fairy-story things. There are more of them than I have ever noticed before. I can tell that this will be a good season for them. All that winter rain, I suppose.

The urge to get on with my plan is hot in me. These past weeks it has often felt like just a dream, something that might never come to fruition, but the sight of those yeasty little heads has confirmed to me it will be done, and done soon.

Henry, usually the first to herald the mushrooms' arrival, hasn't mentioned their appearance yet. I don't think that I should; it might look a bit suspicious later. I know that he'll get around to it, though. He can't resist the idea that they are free for the taking. And he doesn't like waste, so I wait.

Now that it comes to it, and despite my studying, without the book I am not sure that I can tell the difference between the edible and the poisonous varieties. That's good, I suppose. They are so similar that I feel confident that Henry won't notice the ones I sneak into his crop. By the time they join his, he won't be inspecting them, his mouth will be watering, his mind on how he will cook them.

I'll wait until he has chopped them up on the thick butcher's block he uses, and then I'll get him out of the room on some pretext or other and add my special little present.

I don't any longer feel the least bit sorry for Henry. None of this would have happened if he hadn't walked into my life, and then so eagerly into Gloria's. It is all his fault, talking Mother into leaving them the house, pushing me out, acting like some jumped-up squire.

The other night, as I sat on the bench in the garden, I looked up at the house and saw him pause at their bedroom window. A waning moon was out, shedding a pale light, but I'm sure that he didn't see me. I sat very still, and the bench, obscured by the twisting branches of the rose arch, is only partly visible from that window. I watched him draw the curtains against the night, against me. I was suddenly full of fury. He inside Pipits, me out; quite the wrong way around. Bloody interloper.

I don't fear God's wrath for what I am about to do to Henry; and I won't seek absolution. I never ask anything of God, not the tiniest thing. What is the point? If he does exist, he is a cold God, not in the least bit interested in me. You only have to look around you to question his existence. I can vouch for the fact that there's no such thing as fairness, and the injustices I suffer keep coming. Now, what kind of example is that if you are looking for followers? If God does exist, which truly I doubt, I cannot see that he is any better than the devil. If he does exist, perhaps they are one and the same being, the shadow and the light.

"HENRY, THERE'S SOMEONE AT your studio door," I say, looking out of the kitchen window, a nice touch of surprise in my voice. "Oh, they've gone around to the back now."

"Really?" he says, joining me at the window. "I'm not expecting anyone."

"Perhaps it's a new customer."

"Maybe," he says, taking off his apron. "I'll go and check. I'll only be a sec, Betty."

"I'm not staying," I say. "Only popped in to see Noah."

"Gloria's taken him to be weighed," he says, heading to the door.

"Oh," I say, as if it's news to me.

Of course it's not. I always know what they are doing. They write it down in the diary they leave on the hall table, the one Henry's mother sends them every Christmas. She has good taste for a housebound pensioner; it is always the V&A one, so beautifully illustrated.

Things are working out well, Gloria at the surgery and Henry jumping to my commands. If Gloria had been at home, it would have made it harder for me to contribute to Henry's delicious meal, which is to be a risotto. He is so predictable. The mushrooms are all nicely chopped on the board, ready and waiting.

So much of luck is about timing, a minute here or there, a missed plane, left or right at the crossroads, and your fate is decided. If I hadn't taken Henry home on that sunny day, or if the weather had been gloomy, rainy, perhaps, would Gloria have glowed quite so radiantly? If I had whispered my love for Pipits in Mother's ear, as Gloria and Henry had dripped their neediness, would the house be mine now?

I don't expect Henry will succumb right away. The information I've gathered claims it will take between six and twelve hours, rather like food poisoning, which I suppose it is. A simple case of food poisoning that could happen to anyone.

Earlier this morning I watched Henry from a vantage point in our woods as he stooped to gather the mushrooms for his lunch. Since the fungi first appeared, I have taken to morning watching in the woods. I needed to know when Henry started his picking. It was a relief to see him there with his basket, all eager, checking the pictures in his book, making sure. He has been so preoccupied with testing out the design for a new line of wavy-edged bowls that I was beginning to fear he would let the complimentary harvest go to ground this year.

When he had gathered enough of the copious crop, he left, whistling to himself. Henry has a way of doing so in moments of contentment, a tuneless sort of fluting. It would be beyond irritating if it weren't for the fact that it lets me know where he is.

I wondered if he was aware of being watched. He showed no sign of it, but we are meant to sense it, aren't we? Sense the watcher. I leaned against one of the big self-set trees of heaven and kept him in sight as he strolled across the meadow swinging his basket, until he disappeared around the side of the house.

I know his habits well. He will put the basket down next to the Aga to allow the damp mushrooms to dry off; then he will go to his studio to work. At around twelve fifteen he will return to the kitchen and start to cook.

On normal days he cooks something up for lunch for himself and Gloria, an omelette perhaps, a dish of oily pasta. During mushroom season, though, Gloria makes do with cheese and biscuits, or some leftover thing from the night before, while Henry indulges in his love of fungi. He calls himself a foodie. Greedy, more like.

I suppose I could just have sneaked into the house and added my mushrooms to his while he was in his studio. I think, though, that if the mushrooms were seen whole, there was the chance, however slight, that he may have noticed a difference in the color of the gills, of the firmness of the flesh. To be sure that Henry would accept them as his own, I had to slice them and replace some of his with some of mine. No sense in being careless.

Once Henry, swinging his laden basket, had made it back to the house, I slipped on the plastic gloves I had bought in preparation and began gathering up the *Amanita virosa* that I had identified, with the help of the book, growing underneath the beech trees in our woods. I couldn't take the chance of poisoning myself through my skin, so the gloves were necessary. The *virosa* is quite the little serial killer. Commonly called the destroying angel, it must be handled with extreme caution.

The mushrooms had the strangest scent, new potatoes with a trace of almonds, although I'm pleased to say that it has faded to almost nothing since I picked them. When I first saw them a couple of days ago, nudging their conical caps up through the moss, I thought they would be hard to disguise. Today though, I see with relief that the caps have opened up to mimic their nearby edible neighbors.

I put them carefully into a plastic bag and stored them in the pocket of my jacket. Then I waited until I was sure Henry would be back at work on his bowls before leaving my spot in the woods and strolling back through the meadow.

Early on there had been fog in the village, a grayish haze

hanging low over the houses, but with the clouds thinning, the sky was coming up clear. It was a pleasant walk, past the swimming hole, past the ancient horse chestnut tree and the big elm that survived the disease that felled so many of its kind. Our childhood swing, the wooden seat rotten now, hung lopsidedly from one of its lower branches, creaking as it swayed in the breeze. I looked at my watch. Henry wouldn't be preparing his lunch for at least a couple of hours. Time for me to shower, time for a prelunch gin.

———————

I WATCH HENRY LOPE toward the studio in search of the non-existent caller, and hear him sing out a cheery "hello" to the empty air. I quickly put my gloves back on, open the bag, and tip out the *virosa*. I refill the bag with a good quantity of Henry's mushrooms and shove it back into my pocket. Then I slice mine and shuffle them through his prepared pile. Tumbled together they look innocent, so innocent that even I, having glanced away, now can't tell Henry's harvest from my own.

As I leave through the front door, I hear him coming through the kitchen. It occurs to me that, if things go according to plan, I might never see him again, not alive, anyway. I hear him clank down a pan on the Aga's burner, hear the knife tap on the board as he slides the mushrooms into a pan. He begins his whistling.

I walk to Cold-Upton's surgery intending to meet up with Gloria. I don't want to be anywhere near Henry. There is no telling how long he will be symptom-free. It could be some hours, but nothing is certain. I gave him a hefty portion of the *virosa*, so it might happen fast.

I'll greet Gloria and walk with her at a sluggish pace, tell her I've just remembered that I need to buy some milk as we pass the garage. I'll take my time while she waits for me. The longer we are out, the less chance Henry has of getting help should things happen swiftly.

Gloria isn't in the surgery, though. The receptionist says that she has gone to have a coffee with the other mums in the tearoom attached to the back of the village shop. It is a regular thing, apparently.

I am put off by the thought of those mums with their boring talk of sleepless nights, their impatient babies always needing something: a drink, a cuddle, a feed; such insistent little creatures, bantam gods tugging at their mother's chains, demanding to be adored. Besides, whenever I have come across those women in the village, they seem ill at ease with me. I am the daughter of the big house, after all. I have an aura of sophistication that makes them nervous. They like Gloria, of course.

It is fortunate that she is with them, using up time. I buy a packet of tea from the shop and wait for a good twenty minutes outside by Noah's empty buggy before she appears.

"Hello, you two," I say. "It is such a lovely day, I thought I'd share the walk home with you."

"That's nice. How did you know we were here?"

"Oh, I needed some tea, and I saw Noah's buggy."

Noah is halfway to being asleep in Gloria's arms, but he's fighting it. He seems to drift off, then just as Gloria relaxes he gives a start, a little whimper, and she sets to rocking him in her arms again. She whispers to me that he is about to go and lowers him gently into the carriage, covering him with a soft new blanket. Blue. Alice's pink pashmina is nowhere to be seen.

Gloria asks me if I want to come to Pipits for lunch.

"I'm sure Henry will make enough for two," she says. "Or there's some soup I made yesterday. Mother's recipe."

She often cooks from Mother's recipe book. It is one of those big hardback notebooks you can buy cheaply from any stationers. Why it should be Gloria's and not mine is an indication of her desire to grab everything. She has never offered me so much as a photograph from the house. It hardly matters, though; I wouldn't accept her handouts anyway. When I take over, it will all be mine, and everything in its proper place.

I don't cook much, it's true, but I will enjoy every page of that book, so redolent is it of my childhood. Splashes of the food Mother cooked decorate the pages, and the notes she made stir the memory of my early years at Pipits.

> *Gloria's favorite. Betty's favorite. Remember it must be butter not margarine, it is the only way Betty will eat it. Tried this yesterday and both girls loved it. We ate this salad outside on the terrace and were visited by a sparrow; it thought my homemade bread so lovely that it cheekily perched on the table to take a share from the board.*

Gloria says she feels Mother's presence when she makes her meals. She's convinced that Mother watches over us. I hope not; I don't like the idea of being watched over, or of Mother hanging around to spy on us.

I say no to lunch, that I am not hungry, which is the truth. Gloria waits outside the garage while I buy milk, pushing Noah's stroller back and forth with one hand. When I come out, she asks if I'm sure about lunch. I say that I am, and a few yards on we part, she to head to Pipits, me to Alice's house with my fingers crossed.

I am on alert all afternoon, waiting for the phone to ring, for a distraught knocking at the door, but all is silent. At dusk I light Alice's wood-burning stove and burn the gloves and the bag full of Henry's mushrooms. I had meant to do it earlier, but the hours seemed to slip away with my thoughts elsewhere. They are gone in an instant, in a puff of sooty smoke that leaves an acrid scent in the air. I feed wood to the fire and watch it catch, watch the flames turn from blue to orange and then settle to a red glow. Still no word.

I sit by the stove and attempt to read one of Alice's books, *Howards End*, but my mind keeps wandering, and the words wriggle and swim away, like tadpoles in a pond.

I make a pot of tea and then decide on gin instead. I haven't eaten for quite a while—I remember having a sandwich earlier, Marmite I think, but I don't remember when—so I make some toast and am generous with the butter. Even with the gin to help it down, I am finding it hard to swallow.

Shortly after six o'clock, the waiting is really beginning to get to me, and I am debating with myself about whether or not to pay Gloria and Henry a visit to check things out, when the phone rings. It is Gloria. She blurts out through sobs that Henry has taken ill. I can tell she is distraught.

"Really ill," she says. "We thought it was just flu earlier, but it's not, it's something terrible. You have to come and look after Noah. I've called for an ambulance."

As I walk in the dark to Pipits I hear a siren in the distance. It gets louder as the ambulance takes the hill through the village. Can this really be happening? My heartbeat amps up as I listen to its shriek. I am excited, thrilled at the thought that I have, by my will, brought this about. I turn through Pipits' gate and have to stand aside in order not to be mown down by the ambulance as it speeds toward the house.

Gloria is standing at the open door with a panicked look on her face. Tears salt her cheeks, little rivulets of them are running into her hair, sliding down her neck. Even in despair she is beautiful.

"Oh, Betty. Thank God," she says, pulling me through the door.

Two paramedics jump out of the ambulance and unload a stretcher. Gloria is asked for Henry's symptoms. One of the paramedics asks her name and then the pair of them repeat it in every sentence as though they are talking to a child. She might as well be, so eager for comfort is she from the big strong men. They tell her not to worry but to try and remember all of the symptoms that Henry is displaying.

"Bloody diarrhea," she says. "And stomach pains, bad stomach pains. And vomiting, too."

"Good girl, Gloria," they say. "Well remembered, Gloria. Anything else, Gloria?"

"He's a funny color," she wails. "And he can't breathe properly."

Henry is put on the stretcher. He is scrunched up in the fetal position, moaning a little. There is terror in his eyes, and his skin has turned a peculiar color, some phosphorous shade between yellow and green. I can smell the sick on him: new potatoes and almonds.

"Oh, Henry," I say. "What on earth has happened?"

I put my arm around Gloria and tell her not to worry. She whimpers a little, then follows Henry on the stretcher into the ambulance, calling out instructions to me.

"Noah's awake in his cot. I've expressed two bottles of milk for him. They are in the fridge, and there's more of my milk in a jug on the same shelf. I'll phone as soon as I know anything."

I hear the pain bleeding in her voice. It astonishes me that in an emergency that might well see her husband out of this world, Gloria has had the forethought to express her milk for Noah. I suppose that progeny comes first, no matter what.

The ambulance guns down the drive, clipping the gate on its way out. I hear the siren wail as it takes the bend on Church Street, then grow fainter as it passes the pub opposite the cricket pitch. The sound dwindles to a soft moan as it leaves the village and heads toward the city, and to the hospital.

Caught up in the moment between the thought of what is and what might be, I shut the door against the night. I switch the lights off and stand in the hall looking out past my reflection through the darkened window, at the immense cloud-mottled sky.

When I go to Noah in his cot, he is walloping the air with his hands and legs, making happy little gurgles. We look at each other, and he blinks his eyes and smiles. I leave him there and go to the kitchen. I will be the good sister and clean up for Gloria. I put on her silly pink rubber gloves with the fake fur cuffs, empty the rubbish bin, bleach the countertops, and put a used mug into the dishwasher that is loaded with the crockery from lunch. I switch it on and it gives a little shudder before starting its cycle.

With the clearing up done, I help myself to a gin and tonic from their booze store in the cupboard above the sink and settle down with Pipits.

———————

THEY HAVE WORKED OUT what the problem is. Once Gloria told them what he had eaten for lunch it didn't take them long.

One of the paramedics has come back to the house, to gather up any bits of the mushrooms he can find in the waste bin.

"It will help to identify them," he tells me. "Although the treatment is pretty much the same whatever they are."

He has that sympathetic look on his face that Gloria does so well: head to one side, a soft expression in the eyes. I guess he is used to comforting anxious relatives, because he puts his hand on my shoulder and gives an encouraging squeeze.

"It is serious, but don't give up hope," he says.

"I won't," I assure him. "One should never give up hope."

Gloria phones. She isn't crying now. Her voice is low, breathless, as though she is in shock. I guess she is. Poor Gloria.

"It couldn't be worse," she says. "They say his liver is failing and most likely his kidneys are damaged, too. If he is to survive, he will need a liver transplant. He has to be on dialysis until a liver turns up. Someone will have to die if Henry is to live. Oh, Betty!"

"If he survives?" I ask. It isn't hard to make my voice soft and full of concern. Over the years I have made the part of false sister my own.

"He may not," she says, and her voice quivers. "I have to prepare myself, they say. He could die. Oh, Betty, Henry could die."

She asks about Noah, tells me what he needs, which includes regular changes to keep his rash at bay, and if she isn't back in time for his next feed, I will need to make up fresh bottles from what's stored in the fridge.

"The jug marked breast milk," she reminds me. "Although there isn't much left in it. And lots of cuddles," she says. "Give him lots of cuddles."

"Of course I will," I say. For the first time in a long time, I don't mind comforting her.

Things don't seem to be going the right way for Henry, although it is too soon to claim success. What is the likelihood of a liver turning up in time? People wait for years, don't they? It is too much to contemplate losing at this stage of the game, so I stop myself from thinking about it and set about seeing to Noah's needs. I give him his milk, and his eyelids flutter with the comfort of it.

Why Gloria makes caring for Noah so complicated is a mystery: milk must be at blood temperature, his bathwater the same; the house must be quiet for his sleep, he won't settle otherwise. I take no notice of Gloria's rules. Apart from the Pampers changes, which are unpleasant, I find Noah a calm baby, asleep within minutes of his feed. I switch off the baby monitor and close the door. He must learn that if he wakes and cries, I will not come running.

In the kitchen I am suddenly overcome with the creepiest feeling, as though some slithering creature is working its way through my guts. It could be fear, I suppose: the fear of being caught out, the fear of Henry surviving. And what if my plans for Pipits elude me? After all I have been through to get to this point.

This slithering sensation is not entirely unfamiliar. I experienced it once before, long ago, when Gloria and I were riding our bicycles around the village.

Hers had training wheels on the back, and it was prettied up with ribbon streamers on its handlebars. Mother had put me in charge of keeping an eye on her: I was to ride beside her and see that she stayed on the pavement.

"Don't let her out of your sight," Mother warned. "And don't let her ride on the road. You know how cars speed through the village."

I couldn't wait to get away from little sister's chatter and from her joy at being out with me that was signaled by her smiling face. I ordered her to stay where she was and geared myself up to freewheel down Cold-Upton's hill.

The village girls were scared of the ride down the steep incline, at least I had never seen one of them attempt it, but I'd been thinking about doing it for a while. It probably looked a mile long to Gloria; no way would she follow me. She would blab to Mother later, of course, but I was so used to Mother's disapproval, it hardly mattered.

With the fear creeping through me at the thought of winding up in a bruised and bloody heap at the bottom of the hill, I had second thoughts, but a group of the village boys had gathered to watch, and, having positioned myself for the attempt, I knew that I couldn't chicken out. It was their territory, their show-off ground. I guess they hoped that I would be taught a lesson, fall badly, split my head open or worse.

I started out well, handlebars steady, gathering speed in a straight line, but before the road had evened out enough I braked early and too hard, somersaulting over the handlebars and landing on the ground in a sitting position. One of the village boys shouted out, "Rubbish," and his friends jeered and laughed.

The humiliation hurt more than the bruises. It taught me, though, not to expose myself, not to rush into things. I should have practiced, taken the hill for the first time without an audience. I should have gotten the move right before attempting it in front of those boys.

I tell myself now that I planned this thing with Henry well in advance. Nothing was left to chance, and no one could have done it better than me.

The creature inside me stops its slithering.

At around four fifteen in the morning, Gloria phones to say she is coming home for a little while. They are taking Henry for tests. He will be off the ward for an hour or two. She can't stay long, but she needs to hold Noah and to express more milk.

I hear her taxi crunch up the drive. Its headlights sweep a white light briefly through the kitchen, where I am sitting at the table in the dark, sipping from my flask. Gin is so soothing.

I pop upstairs and put Noah's monitor back on. He is sleeping peacefully, taking deep, even breaths, one hand clasping the satin hem of his new blanket. Good boy.

On my way back down the stairs I hear Gloria's key in

the door, and I am there on the other side of it to greet her. She practically falls into my arms.

Henry has had a seizure. He has ferocious back pain and jaundice. Even the whites of his eyes are yellow, apparently.

"There's nothing I can do," she sobs. "I want to help him, but there is nothing I can do."

"He is in the best place," I say. "The doctors at the hospital are the only ones who can help him now." Platitudes are useful in these circumstances.

"My little Noah," she says, taking the stairs two at a time.

She brings Noah to the kitchen, where I am heating her some of the soup she offered me earlier in the day. It's been a long night, and the conversation we had then feels like it took place weeks rather than hours ago.

"Oh, Noah," she says, kissing his head. "Daddy's lovely little boy."

Noah starts to whimper. Who can blame him? He has been woken from his sleep and brought into the bright lights of the kitchen. And besides, Gloria is hugging him far too tightly.

"I can't believe Henry could make such a mistake," I say. "He is usually so careful."

She shakes her head in disbelief, hands Noah to me, and starts searching for the board and knife that Henry used to chop the mushrooms.

"I thought the same, Betty. I can't imagine how he got it so wrong. Oh, my poor darling boy." Gloria's eyes fill with tears which she wipes away with the back of her hand.

I find her language irritating. Henry is hardly a boy, but

I don't say as much. I pat her on the back, say that I guess maybe he wasn't concentrating, that we all have off days, and these things can happen to the best of us.

She opens the dishwasher and takes out the knife Henry used to chop the mushrooms.

"This has to go," she says, brandishing it like a weapon. "Everything that Henry used has to go, we can't take the chance of contamination, however slight."

"No, of course not," I agree. "I should have thought of that myself."

"We should burn that thing," she says, indicating the board.

"I'll do it in Alice's woodstove," I say. "Don't worry about that now."

She stands holding the knife, tears welling, her lower lip quivering as it did when she was a little girl and something had upset her. She is a study in pain.

"Why Henry?" she cries.

Why not Henry? I think. But I keep quiet.

15

I NEEDN'T HAVE WORRIED ABOUT the police getting involved. Apparently, the local authorities only have to be notified about food poisoning when public risk is at stake, as in the case of restaurants and food outlets, anywhere the chance of further victims is a possibility. Unless suspicious circumstances are suspected, it seems that only gun and knife crimes must be reported to the police.

Gloria has confirmed that Henry picked the mushrooms himself. He had told her that it was a good crop this year, and that the risotto was delicious.

"If he gets through this," she sobs, "I'll never let him near a mushroom again."

As Henry poisoned himself, it seems that his story stops there. I couldn't have hoped for better.

I tell Gloria I will move into Pipits so that I can look after Noah.

"Bless you," she says.

I will inhabit my own dear bedroom, have the run of the house. Things are already looking up.

Don't come back, Henry, don't ever come back, drown in the dark waters of a coma.

"He loves you, doesn't he," Gloria says now, gazing wistfully at Noah. "You can't beat blood."

The truth is, Noah would love anyone who looks after him. Whatever Gloria thinks, it has nothing to do with blood. Helpless creatures are wired to love those they depend on to exist. It is simply a case of survival.

ONLY FOUR DAYS AFTER Henry was put on dialysis, and in a stroke of unbelievable luck, a liver has turned up. Because Henry has a blood type that matches the donated liver's antigens, and the liver has only a few miles to travel to the hospital, it is to be his. It came from a man of similar age, killed on a motorbike as he overtook a school bus going down Lansdowne Hill, and met head-on with a four-by-four. What are the odds against that happening at just the right time, and place?

"It couldn't be a better match," Gloria says. She shakes her head in wonderment, her eyes moist at the thought of the kindness of the dead man, who had thoughtfully signed away his organs while he still lived, while he could hardly have imagined his own death at so young an age.

"I'm going to do the same," she says. "Donate my organs. I can't think of a better way to repay this wonderful gift." She is faint with relief; a touch of color has returned to her cheeks. Don't tell me there's no such thing as a Beloved.

Even though Henry has a long way to go to recover fully, I am not optimistic. If he survives this transplant, as now seems likely, my plan will have come to nothing. It will all have been for nothing.

For now, though, there is little I can do but wait. Wait and hope that things will go my way in this duel between Henry and me. At this moment, if I believed in the soul, I would be summoning the devil. Make me an offer, I would tell him. Take my soul for Henry's life.

More people are in the house these days. They come to console, to offer help, to express their shock at what has happened. Neighbors and friends phone, send flowers, forget their manners and ring the bell at all hours. St. Agneta, Miss Goody Two–shoes from the village store, calls at the house, offering to deliver Gloria's weekly groceries.

"Please tell Mrs. Bygone that it will be no trouble. I would like to help."

The him and him couple, potters of little distinction, have set to work in Henry's studio. They will fulfill his orders, keep things running smoothly while he is out of action. What are friends for, after all? They have copied to perfection the mugs and the *HB* signature that Henry uses to mark his work. Surely that is fraud.

I can't walk in the village without being stopped every few minutes.

"How is the dear man doing?"

"That such a thing should have happened."

"If I can help in any way, just ask."

I cluck along with them, smile and thank them as if I am grateful for their concern.

I am tired, so very tired. Looking after Noah doesn't help; the juggernaut of his demands just keeps coming. I'm tailoring his needs to meet my own, though. I refuse to go to him after I have put him down for the night, no matter how much he cries; and whatever the weather, I wrap him up and put him outside in his buggy for his morning sleep at the same time every day. He is stubborn, not always ready for sleep, but given time, he would learn—if it weren't for Gloria's flying visits home, turning my routines upside down. She responds to his smallest whimper.

Spending my days with my lovely Pipits has been wonderful, but the glory of it is tinged now with the likelihood of loss. And it's disturbing that House remains mute, shocked into a hopeless silence. If Henry survives, how totally I will have failed.

I join Gloria in the hospital. Now that a liver has been found for the transplant, things are moving fast, and she cannot be left alone to wait while Henry undergoes the onslaught of the knife.

Noah has been left with Mrs. Lemmon. She will spoil him, of course, feed him sugar from her finger, coddle him with baby talk.

If the transplant works, Henry will have to be on drugs for the rest of his life, but he will be up and about after the operation in four to six weeks. Four to six weeks! Such a trifling stint out of a whole lifetime.

"Things will never be the same," Gloria says. "But keep your fingers crossed, Betty. We need all the luck we can get."

"My fingers are permanently crossed these days," I say.

I groan at the thought of their luck. They may already have had more than their fair share, but that doesn't mean it has run out.

Henry is wearing one of those hospital robes that tie at the back, all prepped and ready to go to the operating theater. His voice is croaky, at whisper level; he has to pause between words to draw breath. He seems pleased to see me.

"You've been a treasure," he says weakly. "I don't know how Gloria would have managed without you."

"She's been wonderful," Gloria agrees.

I allow myself a touch of hope. Henry looks fragile, so very pale with purple shadows under his yellow eyes. Too fragile to survive the onslaught of this operation? I would like to be optimistic, but it feels like I'm panning for gold in a worn-out seam.

"He'll be glad to see the back of the hateful dialysis," Gloria says.

"Getting stronger every day," Henry gasps, raising his arm as if to bunch a muscle. He looks so awful, I can tell that even my silver-lining sister finds that hard to believe.

"Back before you know it," he croaks as he's wheeled out of the ward.

Gloria follows him to the door and out into the corridor. I see her bend and whisper something to him before she kisses him full on the lips. Henry touches her hair, holds on to her hand until they are pulled apart and he's wheeled away.

I see her back crumple before she takes a deep breath and shakes her head. I join her and take up her hand. She squeezes mine hard; I squeeze back. We watch Henry flying down the hallway toward his new liver. Is that celestial light or just dust motes I see dancing around his bed? I am distracted from the image by Gloria bursting into tears.

16

S EVEN WEEKS DOWN THE line, after the transplant, following a small bleed, and an infection that looked as if
it might finish him off, Henry has come through and is on
the mend. The medics say, with admiration in their voices,
that he is made of strong stuff, that he is a fighter.

Gloria has started singing again. "My prayers have been
answered," she says. "We have been blessed."

She purrs along to the music with an idiotic smile on her
face as she cozies up to Noah or makes tasty little salads and
pastas to take to Henry in the hospital. Death visited her
world, spun her around for a moment. *Coming, ready or not*, it
chortled. But it was only teasing. Now, with the tease ex-
posed, Gloria is back to her infernal humming and—no
doubt when Henry is up to it—to breeding.

I have been visiting Henry twice a week to give Gloria a
break and allow her time with Noah. I take him clean pajamas, shaving foam, magazines. I am the good sister-in-law.

Last week, during one of my visits, he was positively
glowing with life. He had showered and shaved, washed his
hair, and was sitting in a chair by the side of his bed, wearing
a sweater over his pajamas.

"I'll be out soon," he said. "I can't wait, and I bet you'll
be pleased to be back in your own home. You like it tidy,

don't you? We're messy, and that's not going to change any-time soon. You've put up with us for long enough. I couldn't be more grateful for all you've done, Betty."

Couldn't be more grateful! Ha!

I am to be pushed aside, denied the only thing that mat-ters to me. This failure leaves me in the wilderness. The fu-ture once again is alien territory. What's to be done?

Back to London for the time being, perhaps? Despite what Bert says about failing galleries, I know that plenty of people would jump at the chance to employ me. But I don't want to repeat that life, and it would be futile to attempt to smother my desire for Pipits, to lock it up somewhere deep inside me; I've tried that, and it doesn't work. Desire won't be denied; no matter how heavy the stone you put it under, it simply crawls out.

When I wake, Pipits is my first thought, the thought that comes to me a hundred times a day. I cannot just up and leave it behind. Love hurts, but you can't abandon it. You must stick with it to the very end.

Would you believe that Bert has been visiting Henry in the hospital? I'm reeling with the knowledge of it. They have kept his visits from me, sneakily accepting all my help, using and deceiving me.

I found out when I called at the hospital the other day just to drop off some toiletries Henry had requested. I was shocked to see Bert getting out of his car, magazines and chocolates in hand. He saw me but pretended not to for a bit, fussing with his keys, debating, I think, whether he could continue with the farce of not noticing me. I could hardly believe my eyes. They all just carry on as though I don't exist.

After a moment's pause, I marched straight up to him and waited for him to speak.

"Ah, Betty," he said.

So I am not to be Lizzie anymore. Yet further evidence of time spent in Gloria and Henry's company.

He stumbled through, "I am so glad that Henry is on the mend. It must have been awful for you."

No apologies, no excuses for his presence. I turned on my heel and walked toward the hospital as Bert kept up alongside, an embarrassed smile on his face.

It was easy to tell that this wasn't the first time he had visited. He knew exactly where he was going. The complicated route to Henry's ward, down long corridors, through three sets of doors, was familiar to him, no need for directions.

The sister on duty greeted us with a questioning look. What were we doing here outside of visiting hours, she wanted to know.

"I won't stay long." Bert gave one of his big open smiles. "But I've come from London specially to cheer up my friend."

His friend! His friend!

"Oh well, it won't hurt, I suppose. Just this once, though," she relented.

I am reminded of how easily Bert can seduce, be it man, woman, or creature. For some mysterious reason, people get pleasure out of pleasing Bert.

Henry had the grace to be embarrassed by the joint visit, which was a cold half hour of banalities and uncomfortable silences. Bert left first. I didn't reply to his goodbye. It is unfair that I should have to go through this, Bert insinuating himself into my family, Pipits still at terrible risk, and me being dealt a losing hand at every turn.

"We should have told you," Gloria says later, when I complain to her about Bert visiting. "We thought it would hurt you, but Bert is so fond of Henry that we couldn't say no. And the truth is, Betty, they—Henry and Bert, I mean— want to continue their friendship."

"Oh, do they? And you think that's fine? You think that it doesn't matter that Bert cheated on me with Helen. You're my sister, but you're on his side."

She said all the usual mealymouthed things; it wasn't about sides; we were all grown-ups, after all. If we respected each other's feelings, we could make it work. Of course I was more important to them than any friendship, but they would make sure I never had to meet up with him, if that is what I wanted.

I wished I hadn't pressed her on it, hadn't shown my anger. The knowledge of their betrayal is in the open now. I gave Gloria the opportunity to confess to the ongoing friendship with Bert and horrible Helen, so now they don't even have to be careful about it. Before I know it, they will be having the Walkers and their cockapoo mutt for the weekend, while I sit alone in Alice's house. They have put me in a box marked duty, only to be let out when it suits them, only when I can be of use. I have no tears, just an icy anger. I question whether I have the strength left in me for another battle. The answer to that question must be yes. What else?

The truth of the situation is that I had a good plan, it didn't work, and now I need a better one. The strategic error was that Henry's death, although likely, was not guaranteed.

For now, though, my head feels mushy with the clamor

of half-formed thoughts. I am not ready for a new scheme; I'm still wired with the hard-knock failure of the last one.

———————

I HARDLY KNOW HOW to spend my days now. I sleep a lot of them away so I can feel more alive in Pipits' garden at night. It is my only comfort.

The Bygones, meanwhile, are back to playing happy families. Gloria the careless housewife, and Henry, having glimpsed the white light at the end of the tunnel, the truly grateful potter. They tell me that I am welcome at Pipits. Visit anytime, they say, their voices mottled with the pride of ownership.

Even the weather is arranging itself for them, giving Henry joy in his convalescence. Clear blue skies, crisp mornings, and the hedgerows capped with frost. There is always a bonfire going somewhere in the village; the smell of wood smoke fogs the air, its top note musky, the drydown melancholy with something of the night in it.

Cold-Upton looks at its best in this weather. The church sits dreamily on its mossy plot, and the houses appear washed clean in the blanched winter sunlight. Better for me if the days were gray; this beauty is heartbreaking.

I'm distracted by the wound that Henry's survival has inflicted on me. How to finish him off is constantly on my mind. People speak to me, and my thoughts wander off, so that I hardly make sense of what they are saying. The other evening, with my head wrestling with how to dispose of Henry, I had driven halfway to my favorite spot beside the river, when I almost hit a cyclist. He wobbled a bit before falling onto the roadside bank. I watched in my rearview mirror as he stood, shaking his fist idiotically at me, mouthing some obscenity. I realized I had been driving the route without seeing it. It shook me up. I'd had a fair amount of gin that day and a handful of the painkillers that I find such a comfort. That may have had something to do with it. Still, I must cut down. And I will. I will think of a way forward. I will not be beaten.

"Am I boring you?" the postman joked this morning as he waited for me to sign for a delivery of narcissi bulbs I'd forgotten I had ordered months earlier.

Narcissus papyraceus, known as the paperwhite, delicately scented and more refined than the common daffodil. I remember thinking, as I wrote out the order for the bulbs in summer, that by the time they arrived I would be in possession of Pipits. In my mind's eye I saw them dancing like Wordsworth's golden hosts over the happy years ahead.

I had sent for them in a flush of optimism, but that optimism, due to the recent run of events, has proved unfounded. But despite the autumn not delivering what I thought it would, I will plant them out between the apple trees in Pipits' orchard. I'll keep to the rhythm of the seasons.

Henry's business is flourishing. I can't work out how it has happened, but suddenly orders are flooding in. He claims that the poisoning he endured, and the liver transplant, dreadful as it was, brought death so close that the beauty of the world came to life with a depth unknown to him before. No more of the potter's pervasive browns and grays; he uses color now: blushing reds and bright blues, saffron yellow and splashes of gold everywhere.

It is hard to believe, but he has an order for his new

range of pots from Barneys department store, in New York. Gloria says Bert showed the buyer his work, and she thought it heavenly. Of course Bert did. Damn him.

In a flush of success, Henry has taken on Fi, the mural girl, to help him fulfill the order. He gets tired these days if he does too much, and the order is a sizable one, so he needs an assistant. It is not her field, but she is eager to learn, loves the painting, and the colors, which she says are life-enhancing. Clichés firing off everywhere.

Henry, as venal as most artists, knows what to charge his clients.

"I think they value it more, the more they pay," he says.

With cash rolling in, they'll be back to cracking the bones of Pipits again before you know it.

And I was right about Bert and Helen. They *have* been to visit at Pipits. Even if Gloria hadn't warned me they were coming, I would have known as soon as I glimpsed the out-of-season peonies and white roses scenting the air, displayed on the hall table: a definite Bert choice.

Feeling guilty, I suppose, Gloria repeats that it was only for lunch, as though that is some consolation.

The days are short, dark before teatime, and I am waiting still for inspiration, for the idea that will finally allow me to take my rightful place as mistress of Pipits. I cannot risk another failure. This time, no matter what it takes, I must win.

Another Christmas will be with us soon.

17

THE SOIL BETWEEN THE apple trees is firm from the morning frost. It takes a bit of effort to break through the crust into the ground, but I'm soon into the rhythm of it, breaking up the shell with the blade of the shovel, then, with all my weight behind it, pushing down hard.

The air is cold, the wind brisk, and there is a buttery light that comes and goes as if someone is flicking a switch on and off. One minute the sun is there, the next the clouds have obscured it for a moment, then . . . click . . . it is back again. It will rain later, which is good for the bulbs; they need to drink deep when they are first planted.

I coat them with the dug-up earth and think of Mother's ashes in the ground under the buddleia, which was festooned on that burial day with cabbage whites. I think of Henry's big hands covering her remains with this same rich Somerset soil. I must prune the buddleia. It's a spring job, really, but no harm to do it early. It is hard to kill off buddleia no matter how roughly you treat it. Ours is old and so tough that I'll have to take a saw to it.

Mother used to hack at it furiously. Her obliging nature was never at the fore where gardening was concerned. Certain flowers would be held back with iced water if a neighboring specimen that would show them to their best advantage was slower to open. Plants that grew too big for their allotted space would be cut to the quick or pulled up and burned. The garden was her passion, and she spared nothing that got in the way of her plans for it. People thought my mother a gentle soul, but I knew different. I was too often the target for her poison darts to be taken in by her soft voice and sweet smiles. I saw her flaws, knew where her fault lines lay.

The mournful song of a bullfinch is in the air, although I can't see any of the creatures about. Their woeful song belies their natty appearance: little housewives off to the shops in their ruddy pink coats and perky black caps. Mother was always irritated with them for eating the new buds on her fruit trees. Personally, I don't begrudge them; they are merely part of the cycle of things.

It takes me some hours to get the bulbs safely tucked up in their earth beds. My back hurts, and there is a welt across my palm in the shape of the shovel handle. I take a couple of aspirins with a glug of gin from my flask and sit on the ground for a bit. I'm feeling low, so low that I could stay here for hours and howl. I won't allow it, though. Misery is clever; it will disarm you if you let it. I must be careful not to indulge these feelings, not to give in to the forces against me.

I decide to make a bonfire. The winter winds have ransacked the orchard, so that the ground is littered with the severed boughs of the fruit trees and with a scattering of rubbish blown in or dropped by trespassers. Everything is braided up with bits of broken bramble. There are rotting piles of leaves and the boxes the narcissi came in. I've put a hundred in the ground and am expecting a good show.

All of Pipits' land needs attention. There are branches

down in the woods, too, and ragwort at the margin of the meadow that will smother the summer poppies if it is not dealt with; the little wings of self-set sycamore should be sprayed with weed killer, and the stream needs dredging. You'd think Henry would take some responsibility for the land, but no; he is content to leave it all to me.

I gather up the debris and pile it, wigwam style, at the bottom of the bank, below the trees. The fire takes a while to catch, but I persevere until the brightest little flare appears and takes hold. The flames crackle, spit out morsels of the damp wood, and rise higher than I imagined they would. Bits of burning box float away from the fire and catch in the trees like bunting, where they morph into ash. A caul of smoke, as gray as Miss Havisham's wedding veil, is taken on the wind and floats away toward the church spire.

I stand by the blaze breathing in the singeing smell until, with nothing left to feed it, the fire dies down to a circle of cinders. My eyes are prickling, my throat raw from the smoke, but I feel better, more settled somehow.

I am taken by how powerful flames are, how cleanly they transform their feed to ashes. I had a dream once, a fine dream, about a bonfire, about the most wonderful show of fireworks. I was standing between my mother and father. Father held one hand, my mother the other. The three of us linked together, laughing and watching the fireworks light up the sky. Gloria wasn't there; she wasn't even in my mind. It was a dream of how things should be, how they would have been if the world were fair. Now I dread my dreams, which have become nightmares: beasts pursuing me, witchy women, and monstrous men, and always the hopeless sense that no matter how fast I run, I will never reach safety.

I pass Henry's studio on the way to Pipits' kitchen and look through the window. He is standing behind the chair that Fi is sitting in with her shoulders hunched in concentration while he explains something to her. Since the operation, Henry never stands quite as straight as he used to. His hand often strays to touch the place where a dead person's liver lives on. He does it now as I slow my pace to watch.

Master and pupil are absorbed, heads down, concentrating. Fi glides her brush across the rim of a bowl, which, under the sweep of bristle, turns into a ring of gold.

"Yes, yes, exactly that. Well done," Henry applauds.

Fi makes a whooping sound and preens, puts the bowl down carefully, then claps her hands, all fluttery like a child receiving a treat.

There's a vile taste in my mouth, a gagging, a something-dead taste. I failed at killing you, Henry, but my hatred for you thrives.

I leave them to it and make my way to the kitchen. Gloria is at the sink rinsing out Noah's bottles, ready to fill with milk for the night feeds, which Noah still cries for.

"Coffee?" she offers.

I accept and settle myself into a chair. I am disappointed that she is here at all. Quite often at this time of day she is out pushing Noah through the village in his buggy. She says it is the only way, sometimes, to get him to sleep.

"I cobble him," she laughs, referring to her habit of bumping the wheels of the buggy over the cobbles on Church Street. "Never fails."

Apparently, he went off easily today, giving her time to catch up with things.

She is bustling about the kitchen chattering away so that

I cannot hear the house. The truth is, though, these days, House seems to have lost its voice. Even when I'm there alone, I can't make out what it's trying to tell me. I feel, though, that it is disappointed in me, maybe even thinking of changing sides.

Don't, Pipits, don't. Gloria and Henry will betray you. You will become a tarted-up, plastic version of yourself, your beauty and sweetness lost forever.

"Wonderful work you're doing in the garden," Gloria says. "It's like having Mother back. Such a comfort."

———————

TWO WEEKS TO GO until Christmas. Things in Bath are crazy. The shops are crowded, people knocking into each other, long lines to pay for purchases, and a frantic must-buy feel in the air.

I am not in the mood for shopping. Nothing catches my eye, nor do I feel particularly generous. I only came to get out of Alice's house. You can be in low spirits in a crowd, it's true, but somehow I find it is less painful than being captive in dead Alice's quarters. The rooms there get smaller by the day. I've never liked her doleful little house, but now I loathe it.

There is the usual Christmas market in Bath, set out in the central square in front of the St. Peter and Paul Abbey. The air, smeared with the smell of hot dogs and mince pies, stirs nausea in me. Jingly music bells out from shop doors to tell us we must be jolly; it is the season of goodwill, after all. Be jolly, and spend, spend, spend.

Outside my bank on Milsom Street there is a man pretending to be a statue. He has painted himself silver and has a basket at his feet with some pound coins in it. His eyes are blank, his mouth a closed chrome gash. I wonder if his teeth are silver, too. And his body, so still as to be ready for the coffin, not the slightest tremble. He has retreated inside himself. It is one way of hiding, I suppose. I don't like the look of him.

I am a regular now at the pub opposite the marketplace. They say "hello, love" and "your usual, is it?" when I order my gin. They sound sorry for me, as if they know something about me that instills pity. I wonder if they talk about me when I leave. No doubt they think me an alcoholic, a lonely unmarried middle-aged woman. I don't care to have judgments made about me, people thinking they know me. I might start wearing my wedding ring again, just to confuse them.

It is hard to believe a whole year has passed since the Christmas lunch that Gloria imposed on Pipits: Alice so ill, Bert still my husband, bouncy Fi, and the other waifs and strays summoned to feed Gloria's ego, to fuel her desire to be the star of the show.

And here we are again, except that now there is Noah crawling around, hauling himself up on the furniture, and Bert has a new wife, and Fi a new boyfriend.

"Ah," he said, when we were introduced. "So you're the big sister of the lovely Gloria."

His name is Barry, whatever that is short for. Fi is an inch or two shorter than him but twice his width at the hips. He is quite good-looking in a milky sort of way: pale skin, pale eyes, a whack of brown hair. He teaches sociology at the sixth-form college in Bath and wears the teacher's uniform:

fawn cord jacket, liver-colored shoes. Henry and Gloria are already fond of him.

I am asked to Christmas lunch, of course, but I shan't go. I'll have one of my headaches at the last minute. The very last minute so that it will keep them from asking Bert and Helen.

I won't be buying presents this year, not even for Noah. He will be getting plenty and will have no idea of who gave him what. I've told them I think gifts are a waste of money. You never get what you want, so what is the point.

"Oh, Betty, you are so right," Gloria gushed. "Better to give the money to charity. Perhaps we should do the same."

CHRISTMAS PASSED. I PLEADED a headache as I had planned to do, and added a sore throat for good measure.

"Come anyway," Gloria begged when I telephoned to give my apologies. "It's Christmas Day. We'll look after you."

There was no way I was going to bow to her demands. I refuse to put on a cheerful face and play the grateful divorced sister. There is something particularly masochistic about watching others make a show of happiness when you are in despair yourself.

Late in the day, Henry came knocking on the door at Alice's mean little house, with leftovers from Christmas lunch packed in a series of Tupperware boxes. They were stacked in a basket with a shiny red Christmas cracker tied to the handle. Gloria had slipped in a net of walnuts and a box of sugared almonds, some tiny tangerines with their leaves still on. There was a note saying she would call that evening.

"Just needs warming through," Henry said cheerfully. "Anything else you need?"

He was wearing a hand-knitted sweater with the image of a Christmas pudding in the center of it. He looked ridiculous.

"A present from Fi." He grimaced.

"I won't ask you in," I said. "Don't want you to catch whatever this damn bug is."

"Have to get back, anyway. I'm chief washer-up."

I watch him stride down the path and get into his car. Despite the liver transplant, Henry still strides, his hair is still golden, his frame still that of a young man. I needn't have taken the trouble to plan or to study homicidal fungi with such keen attention.

Pipits is less than a five-minute walk away, but I suppose Henry is in a hurry, hence the car. He hardly bothers these days to disguise the fact that he is uncomfortable being in my presence. Well, the feeling is mutual.

I take the Tupperware boxes to the kitchen and empty their contents into the waste bin. I cannot eat that sort of food; meat and gravy sickens me. I mostly survive on toast these days, but I will have a couple of the nuts later, after a sleep and before my outing to the river.

At the river I will be able to think clearly; my mind works better there. Surely, the law of averages means it will be my time soon, my time for fairness, for things to go my way. There is no question that I have paid my dues to life in bad luck, not to mention the wrecking of my plans, the lost crusades, one following the other. Whatever it takes, I am determined to be the cause of, and a witness to, my sister's ruin.

ALICE'S HOUSE DOESN'T HAVE a voice. It never speaks to me. No chorus of joy, no babble of discontent, nothing. To break its dreary silence, I must keep the radio on all through the night. Pipits has always been company enough. It needs no such embellishments, no voice other than its own.

This house witnesses my rages, my despair, but has no capacity to comfort. It has no grace. Things are always going wrong with it; fuses pop when the kettle and the toaster go on at the same time, cracks appear in the bedroom ceiling, strange smells leak from the drains.

A stray dog has begun to visit Alice's garden. It is a he, easy enough to tell. He comes each morning at the same early hour and sits on the path a few feet from the front door. He is a big hoary-haired thing, wet nose, begging eyes. I have asked around, but no one seems to have seen him or know who he belongs to.

Yesterday he followed me to the village shop, and I had to shoo him away. He was reluctant to leave until I shouted at him. One of the young mums on her way in gave me a questioning look. These days you are not allowed to shout at children or animals. Anger in all its forms is frowned on; life must float safely above the Plimsoll line, sail on calm seas. But although people talk of passion all the time—he is passionate about gardening, she is passionate about her job—they have castrated the word, watered it down so that it has no danger, or power. They wouldn't recognize real passion if it up and knocked them off their safe, spread-out feet. My sister uses this newspeak all the time. She is a true daughter of this ridiculous century.

I am beginning to feel stalked by the damn dog. I don't like the way he looks at me, all begging and sorry for himself. I make myself stare back at him until he looks away. That's what you're meant to do, isn't it? Show them who is pack leader, top dog?

I mention the stray to Henry, and he says that the poor thing is probably lonely. Why don't I adopt him, he suggests.

"You haven't seen him," I say. "He is the ugliest thing."

"Still, he would keep you company," he says patronizingly.

If the unlucky creature doesn't give up, I'll be forced to use Mother's old trick and go looking for some toadflax plants to fix him a nice warm bowl of milk. I don't want him following me to Pipits' garden at night. It is hard enough as it is to be discreet on that little journey, to go stealthily, unnoticed, without some hulk of a thing following. I cannot take the risk of Henry catching sight of me, wondering why I am in the garden at night. Questioning and disapproving of my being there while he sleeps. He will never understand my need to be near Pipits. Oh, Henry, you are a man of such little imagination.

It would be too obvious to simply walk up the drive and skirt around the house into the garden, as I do in the daytime. Sooner or later I would be seen. So I have to hurry down the side lanes and cut through our woods to the meadow, hem around its perimeter, and enter the grounds through the orchard. Quite ridiculous! Look, Mother, look at the fallout from your will. Look how Henry and Gloria are lording it over me.

I don't stay in the garden long on these cold winter nights, even well wrapped up. The cold eventually enters my bones and forces me off. There have been some hard frosts, a few flurries of snow, plenty of rain. The land in this season resembles a photograph, flat, all surface, as though—like me—it is waiting for life to resume, to burst into color.

I rarely go into the house on my night vigils now, since I narrowly missed being discovered by Henry a few weeks ago as he unexpectedly came downstairs to get something from the kitchen. If it hadn't been for the creak on the landing, a warning from Pipits, and just in time, he would have found me out.

THE DOG KEEPS COMING. It's not as if I encourage the shaggy-haired thing, with its man eyes and blunt wet nose; quite the opposite. He simply will not take the hint to be gone.

And he has an unsettling knack of knowing where I am. I was shocked the other evening, as I sat in my car by my reach of the river, to see him come trotting across the little bridge. He stopped right at the point where I had disposed of the builder's tools and sat staring at me as though he was expecting something: hoping, perhaps, that I would open the car door and invite him in. If he's waiting for me to adopt him, he's dumber than I thought.

I observed him for quite a while without blinking. I think my stare embarrassed him, because he went down on all fours and put his head between his paws.

There is something familiar about the beast, something more human than dog. He reminds me of those illustrations you see in children's books, of wizards with long beards and straggly hair.

I opened my car window and snapped at him to clear off,

and he backed up and disappeared. It was a bit unnerving seeing him there in my special place. The bridge is less than a mile from the village, but still it felt as though I were being tracked.

Now, of all the stupid things, I have to go to court. I was stopped the other day on my way out of Cold-Upton, by a police officer whose car I hadn't noticed parked in front of a van in the pull-in by the pub. According to him, a man so heavy that he wouldn't stand a chance chasing even the most unfit of criminals, I was driving erratically and above the speed limit.

I wondered aloud if he might be mistaken. It is hard to go above the speed limit on that road; you have to drive carefully to avoid the parked cars while constantly slowing down for oncoming traffic.

I could tell he didn't like me questioning him. He raised his eyebrows, walked around the front of the car and got into my passenger seat.

"I should warn you," he said, "that I have you on film. The speed limit is twenty on this road. You were driving at almost double that."

I didn't answer. For one thing I didn't care for his tone, and for another, I wasn't going to play the little woman game, all fluttery eyes and apologies. That is just the sort of thing that Gloria would have done. If I had, I suppose he would have let me off, but I don't hold with that sort of trickery. It is demeaning.

He must have noticed my flask on the dashboard, because although I was perfectly in my senses, he asked me to step out of the car and be Breathalyzed. I was over the limit, well over, it seems. So now I have to appear in court to defend myself.

This limit thing seems quite foolish to me. Of course alcohol affects some people more than others, but I can honestly say I have never been drunk, not really drunk. The police are trained to observe things, aren't they? You would have thought he could see that I was in complete control of myself.

I'm sure that bloody dog's plaguing presence is adding to my bad luck. I am going through troubled times, all due to other people's nonsense, and now, out of nowhere, this court thing.

Noah has just passed his first birthday, and next it will be Gloria's. She's a March girl, late March, the bit that "goes out like a lamb." I couldn't be bothered to drive the five miles into Bath, so I picked up a card for her while I was in the village shop. It was a choice between a horse with its foal or the usual boring flowers in a vase. I chose the flowers. My mind must have been elsewhere, as it so often is these days, because I was followed out of the shop by its owner, Agneta. Such a silly name, after Saint Agneta, she boasts. She was in a fluster, calling after me in her put-on posh voice.

"I'm so sorry. Mrs., um, Miss Stash, but you forgot to pay for the card."

Of course I gave her the money right away. She was more embarrassed than me, making a big deal of how she was sure it was just an oversight.

"We are all so busy these days, aren't we?" she said. "It's hard to keep our minds on things."

Honestly, what a fuss about small change. She could just as easily have taken the money from me on my next visit.

Nothing, it seems, discourages my shaggy intruder, so I have picked the toadflax, chopped it up, and boiled it with milk. It smelled bad, so I put a big handful of sugar in it to sweeten the bitterness, and a vanilla pod to disguise the smell. I added melted butter, which gave it the silky appearance of a rice pudding.

I seem to remember that Mother used both the flower heads and the stems in her concoctions, but it is too early in the year for the blooms. I'm pretty sure, though, that if I use enough of the dieback stems I found by the compost heap, my brew will be just as effective as Mother's.

I came down early this morning, my bare feet dusty from the bathroom floor, and put a nice big bowl of it on the path just outside Alice's front door. It looks tempting, a lovely creamy farewell of a dish. The hound's bound to go for it.

The dust that my feet picked up in the bathroom is everywhere inside. I guess it must be time to clean. I hardly have the heart for it. Cleaning this house seems pointless; no matter how I tart it up, it will always be ugly. I must make the effort, though. I do not want Gloria commenting.

As usual, the house was mute. I heard no morning hum from the stairs, no greeting of any kind. Another crack appeared overnight on the bedroom ceiling; a long thin one running west to east. I wonder sometimes if the whole building will come tumbling down and I will end my days in Alice's bed, under a pile of rubble.

I made a cup of tea and half a slice of toast and looked longingly at the gin bottle. I avoided the temptation and congratulated myself. It is good to be disciplined. The tea helped the painkillers down, although they stuck in my throat long enough for me to experience a chemical sort of prickle. Then I went back upstairs and took my shower.

The infernal dog is there at his usual time, sitting on the

path, my offering untouched. I catch his eyes, willing him to slurp it up, but he just stares at me reproachfully. It is as though he knows what I have done, knows the milky brew is not given out of bounty. He is craftier than I thought.

The dish is still full when the postman comes with the usual junk mail, circulars and catalogs. More often than not, they're addressed to Alice.

"Ah, that's kind," he says, indicating the bowl. "Fond of cats, are you?"

"Hedgehogs," I say brightly.

I leave the bowl out. Shaggy might lap it up later, or it might see off a cat or two.

———

APART FROM PIPITS, THERE are only two places that I care to be lately: alone by the river or in Bath, among people who don't know me. It's a relief to me that just a few miles from my village, I can be anonymous in the city crowds. Although I have twice had to duck into a shop to avoid Bygone friends.

The other day as I was leaving a department store on Milsom Street, a woman spoke to me, and then apologized.

"Oh, sorry," she said. "I thought that you were talking to me."

I had been caught out talking to myself. I must be more careful. People will begin to take notice of me, the very thing I come to the city to avoid.

Our local GP has remarked that I don't seem my old self. How on earth would he know who my old self was? I didn't choose to visit him. I was called in for a prescription review and had to go. If I hadn't, he would have stopped the painkillers, and the sleeping pills I am hoarding. I like to have a cache of them; you never know when they will come in useful. The headaches are not so bad lately, still there, but low on the dimmer. I can buy over-the-counter pills for those, anyway.

"You seem on edge," he said. "Are you sleeping all right?"

"Only when I take the pills," I told him. "Without them, I simply lay awake for hours."

He would like to stop prescribing them, but I'm more than a match for him, know what he is up to.

"You still need the pills to sleep, then?"

"Oh yes, it would be terrible without them. I doubt I would sleep at all."

"Something worrying you? Things on your mind?"

Well, I said, although it had been a while, I was still grieving for Mother.

"Such a lovely lady," he said.

"Mmm."

It would be nearer the truth to say that I am somewhat bruised by how easily Bert has moved on, that the ridiculous upcoming court case over my driving under the influence and my simpering sister and her formerly dying, now recovered husband, are the things on my mind. Why should I indulge his prying, give anything of myself away to him?

"Would you like to see a counselor?" he offered. "Someone to talk things over with?"

I had to stop myself from laughing. I can only imagine what a local counselor would be like: some well-meaning housewife, with a nosy nature and too much time on her hands. Probably someone who has taken a two-week course and thinks she knows it all. Gloria trained for three years, and look at her! She's hardly Freud.

"Sometime, maybe," I said. "I'll be in touch."

———————

DESPITE MY EFFORTS TO impress the officials at court, they have deemed me unfit to drive. They have taken my license from me. Two years before I will be allowed to get behind the wheel again. Well, they say two years, but how will they know if I do or I don't obey their dictate?

I haven't mentioned either the case or the ban to Gloria and Henry. I don't want them to know. Why should they be allowed an opinion on what happens in my life? I will still be driving to the river at night, and anywhere else I want to go. The police won't be hard to outwit. No speeding, obviously, check that my lights are working, give them no reason to pull me over. That's only sensible.

Fortunately, there is a big fraud case going on in the Bath courts that is sure to distract them. It's taking up news time and column space in the local media. A well-known Bath businessman with contacts in high places has been found out and is heading for disgrace. In a frenzy of gluttony, the journalists are after his blood. How they love it when the mighty fall. Pictures of him, of his wife and children, even of his mother, are daily splashed across the local rags and flashed up on television screens. As far as I know, my minor misdemeanor was not reported anywhere.

My first trip to the river after the court ruling against me did not yield what I hoped for: peace and quiet and a clear head. I was surprised to find myself a bit nervous about the possibility of being caught, so I made a detour that avoided the pull-in by the pub, in case a police car was hiding there again. I don't go along with the common belief that lightning never strikes twice in the same place.

The dog was at the riverbank before me, sitting where I usually park, looking insolent. I accelerated toward him, and he shot off, running past me in the direction of the village. I looked in my rear mirror, but he had already disappeared from sight.

"Next time," I said out loud. "I'll get you next time."

WE ARE WELL INTO March, so there is plenty to do in the garden. But I feel lethargic, strangely disenchanted with the work. I'm exhausted by being on my guard, bored with watching what I say. And I'm convinced that, while Gloria has House, I will never sleep again. Still I will force myself to it, refuse to allow things to get out of hand. The weeds would turn the garden into a wasteland if I let them.

I must trim back the *Hypericum*, which I should have gotten to a month ago, pot up the annuals, deadhead the hydrangeas of their old brown blooms. Mother taught me that trick. Left on through the winter, the spent blooms act like overcoats to keep the frosts from the new buds.

I have dug up the big patch of lupines that grow beside the long-suffering willow, so ancient that it must be staked against collapse. I'll put them on the bonfire. I have never cared for lupines. Named for the wolf because they suck the goodness out of the earth. I'm annoyed to see them prosper.

Gloria came out for a chat while I watched them burning.

"But I love lupines," she said. "How can you burn such beautiful things?"

"Eye of the beholder."

"Even so, Betty. They could have gone to someone in the village. Lots of people like them, you know."

Her cheeks are flushed, she has a tendril of silky hair falling just so, and the soft cushions of her lips are rose pink. Lovely, lovely Gloria, step into the fire, why don't you?

Henry is planning a trip for Gloria's birthday. Three luxurious days in a child-friendly, country-house hotel in the Wye Valley. On-call babysitters for Noah, a romantic dinner for the two of them, and a lovely walk through the Forest of Dean. He has bought one of those front-pack things to carry Noah so that the child can look ahead and enjoy the walk, too. Noah can walk all by himself now, but his legs are short, and he gives up easily. Henry says Gloria deserves a break, and he wants to spoil her.

At last, something for me to look forward to! Their absence, and Pipits all to myself. I think of changing the locks, boarding up the windows, seeing them off with a gun when they return. Kids' stuff, I know, and none of it would work anyway. Ridiculous thoughts. But they occur to me because I am sick with the longing to win, to have my way.

18

I WOKE THIS MORNING HUGGING my new scheme to myself. What joy. I have a plan, a wonderful, brave plan. For some days now I have despaired that a good enough solution might never occur to me. And then it came, unforced, gracefully giving form to what had previously been just fragmented notions. It came in a series of images, like stills from a film, a picture board of the story from beginning to end. I see so clearly now what must, what *will* happen. And what with Henry and Gloria soon to be off on their little trip, the timing couldn't be better.

They have driven me to it, but that hardly matters anymore, since I am so entranced with the idea. I know now that from the moment Pipits and I found each other, we were destined for this ending, entwined together at the last, the one never to be parted from the other.

After it is done and there is no going back, Gloria and Henry will understand at last the true value of what they stole from me. There will be worthless regrets and futile tears.

I cannot claim originality. It is an age-old solution for star-crossed lovers; Cleopatra and Mark Antony come to mind, Tristan and Isolde, Pyramus and Thisbe, and, trite though it may be to include them, Romeo and Juliet.

If I cannot have Pipits, then no one can. We will go down together, House and me, become the story Cold-Upton people will tell their children. They will remember the beauty of the Stash house, search in our ruins for an answer to the disaster. There must always be an answer, mustn't there? I will be the heroine, and Gloria will be pitied. The tragedy will damage her, wipe from her face her white-toothed smile.

No matter what comes after, Stash land will forever be a shrine to love. There will be no grave, no stone to memory, but people will pass by and think to themselves, Elizabeth Stash. They will make up stories about me, imagine, perhaps that I haunt the land where Pipits once stood.

The ancient Greeks had it right. They did not shy away from tragedy as a solution to their problems, and neither will I. I do not see it as a tragedy. In fact, I am in a sort of ecstasy, buoyed up with anticipation. Very few humans are capable of committing murder; it's the same for suicide, but I have the strength for both.

As I sat in Alice's bath, the water cooling to tepid, I thought of how bad luck has followed me all my life. It has been a constant, defying the law of averages, the rule of chance. Despite my efforts, Henry is alive and well, back to good health, and Gloria is still a nauseatingly contented wife and mother. And I think of Bert, who so easily gave up getting a fair slice of our cake but now has a whole other one all to himself.

I have begun to wonder if luck is born in us. Is there a gene for it, perhaps? Or is it the soul that determines our fortunes, preordained by some outlandish force? I don't like that idea; it would mean that we have no power to act for ourselves, that our will has no point or purpose. In any case, it is hard to believe there is such a thing as a soul, a phantom in our bodies that exists without weight or form. Science informs us that within our bodies, swimming in our blood among our organs, there is not even something the size of the tiniest bean unaccounted for.

I wander through Alice's deficient house, counting down the hours until I will take my leave from it. I go from bathroom to kitchen, through all the rooms that are dim now in my self-imposed twilight. Lately, whatever the time of day, I keep all the curtains drawn, the doors locked. I know that I am being spied on by that dog creature. If I so much as open a window, he is there trying to catch my eye. And I've noticed people in the village staring at me lately. They are too curious for my liking.

It hardly matters now, though. None of the old concerns matter now. Nothing is forever, after all, not for any of us. People are scared to focus on their own deaths; the end of the world might come before then, and they will be saved.

People are fools.

I would rather sacrifice my life in a grand design of my own making than wait for death to tag me. I will cheat fate out of whatever ending it had planned for me. It would not, I think, have been a kind one. I choose to fast-forward, to take my own route to sweet oblivion.

Gloria doesn't call in on me much these days. She prefers me to visit her at Pipits. She says I keep the woodstove so low at Alice's house that it's too cold for Noah.

"And why are curtains drawn?" she sighed at her last visit. "Why not let the light in? Are you sure you're all right, Betty?"

"I'm fine, never better. I'm just fed up with looking out at that bloody dog."

"He's obviously decided you're the one for him. Why don't you give him a chance, let him in, feed him up, get to know him?"

Her advice blows through me, a mean little wind that leaves a twinge. Who does she think she is? I will not change my way of life to suit Gloria. I won't house the dog or fire up the bloody boiler. The cold helps to lift the fog in my head. In fact, the cold helped to clear my mind, so that my beautiful plan just floated in on my shivers. It was wonderful how it took root, grew stems, flowered.

"I hope you know that you can talk to me about anything," Gloria said with her therapist's hat on.

She implies that I am drinking too much, that a little intervention might help. There is, as always, a down-to-earth practicality in her voice, but I hear the criticism in it.

Henry is not much better; he makes no genuine effort to be nice to me. He is a touch tart in his comments, and there is usually something he must urgently attend to in his studio when I am around.

It's all to do with their guilt, of course. Without my presence reminding them that they have stolen my inheritance, they wouldn't need to feel guilty. They could revel in their ownership of Pipits, indulge themselves in knocking it about, without me hindering their plans.

Fate has shoved me into a corner, but it is not in my nature to squirm there while it prods at me. I am a practical person, I take note of the facts, and the facts are clear: my hunger for Pipits will never be satisfied while Gloria is allowed to play at being its mistress. I must, and I will, take action.

Gloria and Henry will get nothing of mine. My will, safely lodged with Poppy Jordan, has seen to that. In it, a stroke of luck for my old college; to Girton, the college of Queens, I leave both my money and my properties.

I have decided on Gloria's birthday for the event. It is fitting, I think, and the little Bygone family will be on the break that Henry thinks Gloria so deserves. Of course you have guessed that it will be a fire. A magnificent fire. A burning that will leave the clean ashes of my bones melded with those of Pipits. It will be more transformation than death, a lit candle to a pool of wax, alchemy. The thought of it makes me moan a little.

Gloria and Henry will never understand the majesty of my deed. They will, though, be sorry for it. Its reverberations will have an afterlife. She will accuse him of turning me out. She will say it never would have happened if I had been allowed to live in our family home. Henry will feel aggrieved at the criticism, insist that she wanted me gone, too. Oh, the guilt of being a bad sister, a critical brother-in-law. They will discover how it feels to live as I have lived, to show the world an accepting face while the grit of loss chews at their guts.

———————

I AM EXPERIENCING PAINS in my chest, fisted-up knots of it that whip at me when I inhale, so that I have to breathe shallowly to resist them. At Gloria's insistence, the GP ordered a blood test, but no inflammation was found. He says, with surprise in his voice, that my chest sounds clear as a bell.

He took an age to okay the prescription of my sleeping pills on his screen, and seemed loath to let me go. I was too thin, he insisted. How much did I drink in a day, he asked. The man is persistent, I'll give him that.

"As much as I want," I snapped. "Some days nothing at all."

"Well, if it becomes a problem, I could refer you to someone who could help."

"My sister offered the same," I say. "But you're both wrong. I can stop drinking anytime I want to."

"Have you tried, Elizabeth? Have you tried?"

I don't recall giving him permission to call me Elizabeth. I do not even know his Christian name. As we part, he reminds me again about the counseling.

"The pain you're experiencing is stress, most likely," he says. "Have you thought any more about seeing someone?"

Honestly, such airy-fairy ideas from a clinician. Physical pain is just that, physical. You might as well say that the stomach is responsible for feelings of happiness. You might as well say a counselor can cure cancer.

When I leave the surgery, the dog is there. He follows me to Pipits, where I am to have lunch with Gloria. I walk briskly up the drive, and he trots determinedly behind me. I attempt to shoo him away, but he follows me to the door and plonks himself down on the grass, looking offended.

"Stress is more powerful than you think," Gloria says. "You've been through a lot, what with the divorce, and Alice, of course."

She doesn't mention seducing Henry, stealing Alice, or the befriending of my ex-husband and his absurd new wife; she never mentions what she has put me through. My sister prefers not to look at the thoughtless side of her nature. That would make her unlovable, wouldn't it? I let Gloria's barb pierce deep and remind myself that soon she won't matter, nothing will matter.

After lunch she pours me a coffee and hands me a paint chart. "For the landings and halls," she says. "What do you think?"

What I think is that it will never happen, but I feign interest in the colors.

"What are you thinking of?" I ask as I look at the samples.

"Well, Henry likes the Russian red, but I want yellow. Yellow like the sun."

"Yellow is good," I say. "Choose the yellow."

Noah is in his high chair, his face plastered with his lunchtime puree.

"Avocado and beef," Gloria says, attempting to wipe it off while Noah struggles.

I am about to remark on what extraordinary combinations she feeds to her child when I feel the floor shudder beneath my feet. Seconds pass as I try to work out what the shaking means. I see Gloria's puzzled face, watch her grab for Noah. Then a great rolling roar like the loudest thunder ever fills the air, and I look in amazement as the kitchen wall buckles, and the room darkens.

Suddenly I am no longer sitting in my chair but on my feet. Dust is filling up the room, the window glass is exploding, and everything is on the move. There is something hot and wet on my feet; the coffeepot has fallen over, and its contents have spilled onto the table and leaked to the floor in a small lake. My blood has stilled and I cannot move. I think of earthquakes, of the ground opening up and swallowing me whole.

It takes an age for things to settle, for the creaking, whooshing sound to stop. Through a huge hole in the kitchen wall, I see the great trunk of the copper beech tree leaning at a strange angle against what is left of the wall; a couple of its branches reach rudely into the kitchen, and one has crossed the room and smashed into the dresser, cracking it in half. There is broken china on the floor, and Noah's high chair is in bits.

My racing heartbeat slows as I realize what has happened. The copper beech has lost its grip on the earth and fallen into the front of the house. It is huge, bigger now than it ever looked when it was upright. Its longest, thickest bough lies across the kitchen, dividing the room in two. Gloria and Noah are on one side of it, and I'm on the other. Extraordinary that it has missed all three of us.

Glass is still loosening from the windows, chinking onto the floor, the sound of ice cracking. Some of the stone flags have lifted, so that I can see the joists and the earth beneath them. Outside, a tribe of crows screeches in outrage.

Henry appears at the kitchen's back door.

"Oh my God," he yells. "Is everyone okay?"

He takes a wailing Noah from Gloria and guides her around the trembling branches to the outside of the house.

"Betty, are you coming?" he shouts. "It's not safe to stay inside."

I am shaken, it's true. Still, I cannot keep the smile from my face. My copper beech, my beautiful tree, my ally has started the process, sacrificed itself. It is on my side, preparing the way for Pipits and me. We will do the job together.

"Why is she smiling?" Henry shouts at Gloria.

"It's shock," Gloria says.

She has tears streaming down her cheeks, and her face is covered in dust. Henry starts to rock Noah, who is squalling hysterically. Gloria touches his cheek, then comes back into the ruined kitchen, climbing over the branch to get to me. I hear her skirt rip against the rough bark and can't keep myself from laughing.

"For God's sake," Henry exclaims.

"She's in shock," Gloria repeats, putting her arm around me. "It's all right, Betty. We are all all right."

Henry can't resist putting me in my place. "I told you," he crows. "I knew the bloody thing wasn't safe."

Two days later and a crew of men are in. Chain saws are buzzing, transforming my beautiful, brave tree into a hill of logs. Drifts of sawdust powder the ground. Soon there will be scaffolding that will go from ground to roof, past the kitchen, past my bedroom, past the attic. The front of the house must be shored up, made safe. I console myself with the knowledge that their efforts are pointless. Soon, very soon, there will be nothing left to shore up.

THERE HASN'T BEEN AS much damage as we first thought," Henry says. "No reason to miss out on our break."

"No, you should go," I say. "You deserve it."

"Three days, three wonderful days," he says. "And the forecast is good. A little sun, and dry. What more could we ask for? In any case, it's too late to get our money back."

"Well, reason enough," I say encouragingly.

They have been cooking in a borrowed microwave, boiling their water on a little camping stove. "Real food," Gloria says. "Can't wait."

On Friday morning, I start putting what I will need into one of Alice's shopping bags. Candles and a box of those extra-long matches, fire lighters, and a cigarette lighter just in case the matches are not up to the job. I put out the flask I will fill with my cocktail of tea, and the Temazepam I have been hoarding, my lovely sleeping draught. I add a square or two of chocolate to take away what is sure to be the bitter taste. Then I slip in the card I bought for Gloria's birthday, unsigned. My reason for going to the house if, by chance, someone should be there. She will never see it, but a nice touch, I think.

The Bygones are to leave this afternoon, but the workmen plan to work through Saturday until the light has gone, so I intend to be with Pipits on Sunday morning, Gloria's birthday. I have decided not to spend Saturday night there, too much time in love's company, and my resolve might weaken.

What a nice homecoming it will be for Gloria and Henry. Such a pity that I won't see their faces when they turn into the drive and view my handiwork; I picture shock and disbelief, a satisfying panic. They will be lost for words, until the words they never thought to speak will surface from somewhere deep inside them, words hard enough to bruise the soft palates of their fickle mouths.

I'm so excited, I can hardly wait now. Sleep escapes me, but I scarcely seem to need it. The occasional snooze in a chair, a moment or two of dozing fills me with energy. If it weren't for the pains in my chest, I would be feeling better than ever.

I am up and about on Sunday morning before the St. Dubricius bells get going. Mother was a regular attender at our village church. She sang in the choir and was part of the flower-arranging rotation. Gloria still goes. She says the congregation is down to ten or so these days, and that's on a good day. Henry accompanies her sometimes, although he claims that he is not a believer.

"I am a spiritual person, though," he insists.

I notice another fracture in Alice's bedroom ceiling. It is deeper than the others, a thick black mark and widening by the hour. Just as well that I am getting out.

I take special care with my appearance. I wash my hair, apply a deep red lipstick, and select the green dress that Bert bought for me in a different life. Slipping it over my head, I feel his presence, remember him sliding the zip, saying that the color looked good on me. I hardly know the person that I was then, hardly remember the life I used to have, the life that is Helen's now. For a moment I am flooded with an overwhelming sense of loss. I take one of Alice's ugly flower vases from the kitchen shelf and hurl it to the floor. The wire inside me unwinds. I feel better.

The postman calls, bringing me a seed catalog and a package from Amazon. I notice that the dog is sitting by the gate, waiting.

"Something nice, I hope," the postman says, nodding at the package.

It's the novel I had preordered, published now and in my hand. I place it among Alice's books on the sitting room shelves. A flicker of regret runs through me. Once there was pleasure in receiving a parcel containing a book; no more time left for reading now. I wonder what the college will do with all these books, who they will sell Alice's house to, whether Bert will regret giving me the Mayfair apartment as part of the divorce settlement. He always loved it. I could have left it to him, I suppose, but then Helen would get her hands on it. In any case, there is little so quickly forgotten in life as a generous act.

Taking a last look around Alice's house, I feel very calm. I won't bother sweeping up the broken vase, making the bed, or dusting. I will not put myself to tidying at all. Let them wonder about the grime, so out of character for me, about the shards on the floor; let them muse over my little scribbles on the bedroom walls, quotes about injustice. Let them wonder.

I slam the front door behind me, and the dog, still patiently waiting for me, perks up, stands to attention. I walk through the patch of garden to the pavement and drop the keys down the nearest drain. The little god of mischief in me, Loki, come to life, delighting in the games I play.

As I walk through the village, the dog follows behind, stopping when I stop, as though we are playing some childish game. The sun is up, and as I pass the surgery I turn to look back at him and glimpse my shadow on the pavement. He doesn't seem to cast one. Curious.

I amble slowly, taking my leave of the village, silently saying goodbye to the dark row of almshouses and to the stone eagle that sits atop the old vicarage, its beak honed by the wind. I remember the face of the boy who clipped the pub sign with his cricket ball, in the days when children played in Cold-Upton's streets. The chip is still there all these years later. I pass the shop and think about how charming it was when I was little, long before Agneta's time. No café then, and fresh-baked bread every morning. Mother would hand over her list, and the lady behind the till would give me a free sweet. That stopped when Gloria began to toddle; one free sweet was good for business, two a touch too openhanded.

I trail past the long stone wall in front of the church-yard and recall balancing on it as a child, arms outstretched, pretending to be a tightrope walker. Gloria tried to copy me, as she did in everything, and fell off. What a fuss was made of such a tiny wound, what a hugging and kissing, what a spoiling. The memory of it puts me in mind of the sly glance she gave to me over Mother's shoulder that day as I watched her being coddled. Like the cat that got the cream. That was the day the child who was Gloria stole away the child in me.

As I turn into Pipits' drive, I see Mrs. Lemmon walking toward me, fiddling with the zip of her anorak. She seems as surprised to see me as I am her. What is she doing here on a Sunday morning?

"Oh," she exclaims. "I have just locked up and put the alarm on."

"Don't worry," I say. "I'll put it back on when I leave."

"I've cleaned up in there best that I can," she says, nodding toward the house. "So much dust. I wonder if it will ever settle. Didn't want Mrs. Bygone coming back to worse than when she left it."

"No, we can't have that," I say.

Well, clearly she is hinting for me not to make a mess. Stupid woman, what right does she have to advise me on anything? She will be out of a job when I have done my work—a fact I don't regret.

"I am bringing a birthday card for Gloria," I say. "And a present, of course."

I indicate the bag. "A surprise for her when she gets home."

"Aren't you cold without a coat?" she asks. But I don't bother replying.

She's looking at my feet now, frowning. I follow her gaze and see that I have put on mismatched shoes, one brown, the other black.

Now, how did that happen? What was I thinking?

"I don't know where my head is these days," I say. "Now look, Mrs. Lemmon, would you do your best to encourage that dog away? It must belong to someone in the village, don't you think?"

"What dog?" she asks, looking around.

"Never mind," I say. "You go home. I'll take care of things here."

The woman isn't with it at all. How can you not see what is in front of your eyes? It wouldn't surprise me if she is a little drunk.

I watch her walk to the road, watch her until she reaches the box hedge where she turns toward the village. The top of her head bobs above the hedge for a bit, then disappears from sight. I listen for her footsteps to fade, then I put my bag down by the door and head to the garden.

I sit on the damp earth by the buddleia, and explain to Mother what is going to happen. This is all her fault: she got things wrong, was too trusting to see through Gloria's tricks. But I am going to put things right at last, clear up the mess she's made.

"It won't be like falling down a rabbit hole, not knowing

what to expect at the bottom," I say. "That was always your way, wasn't it? Such bad planning. My way will allow no uncertainties, only resolution."

On my way back to House I do a bit of deadheading. I tighten the loosened ties on the Albertine arch, spilling over with buds, pull out the weeds in the strawberry patch so that when the fruit comes, it will have space to spread out and ripen in the June sun.

IT IS QUIET IN the hall. I say hello, and the clock ticks with kindly comfort. "Here you are. Here you are," it tells me.

I walk around the house opening doors and windows, letting the light flood in. A through breeze should whisk the flames nicely. Mrs. Lemmon has not done much of a job cleaning, to be honest. There is dust everywhere. Never mind, though, Pipits glows despite the dust, wounded but more beautiful than ever.

I can tell that House is happy, hear its murmurings of pleasure as along with me, it prepares itself. I chatter to it as I go about my business. In the drawing room, I drag the fire basket forward and add a dozen firelighters to the logs inside it. I use the bellows to get the flames going. I pull the Indian rug into the grate and place it close to the blaze. Before I know it, it has sopped up the flames and begun to smoke.

The candles placed around the room look so pretty, sweetly glowing. I have arranged some on the window ledges so that the curtains will catch, others on the tables beneath the tapestries that hang on either side of the fireplace. One each under the pair of fringed lampshades, and, just for fun, I set a little tableau on the sofa table: four thick perfumed candles, neroli and frankincense, the birthday card propped against them, already singed with flame, along with the back of the sofa.

I had plans for the kitchen, but what remains of it will be hard to ignite, since it is an empty space. The stove lies in bits on the floor, waiting to be reassembled. Sheets of blue plastic are tacked over the missing windows, and the plaster on the new wall is still wet.

I make four attempts to set fire to the edge of the rag rug in the hall that Fi made as a present for Gloria, but it won't catch. The fabric just melts. So typical: man-made fibers, cheap as chips. It occurs to me that I should have brought petrol or some accelerant to help things on their way. Well, too late now.

As I head for the stairs, I turn and see through the open drawing room door that Mother's chair has caught fire, fallen over, and turned into a rolling orange ball. Flames have begun gobbling up the curtains, licking at the walls. Soon they, too, will take the stairs, reach Mother's bedroom, eat up Noah's cot and his mobile, wipe out the hateful mural that caused me such pain. The flames look so pretty, like deer leaping at play. How I love bonfires. This one will be the biggest, the most beautiful I have ever made.

With paper and matches and the last of the fire lighters, I set a neat little fire under the mahogany stool on the first-floor landing. I feed it with pages torn from a book chosen at random off the shelves there; some old tome of Father's on land management. It's ablaze in no time. Smoke is swirling around my feet.

In my bedroom I take my clothes off and sit on the edge

of my bed. I can feel a pleasant heat on the bare soles of my feet as they rest on the quivering floorboards.

"Don't be afraid," I tell Pipits. "Nothing can part us now."

I open my flask and drink down the laced tea that I made earlier. I may have been too generous with the medication—the brew is very bitter—but I wanted to be sure it would work quickly. The chocolate helps, but the swig of gin I gulp down afterward leaves my mouth tasting of metal. I settle myself under my patchwork quilt. The scent of it is familiar and comforting.

"Speak to me," I say, and Pipits does.

I'M GETTING DROWSY, DRIFTING into the dark. I feel as though I am melting from the inside out. My head feels heavy, and the world is tumbling, dipping up and down. I hang on to my quilt, suddenly fearful of falling into space. And then my bed begins to spin like one of those cup and saucer rides at the fairground. Around and around I go, hearing from far away what sounds like lions roaring. How can that be?

I must be having one of those dreams, where you know you are dreaming but you don't wake. The lions come swaggering into view, their greedy yellow eyes wide open, and then two people come walking fearlessly through the pride toward me: Mother in her mink coat, with her arms crossed against me; and Alice, still ill, shaking her head, mouthing something that I strain to hear. I can hear my heartbeat, and a booming sound, and then my dream is washed away by a tide of muddy waves beating on a blood-red shore.

I must give in, let go. Someone is calling me back,

though, calling from far away in a grating, insistent voice. I know that it isn't Pipits; our voice is one and the same now.

"Betty? Come on, Betty, wake up. Stay with me."

There is a harsh chemical smell, and suddenly I am hanging over the side of my bed vomiting, my throat raw with the force of it. Some person, big and shadowy, has come through my window and is looming over me.

I wake in the ambulance with a piercing pain in my lungs, everything hurting. A woman is pumping my chest with her hands. I attempt to push her off, but I can't seem to move. They are taking me away, saving me, they think, but they are wrong. Take me back, I scream at them. I must go back. But I cannot hear my voice. I smell roast meat, and my saliva tastes burnt. "Hold on," says a disembodied voice. "The pain will ease in a moment." Then, something cool on my arm, and I feel a pumping pressure there before I black out.

19

IN THE HOSPITAL I drift in and out of sleep. Even with the oxygen, breathing comes hard. The skin on my chest is tender, bruised where the woman in the ambulance attempted to inflate me. Everything hurts. I cough up black sputum.

They tell me I am lucky, that I could have died from the smoke inhalation alone. The burns I sustained while being carried out of the house are only second-degree. I am meant to be grateful for that. Apparently, I had grabbed onto the scaffolding that was shoring up the front of the house, and the fireman had to prize me off it.

"It was red-hot," the nurse who never stops talking says now. "Red-hot metal. Lucky you weren't wearing clothes; they would have bonded to your skin. Nasty, that."

There are clusters of blisters on my face, maps of them on my legs, and my bandaged hands hurt like hell. I haven't looked in a mirror yet, although I'm told there is nothing there that won't heal.

Gloria and Henry hang around the hospital. Always one of them on duty. They are full of concern, selfless as always.

Henry was there when I first woke.

"Pipits," I croaked. "What has happened to Pipits?"

"Don't worry about that now," he said. "Think about getting better first."

How is it that I am here, and he is standing at my bed-side, ruddy cheeked, unharmed, telling me not to worry? I couldn't hold back the words. "Tell me, you fucking stupid man. Pipits?"

He went white and screwed his eyes up as though I had hit him. I guess he thought I was going to lose it. I have history, after all.

"It's completely gone," he said flatly. "Nothing but rubble and ash, hard to believe how horribly everything has been destroyed."

"Everything?"

"Yes, we have lost everything, Betty."

"Everything but me," I say.

"Yes, we should be thankful for that," he says.

IT'S GRIM BEING SAVED. Pipits is gone, and I've been left behind. It's not the way it should have been. Nothing is as it should have been.

"The police want to talk to you, Betty," Henry says. Do I detect accusation in his voice?

"What about?"

"About the fire, of course. How it started. What you were doing in our house while we were away. Not that we mind, of course. That sort of thing."

"It's nobody's house now," I say, and turn from him.

The police visit me in the hospital, accompanied by a nasty little man who calls himself a fire investigator. Their questions come fast, and they repeat them at intervals, as though trying to catch me in a lie. But I stick to my story.

Apparently, they know that there were candles all over

the house. They are clever about that sort of thing these days. I tell them I wanted to surprise Gloria. That I thought it would be nice for her to arrive home to the fire glowing, with me there to celebrate her birthday with her.

"I am her sister," I tell them. "Of course I wanted to celebrate with her."

"Rather a lot of candles for that, wasn't it?"

"Oh, do you think so? But that is what we do these days. Candles everywhere. It was meant to be festive. I wanted to surprise her."

"So you placed the candles around, and then you went upstairs to bed?"

"I hadn't meant to go to bed. I was feeling cold, so I went to my room to change into something warmer."

"Your room?"

"Well, my room when I lived there. I still have some clothes there."

"But you went to bed instead?"

"I don't know why I lay down. Maybe the smoke got to me. I can't remember undressing. Can't remember much, to be honest."

"And the fire lighters? You took them into the house, didn't you?"

I wonder briefly if they can really tell. Fire eats everything, doesn't it?

"Yes, I thought it would be cheering for them to come home to a nice warm fire. I didn't know if they would have any fire lighters in the house. I knew that I wouldn't get a fire going without them. The chimney in that room doesn't draw well. Never has."

"And you had been drinking quite a lot that day?"

"What makes you say that?"

"Blood tests confirm alcohol and drugs in your system."

"Well, I had taken my prescriptions, if that's what you mean. I was feeling unwell—I had pains in my chest, rather more so than usual—and the painkillers didn't seem to be helping, so I thought a shot or two of alcohol might help to ease things."

"And the drugs? What do you take them for?"

"Codeine for the pain, Temazepam for stress."

I have no idea if they are going to take this line of questioning any further, and I don't much care. Pipits has gone without me. It's a bitter blow.

Grief takes people in many ways, I know. It has set a brick in my heart. I am angry with fate and furious with Mrs. Lemmon, who took it upon herself to save me.

Gloria has explained that Mrs. Lemmon thought I was behaving so oddly when she spoke to me that she just had to return to see if everything was all right.

"The house was ablaze by the time she got there," Gloria says, shuddering a little. "She called the fire brigade, but it was too late to save it. We were lucky that they were able to save you."

"Behaving oddly?" I questioned. "What on earth does she mean by oddly?"

"Well . . ." Gloria hesitates, as though debating with herself about whether or not to report what Mrs. Lemmon has told her. "Apparently you were wearing a cocktail dress, and the shoes on your feet didn't match. And you were seeing things that weren't there."

"What things?"

"A dog."

"Oh, him. He was there, all right. But he's clever at disappearing when the need arises."

Gloria is on her psychotherapy box, all concern, her voice low and syrupy with sisterly concern. She tells me that she and Henry have moved into Alice's house, and that they can't wait to look after me there when I'm released from the hospital.

"You don't mind, do you, Betty? It seems the perfect solution for the time being. We had to get the locksmith in; so much lost in the fire, things we haven't even thought about yet."

She tells me they have had a set of keys made for me, as though I am the guest now.

"You will have to get someone in to fix the cracks in the ceiling," I say. She looks confused.

"I haven't noticed them," she says.

"Well, you were never very observant about such things." I meant my words to wound, but she takes them as a tease and laughs.

"Betty," she whispers, putting her head close to mine, "what is that writing on the walls all about?"

"Oh, nothing much," I say. "I was getting ready to paint them. It was just a bit of fun."

"What color?" she asks pointlessly.

"What?"

"What color were you going to paint the walls? We could do it for you."

"Yellow," I say. "Yellow like the sun."

———————

A HOSPITAL PSYCHIATRIST HAS been to see me. Obviously Gloria has opened her mouth. He knows my story, knows about the Beachy Head episode. I bet she has mentioned the mismatched shoes and the bloody dog that everyone seems to think is a figment of my imagination.

"It is just that you must be in shock," he says. "It is a shocking thing to have happened. You might find it helpful to talk."

"I don't think so," I say.

He says he is happy to come again if I change my mind. That perhaps I am too close to the incident to be going over it in detail just yet. He warns of flashbacks, of how after a fire some people suffer from— He hesitates.

"From what," I say irritably.

"Well, the best way to describe it might be that they suffer from the primal fear of being eaten."

I can't stop myself from sneering. "Why on earth would someone feel that way after surviving a fire?"

"Well, flames consuming everything," he suggests. "A metaphor, of course."

"A bloody stupid one," I say.

I can tell I have offended him. But I don't care, I want him gone. As far as I am concerned, he might as well be a witch doctor shaking a bag of bones. I am an educated, rational woman, after all, and I will not be patronized.

"No one is immune from suffering," he warns. "It's only human to feel traumatized after such a frightening event. Not a good idea to bottle up those feelings; it can make recovery harder."

Henry visits me, too, with pictures on his phone of the

haunting empty plot where Pipits once stood. It is a moon-scape, a dark obsidian patch, a crematorium. Cracked stumps of the drawing room's blackened mantel lay among the ruins; the remains of the stove, a twisted metal heap, smelted and blackened like some brutal bit of modern art, squats on what once was the kitchen floor but is now a carpet of carbon; the exterior walls are burnt to within a few feet of the ground, and the whole wasteland of it is open to the sky.

I am in agony, but I have no tears. How dare Henry show those pictures to me, as though they are holiday snaps? I want to scream and scream, lash out at him with my fists, smash his complacent face. I hold it together, though. He is only allowed to see Betty, dear saved-from-the-fire Betty.

"Look," he says. "The lawns are as black as tar, and the turkey oak has been devoured by flames, its roots sucked from the earth."

Henry points these things out to me with a gruesome sort of pleasure. He crows that in a stroke of good fortune, his studio is untouched by the fire, apart from a bit of smoke damage to the bricks.

"I thought you said everything was gone," I say.

He shrugs. "I meant the house, of course, not the out-buildings. It's rather wonderful that we have been spared the studio, don't you think? At least now I can work, fulfill the orders."

And there it is, the Beloved's gift. I knew that there would be one.

"A yard or two closer to the house and it would have been gone, too," he says.

"Just a yard or two," I say. "Lucky you."

20

I SMELL SMOKE IN EVERYTHING. In the ointment they use to treat my burns, in my newly washed hair no matter that I made the nurse who was shampooing it rinse it twice. I taste it in the water I swallow, the food I eat. They assure me that these things are normal, that they will go away in time.

I looked in a mirror the other day at the hospital, and I won't be doing it again for a while. My face is a mess, weeping and puffy, a dark scab on my chin, shiny red patches above both eyes.

"Your eyebrows will grow back," I'm told. "The burn scars will fade to nothing."

Both my hands are still bandaged, so I have to be helped in the toilet, the nurses have to brush my teeth, smooth my hair. It is humiliating.

Despite all this, they say they will be sending me home soon. Home! I don't want to go. I want to be left alone. I need silence; every sound is an assault. The worst of it is the sick sort of excitement the fire has left behind its run. My sister and brother-in-law are infected with the buzz of it and cannot let it go. They visit, and the air they bring with them is hyped-up, full of nervous energy.

No visiting hour passes without Gloria's endless lists of

what was lost in the fire and Henry's ongoing display of photographs.

"I don't want to see them," I insist. "They all look the same to me."

I do not tell him that to me they are pictures of a grave. Who wants to look at endless pictures of a grave?

"Not really the same, Betty, different angles. And we should have a record, don't you think?"

"Why?"

"Well, for us, to remember. To show our children when they are grown, perhaps. And maybe the insurance company will want to see them, too."

Why did I not think of insurance? Of course they have insurance. It will be their solace, their chance to move on. I see in them no sign of the pain I suffer, yet still they are to be consoled, compensated.

"The holdup in the insurance payout is something to do with the police inquiry," Gloria says. "They have to wait for the results from that. They are sure to report that it was an accident, though. And that's what insurance is for, after all, accidents. Henry says that we shouldn't worry, that it will all be okay in the end."

"What will you do if they don't pay up?" I ask.

"You'll have to take us in for keeps," she laughs. "Orphans of the storm."

They both avoid saying what must be on their minds. What is an inquiry for, other than to place blame? Or does it always happen after a fire? Is it just a formality?

I allow myself to imagine being charged with setting the fire. I summon the possibility of newspaper articles naming me an arsonist. I picture prison, which I don't think I would mind so much, if it weren't for the lack of privacy. Henry and Gloria would visit, of course, forgiveness lighting their eyes, bringing a glow to their cheeks.

I blame myself for not getting it right, although I don't let the Lemmon woman off the hook. I should have known she would be back. I should have posted the card through the door and walked down the drive with her, so that she could see that I was leaving. All that business about me behaving oddly was just an excuse for her to return and check that I hadn't left a mess.

I send a request through Gloria for Mrs. Lemmon to visit me. She comes ten minutes before the end of the afternoon visiting hour, dressed in her horrible anorak, her hair scraped back in one of those scrunchies that her kind wear. I can tell by the big smile on her face that she is expecting me to thank her. I won't, of course. No thanks for her interfering, for her do-gooding, or for the cheap bunch of flowers that she has brought with her to the hospital.

"Mrs. Lemmon," I say. "I hear that you have been spreading lies about me."

"No," she says nervously, the smile falling off her moon face. "Of course I haven't."

"Well, apparently you don't approve of the way I dress. You think that I behave oddly. You tell people that I see things that are not there."

"Well that's not—"

I cut her off. "I have asked you here to tell you to stop your gossiping. I won't stand for it. It is not your place to talk about me. Stick to your cleaning and mind your own business."

It amuses me to see how her eyes dart around the ward

to check who might be listening, how her mood so quickly turns from nervous to offended.

"If it weren't for me, you would have burned in that fire."

"Don't you dare ever mention the fire or Pipits to me again. If it weren't for you—"

I catch myself just in time from blurting out how she had ruined everything. It is never wise to confide in her sort. Finer feelings are unfamiliar to people like her. The Mrs. Lemmons of this world delight in gossip, are strangers to discretion.

"Take your flowers," I say, throwing them to the end of the bed. "You can leave now."

I watch her walk from the ward, the flowers dangling from her hand, her back stiff with outrage.

AT LAST I HAVE gotten my hands on some gin. I paid the young woman in the bed next to mine to bring it to me. She was discharged yesterday, and I took the opportunity to bribe her. I thought she would be up for it; she appeared a truculent sort of person, not one to care much for the rules. In her short stay she has set the alarm off twice by smoking in the lavatory, and her visitors were of the rowdy sort.

She cleverly put the gin in a water bottle and handed it over with some apples. She did it so easily, I could tell that she is no stranger to deception. The alcohol has eased my mind a little, although it seems to have roused the headaches, which have sneaked back to plague me.

Everything in life that once had a point seems meaningless now. I cannot imagine ever bothering with gardening again, or reading, or going through the daily rituals of bathing, putting on makeup, choosing what to wear. I will never hear the sweet voice of Pipits again, or dream the dreams that only came to me in my room there, dreams of possession and togetherness. I will never again smell the cedarwood of my wardrobe, never experience the perfect light that dusts the hall at dawn. Pipits has gone before me. What's left in the wreckage is not enough, not nearly enough.

Without invitation, the psychiatrist visits again. He has questions. How do I feel about the investigation? Perhaps I would like him with me if the police come again. I might find his presence comforting at such times.

"I'm fine," I tell him. "I'm not a child; I can deal with disaster."

He looks dubious. "The brain attempts to reassure," he says. "The emotions won't be ruled, though. You have been through a terrible experience. It might help to talk." That again!

I am discharged, given an appointment for a checkup three weeks from now. Gloria comes to collect me. As usual, she has made no effort. There's a small hole in the elbow of her sweater, the hem of her jeans are frayed, her long hair is messy from running her hands through it. Even so, as she breezes through the ward, she gathers admiring looks.

"Of course we have nothing left," she says. "Only the clothes we stand up in and the few things that we packed for our weekend away. It is extraordinary how people have been so kind. We live in such a good village, don't we? Noah has been given a cot and lots of clothes and toys. He has everything he needs, and more."

She has selected the oddest assortment of my clothes for

me. A pair of dark red trousers that no longer fit me, since I have lost weight. They slip from my waist and sit on my hips, and the hems brush the floor. And to accompany them a green top, fraying at the sleeves, that doesn't go with them at all; I had been about to discard it. Both items were rolled up at the bottom of the wardrobe at Alice's, so they are as crumpled as Gloria's own clothes. It didn't occur to her to iron them, of course. I have perfectly good clothes hanging in the wardrobe that any halfway rational person would have chosen. I say as much to her.

"Oh, but they are such pretty colors. I thought they would cheer you up. Never mind, think of all the fun we will have shopping for new ones when the insurance money comes through," she says.

I give her a look.

"Well, what can we do but make the best of it?" she says.

I CANNOT BEAR IT. I cannot bear being in this poky little house with the Bygone family appearing at every turn. Their clutter is everywhere, so that there is hardly space for me. My hatred for them is a constant stream of acid eating away at me, wolves and sharks. But what is to be done? What is to be done?

Gloria says she doesn't mind the huddle. "I will miss it when things sort themselves out," she says, as though she has convinced herself that she will. Little Miss Pollyanna.

I visited what used to be Pipits and was overcome with a new kind of misery. Poor dead House. Gone without me House.

"You will be avenged," I promised. "This is all Gloria's fault."

I collected some of Pipits' precious ashes, most of which have been scattered far and wide by the wind. I have them in a small leather jewelry box, which I have secreted in my car. It's a comfort when I'm alone, to talk to them.

To get away from the making-the-best-of-it Bygones, I daily walk the village trail through our woods and across our meadows. The meadows hold less pleasure for me these days, since there is no Pipits to be seen in the distance anchoring the view. Now there is only the patch of festering earth where it once stood, the sight of which feeds my anger.

I prefer my time on the riverbank, where I can commune with House in peace. Naturally, I drive there. Why not? I see no reason to obey stupid rules. Gloria has no idea that I lost my license. How it would shock her to know. I still take the longer route, keeping an eye out for the police, being the most considerate of drivers.

Two months since I left the hospital, and still no sign of the dog. In my absence, he must have found himself someone else to moon with his doleful eyes. Unless he somehow got caught up in the fire. I shouldn't think that is the case, though. He looked a cowardly hound to me, the kind that would run at the first whiff of smoke.

In May's warm wetness, this new unlooked-for life is a punishment I endure. I stoically bear Noah's crying, the mess, and the relentless company. My dreams are broken up with Noah's keening. He has turned into an irritable child.

"It's a stage," Gloria apologizes. "Frustration that he can't get into things."

Alice's house has been toddler-proofed. There are covers for the plug sockets, locks on the kitchen cupboards, even a fastener on the toilet seat.

Gloria spoils him, so his fussing is not likely to get any better. I dwell more than ever these days on how it would have been had I never had a sister. I dwell now on too many things.

Spring storms come and shake the window frames, the wind rattles down Alice's chimney, and more cracks appear in the ceiling. Gloria looks upward, screws her eyes up as if to see better, and stares for the longest time.

"Hairline at best," she says. "Nothing to worry about."

So little in life bothers my optimistic sister. It comes of having a limited imagination. She has started to paint over my graffiti in a wash of yellow, the wrong shade obviously, egg yolk, when citrine was what I had in mind. Is she trying to wipe me out? Does she resent me without knowing it? Even if that's true, it is not something she would ever admit.

They spent last weekend with Henry's mother. Oh, the beautiful silence. I found a letter from Bert in their bedroom, his words thick with sympathy. He can't believe what they have had to suffer lately, the mushroom poisoning and now this terrible fire. He says thank goodness I made a complete recovery, and to give me his best wishes.

What luck Mrs. Lemmon returned in time, he writes. *You might have lost her otherwise.*

I guess they decided not to relay his message, thinking even the mention of his name would scratch the sore. How feeble they must think me. I was surprised at his reference to the mushroom episode. I had forgotten it. It is odd how these things slip my mind, how I don't remember the details anymore. The mushroom episode has become just that, the time when Henry ate the wrong mushrooms. I do not give myself enough credit.

———————

JULY, THE FLOWERING MONTH, and the weeds have taken over Pipits' garden. It has become an allotment of nettles and ground elder; the paths are muddy, their edges tufted over with uncut grass. I have neither the energy nor the desire to do anything about it. The garden cannot now complement Pipits' beauty or serve as a memorial to us.

As anger and grief pace side by side in me, another privation adds itself to the total. My spot by the river has been invaded by newcomers: three lads in hoodies, parked up in my space in their rust bucket of a car, smoking weed. I've inspected their cigarette butts scattered about and recognize that Moorish aroma of sweat and honey. It is not uncommon in the art world.

The river has been my haven, a place away from the wreckage, but now I never know when I will find the intruders there, so I have been forced to give up going. I do not like the idea of being in a city, the thought of noise, and crowds, quite sickens me. But there's no other option I can see for the moment. I decide that I must return to London.

I have put off even visiting my apartment there, because I didn't want people staring at me. But my eyebrows have begun to grow back, and the burn scars have faded. I'm looking about as good as I'm going to get. And if I wear makeup, the scars are hardly noticeable.

At least in the apartment I can be alone.

21

I HAVE BECOME, BY DESIGN, one of those women that you see around Mayfair: smartly dressed in Chanel or Dior, her coral lipstick on straight, and walking alone, always alone. Mother's pearls and a black velvet headband in my hair, which now skims my shoulders, add to the look. I wear silk blouses under boxy jackets and carry neat chain-handled handbags, nothing squashy; the look is all about smart, finished edges, well-applied makeup. I am pretty sure that I have nailed it. You would take me for a good ten years older than I am. I'm an actress playing a part, disguising myself in an alter ego.

My creation of Mayfair Lady has the desired effect. Because I am a type, and therefore unremarkable, I am rendered anonymous. I do not wish to be seen. A small dog of the embryonic sort would add to the look, but I am not prepared to go that far.

I have taken up smoking. It goes well with the gin and helps with the boredom. I am never lonely, but I find that there is little worse than being bored, little worse than the dread of the empty hour. I have thought about getting a job, returning to work, to the world, but I don't feel fit for it anymore.

The insurance money for Pipits has come through. The inquiry came to nothing in the end. The investigating fire officer's report put it down to an accidental fire caused by unattended candles, a not uncommon event these days. I am not surprised; what was there for them to prove? It was obviously an accident, a kindly sister wanting to celebrate her sibling's birthday.

Gloria and Henry offered to pay me for the Miró that wasn't a Miró, made charcoal in the fire.

"It's the insurance who are paying," Gloria said. "So you don't have to thank us."

I told them to keep the money. They think me generous, but the truth is I cannot bear the thought of profiting in any way from Pipits' demise.

Another Christmas has passed. I was invited to spend it with the Bygone family but didn't. Christmas with them, in Alice's house, was a penance I had no intention of paying. I told them I was invited to visit friends in London, that the invitation had been given with so much notice that I couldn't get out of it. They don't need to know I have not kept up with any of the people I once knew in this city. I expect Bert and Helen count them as friends now.

Gloria and Henry plan to build a modern house on Pipits' land. The nerve of them. Hatred for the happy pair coursed through my body. They say they are grateful for the use of Alice's house but hope I will come back to live there when they vacate it. Well, Gloria says it. I doubt that Henry hopes for it.

I may be distanced from Pipits, but it is not forgotten. I have its ashes on a chest of drawers at my bedside. We lie together as though in state, like those stone effigies of kings and queens, slumbering in the great cathedrals. At night, I light a candle and talk things over with House.

I think of the land that is left, the land that should be mine. I think of Henry, building a new home on that land, and the desire to be rid of him is still strong in me. "Third time lucky," I say to House. "Goals to aim for."

Noah has passed his second birthday. He walks, and talks, and I see from the photographs Gloria sends that he has her mouth, Henry's halo of golden hair. I sent him the best soft toy that I could bag for his birthday: a polar bear with a black velvet nose and pink paws. It had a fifty-pound price tag hanging from its ear. Pretty steep, I thought. I decided not to pay it.

So, while I wait for inspiration of how to dispatch Henry, I have taken to shoplifting, such a crude way to describe what I have turned into a kind of magic. Now you see it, now you don't. It is not about the stealing but about the game, about outwitting the store detectives, about reading signals, about giving the heart a workout and enlivening the day. It is about the hot blast of excitement as I exit a store with my prize. I am skillful at analyzing the shop assistants' body language, at seeing what lies beneath their made-up faces; this one dense, that one sly.

Taking things that catch my eye helps with the boredom, makes me feel alive, if only for an hour or so. My first stab at it was in Liberty's jewelry department. I had been wandering around for an hour or so, and had even bought some makeup with a credit card, so it wasn't on my mind to take something without paying for it.

It was no surprise, though, that I took umbrage against

the woman who was serving me. She was uppity for a shop assistant, the kind who pathetically associates herself with the class of her customers. I doubt that she could have afforded any of the items she was hired to sell. Her eyes scanned me from head to foot as though adding up the sum of me and finding that it didn't amount to much.

I decided to give her the runaround, to put some trouble into her day. Like the jewelry she was selling, she was a piece of design herself: smart with a touch of the arty about her, blunt-cut hair, big statement necklace, dark brown nail polish, heavy man's watch on her slim wrist. She spoke to me as though I were in need of her advice.

I attempted to slip one of the bracelets she was showing me into my bag while her back was turned, but I wasn't quick enough. I think that she knew what I was about, because she became very haughty and offhand with me. I gave her back as good as I got, requesting to examine a half-dozen things I feigned interest in before strolling off without thanking her.

The failed attempt thrilled me. Hardly a day goes by now when I don't return to my apartment with some prize. I keep it all in the big coat cupboard in the hall. It gives me a warm feeling to look at it, to know that I have left my mark somewhere.

I confess to but don't complain about feeling excluded from everything in this new life. People in the street pass me without a glance, waiters forget my order, cabs sail past despite my flagging them down. I guess my disguise is working. I had thought the Mayfair Lady type so ubiquitous in the city as to be anonymous; it seems that she is invisible, too.

I keep myself busy. I read a bit, troll the shops in daylight, and drive the neon-lit streets at night. The driving ban is over now, not that it ever made the slightest difference to me.

There are times when I catch sight of my reflection in a shop window and have to hunt for myself hidden beneath the painted veil I have contrived. I hug to myself the knowledge of how well I am concealed. Even Gloria would walk past this overdone woman without a second glance.

Sleep, as usual, is hard to come by. I pace around the apartment in the early hours with only the radio and London Dry, my favorite brand of gin, for company. The little catnaps I take are plagued with dreams of endless corridors of white space: no sound or color, only vistas of bleached-out nothingness.

When I first returned to the city, I took long walks by the Thames. So many convenient bridges above deep enough water, such a powerful pull waiting to embrace me, to reunite me with House. But the secret weapon of my own death has no target now. I don't believe the Bygones would mourn me for long. And, besides, I am a good swimmer, and instinct would probably have kicked in, making a fool of me. I gave up the notion and decided to stick out time here for a bit. Life has meaning while there is land, Stash land, and Henry still to deal with.

Nothing lessens my loss, however. I feel it as I cross the road dodging the traffic on a green light, as I take my last drink at night, speak on the phone to Gloria: especially then. In Gloria's voice, her giggle, the lilt at the end of her sentences, I feel my childhood come to life. I don't thank her for it.

———

THIS MORNING I WAS caught out in my little game of lifting merchandise from stores without paying for it. I confess that it was my carelessness, and not their cleverness, that gave me away. It was early in the day, so it was just a warm-up as far as I was concerned: a lipstick tester from the Dior counter in Harvey Nichols; not my color, a pale frosty sort of purple. I cannot imagine whose color it would be. I dropped it into my bag as I called over the assistant. Boldness is the thing. Do it right in front of them and they don't see.

I think that at some level I must have sensed that I was being watched, because I felt a bit hesitant about leaving the store. I took the escalator to the fifth floor and spent longer than usual over coffee. Afterward, at the beauty salon on the ground floor, I decided on impulse to have my eyebrows dyed. They have struggled to grow back as thick as they were before the fire and have lost something of their previous shape. I thought about a manicure but decided against it.

"More arched," I told the girl. "Much more arched."

I paid, looked around me, and when no one seemed interested, I headed for the exit. I intended to make my way along Brompton Road to the Armani store to take a light lunch in its restaurant, more for somewhere to sit than to eat, but as I left through the big glass doors onto Sloane Street, a woman put her hand on my shoulder very firmly and spun me around.

"Would you mind coming with me, madam? I am a store detective."

It was so corny a statement, I couldn't resist a smirk. I went without a fuss. I didn't want to attract an audience.

I followed her to a tiny room where she offered me a

seat, which I declined. I was an inch or two taller than her, and sitting would have deprived me of that advantage.

"Empty your handbag please, madam. Onto the desk."

I didn't like her tone, or the sour whiff of her breath, and I don't take orders, so I passed my bag to her, shrugging as though I didn't know what she was talking about.

"I'm rather late for a lunch meeting," I said, looking at my watch. She didn't reply.

I feigned surprise when, routing through my things, she found the little bullet of purple with the tester mark on it. She looked disappointed, as though she had been expecting to find something more substantial.

"It must have fallen in, as I was trying out the colors," I said.

"Mm . . . or possibly intentionally taken?" she questioned in a flat south London accent.

"Oh, surely you cannot believe that anyone would wish to steal such a silly little thing." I said it with the sort of posh disbelief that I thought in keeping with Mayfair Lady. Friendly enough but with a touch of formality that indicated I was not about to play her victim.

The windowless room was very stuffy, and the palms of my hands had begun to sweat, but I stood with my shoulders back, composed in a way that I imagined might intimidate her.

"You'd be surprised what people will steal, madam."

"Yes, I suppose so. I can't say that is something that I have given much thought to."

"I could call the police in, you know. It would be very embarrassing for you."

"You could, of course. I imagine, though, that they have

better things to do. In any case, just look at me. Is it likely that I would even wear that color?"

"I don't wear lipstick myself, madam. I have no idea what color you might wear, but that is hardly the point."

Odd as it seems, I was enjoying our banter. She was no match for me, but it felt good to fence. No way would she be taking it further. She obviously thought I had stolen something new, something of value. Holding up the little purple tester to the police would have made her look foolish.

"You seem like a nice lady," she said. "So I'm going to let you off with a warning this time. You wouldn't want your name in the papers now, would you?"

"Isn't that what everyone wants these days," I said with a smile. "STOP PRESS. Police find used lipstick in woman's handbag."

"Yes, madam, very droll." She couldn't resist a smile herself.

I must be more careful. It has all been so easy that perhaps I was getting overconfident.

———————

GLORIA AND HENRY HAVE engaged a prize-winning architect to build them a new house. It is to be a confection of steel and glass, a modern-day palace to stand where "the old house," as they so pitilessly call Pipits now, once stood. It's as if Pipits were some useless saggy thing they are glad to be rid of. It is no surprise to me how bereft of true feelings the Beloveds are.

I looked the architect up online, and she is indeed a prize winner. Rather beautiful, too, if you like the pale and fragile look. There are pictures of her with some minor celebrities, and one of her standing in front of a house she designed that looks more like an arc, a rainbow of silver and white, than someone's home.

I have to say her work is better than most of the modern stuff you see around and rather masculine to have come from such a delicate-looking woman. I wonder how Henry and Gloria came across her. She won't be cheap, but Henry's mother has offered to pay for her services, in lieu of leaving them the money in her will.

They are free now to do as they wish, to build whatever ghastly vision appeals to them. Blithely unaware of their part in it, they take no responsibility for the misfortune of losing Pipits. Still, I keep my agony hidden. My voice is calm when I speak to them. It is wiser to charm than to rage, and on the phone they cannot see the expression on my face.

Gloria says she has never seen Henry so utterly absorbed in a project. He is elated at the thought of the innovative building that is to be their new home and is involving himself in every little detail, choosing with care the doorknobs and showerheads and even the light switches, which are to be sensor operated.

"Just a wave of the hand," Gloria gushes on one of her endless calls.

"And let there be light," I join in, as if I care.

"Yes, and all this, Betty, before even one brick has been laid."

I ask her where she and Henry found this just-too-wonderful architect. There is a noticeable pause, a ladylike little cough.

"From Bert," she says brightly, recovering herself. "She is building a house for them in Spain."

Of course she is. No call with Gloria ends without her picking at my scabs.

She thanks me for letting them live at Alice's house, invites me to come and stay. I am not ready for that yet. Will I ever be again?

22

A COCKY NEW COUPLE HAS moved into the first-floor apartment beneath mine. I had a letter from the agency that takes care of the apartment's communal areas, informing me of their arrival. They are newlyweds. He is something to do with finance; she is a buyer for some upmarket catalog, so she travels a lot.

I watched them move in from behind my sitting room curtains. A smart moving van, men in uniform, boxes all labeled nicely. No shortage of money, then. They are a tall and short pair. Wifey is the tall one, athletic-looking, with a halo of corkscrew curls around her freckly face; and Hubby a bit overweight, but quite good-looking in that city-boy way, striped shirt and short messed-up hair.

It took no time at all to discover they are beyond noisy: every kind of music played at full blast so that the bass note beats its mindless way through my floors until I think I will go mad; the volume on their television is stuck on maximum so that I can hardly hear my radio, no matter how loud I have it. Doors cannot simply be closed but must be banged shut.

They chatter boisterously in the hallway, where they leave a folding bike and a bright red helmet. I intend to speak to them about that. They have no right to park anything in the communal area.

They are not the first occupants of the flat downstairs I have had to have words with over similar annoying habits. The owner lives abroad and rents the place out so that one is always meeting strangers in the lift. A good enough reason for me to take the stairs, which I prefer to do anyway.

Bert was very friendly with the last lot of tenants, although I found them nosy in the extreme. When I moved back in on my own, I had to snub them to keep them at a distance. I suppose when they left, I should have returned the set of keys they gave into Bert's keeping, in case of an emergency.

"Fire or theft," they had joked. "Rape and pillage."

They must have forgotten they had given them to him, I suppose. I found the keys when I was clearing out the drawer in the desk where Bert had left a mishmash collection of pens and rubber bands, aspirins, and the like. They were in an envelope clearly labeled in his bold writing.

I don't suppose I would ever have used them if the catalog and city-boy couple hadn't complained. Not in the place five minutes, and they are already acting as though they have rights over the entire building. They cannot stand my walking the floors during their sleeping hours, apparently. My radio, they say, is on all night and is so loud that it keeps them from their slumber. My radio is loud!

"We want to be good neighbors," the husband says, standing solemnly at my door. "But if you could just keep it down."

Can you believe it? They are the noisiest people imaginable, and they have the cheek to complain about me keeping them awake with what they refer to as my "patrolling."

I have no desire to charm them, so I will be ignoring

their complaint. If I want to keep the BBC World Service on all night, I will, and at whatever volume I choose. Why should I change my habits for them? If they are that bothered, let them rent somewhere else.

They phoned me once at three o'clock in the morning to ask if I would mind stopping my pacing and turning my radio down. I could tell that they were on loudspeaker: I heard the wife sigh, and there was the tiniest echo on the line. He had an early meeting, he said, and she was recovering from jet lag, and they needed their sleep. I told them I would do what I liked in my own apartment and not to call me again.

I reminded myself that they were merely annoying transients. I should not have to change my habits to suit them. I began wearing my high heels as I pottered around in the evening, and copycatting the banging of their doors.

Then, a month or so later, the letter—the-first-real-shot-of-the-war—came from their lawyer, and the battle lines were drawn. I was damaging their peace of mind, their right to a stress-free life. What about their intrusion into my life, what about my rights?

I must say I was engaged more than upset at the letter. It felt good to have a skirmish that was nothing to do with Gloria and Henry. Getting the Stash land into my keeping, no matter what ultimately gets built on it, is my priority, but this fracas with the downstairs tenants was a not unwelcome distraction.

I lit the candle, put my hand on the box that contains the ashes of beloved House, and explained what I was about to do. I could tell that House approved of my plans.

"Sleep, now," I said. "When the time is right, I will win the war for us. You will be proud of me."

Two days after I received the letter from their lawyer, I let myself into their apartment with the previous tenant's keys. I am not sure what I intended to do that first time other than to find out what kind of people I was dealing with. That they were loud and brash I knew. But I needed to know more.

There are four apartments in this building, but quite often I am the only person in residence. The penthouse above me belongs to an American businessman who is hardly ever in occupancy. The complainers are below me on the first floor, and the ground-floor apartment is empty and up for sale. It has been on the market for some time now, due to its lease running out and the cost of renewing it, let alone the poor state it is in. All somewhat off-putting to prospective buyers.

Despite the fact that I had watched them leave, and had checked to make sure their car was gone, I took the stairs down to their hallway and stood listening outside their door until I felt sure of their absence. At first the key didn't seem to work, and I felt a moment's disappointment before realizing that they had double locked the door. I turned the key again, and the door swung open.

I had been in the place a couple of times before when Bert and I were invited for drinks with a previous tenant, so I knew the layout. It was not dissimilar to my own apartment: higher ceilings, though, and longer windows, the light brighter. The first floors of these Regency houses were the original reception rooms, so space and light are better in them than in the rest of the house. I had always envied that Bert hadn't got to this apartment first, even though he said he preferred the coziness of ours.

It was easy to see they were a messy couple. They couldn't even be bothered to put their breakfast dishes in the sink: toast crumbs on the table, bread bin open, sticky marks on the work surfaces.

Their bed, an ocean of white, was unmade, the duvet rumpled up as though they'd had a fight on it. There was a pack of contraceptive pills on a nightstand, clearly her side, and a nail clipper and a flashlight on his. Not readers, then.

Their bathroom looked like it could do with a good clean, too: half-empty products scattered about, a brownish soap ring forming in the sink. In the sitting room, wine-glasses had been left on the coffee table, and an iPod was slotted into the top of a radio. I slipped it into my pocket. They would buy another one, of course, but its loss would keep them from their jingle-jangle music while they hunted for it.

I stood for a few minutes in their hall breathing in the quiet air of the place. As I looked around, my skin tingled in a way that reminded me of the old days, when I had enjoyed an interest in life. There was a strange crunching sound in my head, like the sea rushing at a shingle shore, and warm exhilaration welling in my chest. I closed my eyes and waited for the sound to retreat.

The idea came to me that I was the fox in the hencoop. I pictured myself running riot, wrecking the place. It was an exciting thought. A tempting idea, but too much in it to give me away. To see them off, I would need to be thorough, to take things more at a drip-drip pace.

With Pipits gone, and no idea as yet how to recover the land it had sat on, or how to deal with Henry, it felt good to have a project, a purpose. Still, I felt a momentary twinge of unease. What if I got caught? I would have to make sure that didn't happen. I would be cautious; my intelligence would protect me.

Whatever occurs from now on will be their own fault. They set this whole thing in motion with their whining and threats. I cannot allow them to get away with it, to meekly oblige them. They are the kind who will never be satisfied. Comply with one thing and they will find another to moan about. I will not have them as neighbors; they have to go.

It will be little things at first, nothing they can prove, and nothing the police would have an interest in. Their lives are about to become unsettled, full of events for which they will have no explanation. They will wish they had never set eyes on the place, wish they had never interfered with their neighbor's peace of mind.

For tonight, at least, there will be no pacing to bother them, not the slightest hum from the radio. They will think the letter has worked, think me scared by their absurd threats.

I guessed they would be congratulating themselves while hunting around for their missing iPod, blaming each other, perhaps, for its disappearance.

In the weeks that followed that first visit, I made sure that every few days something went wrong: a split pipe under the sink so that they returned home to their kitchen under an inch of water, a dribble of bleach in their mouth-wash, a feed of gin to their expensive bright pink orchid, so tasteless in its shiny black pot, and their framed wedding photograph fallen from the mantelpiece to the floor, the glass split into three shards, tiny splinters of it sparkling like ice in their snow-white sheepskin rug.

It occurred to me that they might begin to think the place haunted, a poltergeist making mischief, perhaps. How funny that would be. I imagined them the sort to believe in such things.

I watched them leave for work every morning from my bedroom window, which looks down onto the private parking area for our house. They aimed for eight o'clock but rarely made it, so that they were always in a hurry; a quick kiss, some calling out to each other, and laughter, always laughter. She, when not getting into a taxi to the airport, unfolding her bike, putting the red helmet on, wobbling off. He in their four-by-four, backing slowly down the slope of the parking lot so as not to hit the big metal refuse bins lined up neatly against the wall.

Driving a four-by-four, especially one with a big ugly bull bar mounted at the front, seems very show-offy to me. What need for it in the city? I still have my old Volkswagen; the same car I have had for years. I like that it doesn't draw attention.

Once, as Hubby drove out of their parking space, giving a brief little toot of the horn to Wifey, I saw her dismount her bike and stare back toward our building. She held her gaze steady for a few seconds as though trying to work something out, then she shrugged and wheeled her bike onto the road.

I am pretty sure she didn't see me looking through the narrow gap in my closed curtains. I know how to stand motionless, to become merely a shadow. Still, I gave it a couple of hours that day before letting myself into their apartment. Perhaps she had simply forgotten something that morning, something that she might return for. I left their front door ajar so that I would hear the lift, although I couldn't be sure she wouldn't take the stairs. If I am ever caught, I plan to say their door was swinging open as I passed, and I thought that they might have been broken into; might have needed help. They could never prove otherwise.

I thought about leaving red roses at their door with a card to one or the other of them, love from A or B or the like. It might help to break the trust between them. Risky, to introduce things from the outside, though. I will need to think about that one.

Today's task will be accessing a girlie porn site on their big shiny iMac. She won't be pleased to see that come up in the recently viewed history. He will be bemused, insisting on his innocence, aggrieved that she could even think it of him. I imagine they will argue about it, and their arguing will not be the harmless bickering that is the stuff of all marriages, but something deeper, something that will fracture their happiness. The thought of his needing such sexual stimulus will hurt her. She will question why, so soon into their marriage, she seems not to be enough for him. The idea that his interest in such things might lead to infidelity will not be easy to dismiss. She will be suspicious.

I was delighted to discover that neither one of them uses passwords for the web or their email. They have set up their computer so that you simply click on an icon and are taken straight through. Such laziness.

Their accounts are very boring on the whole: gym fees due, her mother twittering on about how she can't wait to see them. Nothing from his parents, though, so I suspect they may be dead, or perhaps they don't have email.

Sometimes I glean a bit of useful information, such as when they will be away, or when they are meeting up with friends—a helpful indication to me that they will be home late. I've learned that he has a hundred and three friends on Facebook, she only eighty. Occasionally I delete something, a payment reminder, or one or two of their favorites on their supermarket shopping list.

Tonight they will return to a neat little hole in the bathroom mirror and a tipped-over jar of honey in the kitchen, its contents drooling through the wire racks of their pull-out food cupboard. The honey was a mistake. I was looking for coffee, as I had run out, and I accidentally knocked it over. They had left the lid loose. Tut, tut.

It's enough for now that I have access to their lives. So I keep off their radar by being the quiet neighbor: my radio on low and bare feet around my apartment. I'll start up again when I'm ready. On-off is the way to niggle and confuse them.

Their habits are not entirely reliable, so I keep a notebook to jot down their comings and goings, snatches of conversations that I overhear, what they are wearing, whether they are holding hands or seem a little apart as though they have argued. It helps to detect patterns, to know your enemy.

They often entertain; people like themselves, people I think of as the Burberry set, designer-labeled, unoriginal. They are, like most people, tribal, wearing the same clothes, driving the same flashy cars, sharing the same cul-de-sac mind-set, no doubt.

They take their rubbish out to the big bins on Tuesday evenings and Sunday mornings. He does Tuesday, she Sunday, wearing a coat over her pajamas and silver trainers on her feet. If it weren't for the hair, she would look quite masculine, with her broad shoulders and long strides.

Occasionally they go away for weekends. I see them put their bags into the trunk of their car, notice the upward lift in their body language, watch the newly washed four-by-four sail away. It is just lovely when they are absent at weekends. I put aside thoughts of Pipits' land, and of Henry, and indulge in the present. House knows that I will get to it when the time is right, when plans fall into place, as they have a habit of doing. Meanwhile, it feels good to be taking on the neighbors.

I stand sentinel at my window for a few minutes in case they return for any reason, and then I allow the pleasure of their truancy to wash over me. If the upstairs American happens to be away at the same time, I revel in the joy of having the whole house to myself.

I take my time getting ready: a long shower to wash away Mayfair Lady, no makeup, no disguising clothes, no jewelry. The real me emerges: straight hair, pale skin, my jawline appearing sharper than ever without the pearls and scarves to soften it, my eyes a little hollow without the makeup. I reclaim my true self.

In their apartment I make coffee, watch their television. I left it on once for them to come home to. I wonder who got the blame for that. I take my own gin with me, since they are not spirit drinkers. Wine is more their thing.

I took a nap on their bed one Saturday afternoon when they were on a break to Paris. But I couldn't settle down for long. Every sound disturbed me. And what if they returned unexpectedly? *Who's that sleeping in my bed?*

A bit of me is always on alert when I make myself at home in their apartment; wise, I think, not to allow myself to relax completely. But I so love it there; maybe because no one in the world knows where I am.

———————

TO ADD TO THE pressure of living in their jinxed apartment, and just when they must be thinking they have tamed me, I have resumed my radio habit and sent them a letter about the bike, reminding them that the hallway is communal property and that they have no right to block it with their things. I've warned them that if they do not remove the bike, I will be obliged to complain to their landlord, who is an old friend and would be upset to think that they were breaking the rules and displeasing his fellow tenants.

I cannot actually claim their landlord as an old friend, although I did meet him on a couple of occasions before he started renting his apartment out. He bought a painting from us once, a rather good abstract by a Camden artist, and afterward, he invited us to the theater; he had tickets for something or other. Bert went. I can't remember why I didn't. I reason, though, that our interest in the building is the same and that he is bound to take my side in any disagreement. After all, I am an owner here, too, and will be in the building long after "short and tall" have left. So I write to him with my complaints, and, just to be friendly, I mention a little of my new circumstances.

My request to remove the bike from the hallway was perfectly polite, but the couple sent no reply, and as yet the bike is still there. It is foolish of them to think I can be ignored.

Whatever Hubby said, it is obvious they do not want to be good neighbors. Their recent attitude to me has proved that. I met them on the stairs the other day, and you would have thought it impossible for "good evening" to sound so hostile. They were dressed in running gear, their faces polished with sweat. He couldn't bring himself to smile, and Wifey gave me a strange look that made me wonder briefly if she could smell her perfume on me.

I heard them chattering on their way up the stairs before they saw me coming down. They mumbled a brief greeting, and I did the same. After we had passed they fell silent. In my mind's eye I could see them exchanging sniggery looks. I wondered in what terms they talk about me to each other: the uptight insomniac, perhaps? The bitter middle-aged woman who could do with a good seeing to by some randy buck? I know how their kind think. They see Mayfair Lady and make assumptions.

Well, I shouldn't be surprised, I suppose. I marvel at how perfectly I have created her myself; everything faultlessly in keeping, the lipstick thick enough to fleck the teeth, the hair so lacquered as to be oblivious to the wind, and the clothes archetypal, right down to the beige fifteen denier tights and matching taupe court shoes. How surprised my brash neighbors would be if they could see the real me.

And my darling sister, Gloria. What a surprise it would be to her, too. She has visited me on two occasions in the last eighteen months, once overnight with Noah, who ran around the apartment dropping his toys, crying the moment he woke, and being so noisy that I thought the couple downstairs might come up to complain and discover the real me. And once with Henry, who was up for a trade fair where he was showing his wares.

Their visits were a strain. I have since put them off coming again, with the excuse that I have engagements, or that I will be away staying with friends.

"How lovely for you," Gloria said. "To have such a good social life."

My sister thinks that she knows me well. How surprised she would be to find that she does not. She knows nothing of my subtlety, my secrets, my true feelings. In her eyes we have a sisterly bond that cannot be broken.

Hah.

23

T HE LATEST OUTRAGE CAME via the owner of their flat, a man whom I felt sure could be relied upon to take my side. He has sent me a letter, in reply to mine, in less than friendly terms. He is sorry to have to say it, but he thinks that I am making his tenants' lives very difficult. They are good tenants, he says, their references exemplary, and they are entitled to their peace of mind. He would hate to lose them.

He writes, *Of course it is not your fault that some unfortunate things have happened in the apartment since my tenants moved in, but your late hours and loud radio are depriving them of sleep. I would be grateful if you could be a little quieter after midnight.*

I was very sorry to hear of the breakup of your marriage, and to learn that Bert is no longer a neighbor. I am sorry, too, to have to write in this vein. I have confidence that all will be well, now that you are aware of the problem.

He adds a P.S. *Do you by any chance have a set of keys to my apartment?*

So they have written to him complaining about me. No doubt accusing me of all sorts of bad behavior. Why would he mention the "unfortunate" things going on, otherwise? They must have put into his head the idea that I am to blame. So now I know they suspect me. And why ask if I have keys to his apartment? His letter has put me on edge. How dare he question me?

I answered him promptly, told him I was surprised at his attitude, that his tenants were troublesome neighbors and that I had more reason to complain than they did. I said he should get them to move their bike from the downstairs hall. And no, I did not have keys to his apartment; if some are missing, perhaps he should ask Bert. But he hasn't bothered to reply.

I bet they are going to change the locks. If not, perhaps they are setting some sort of trap to catch me. I am furious enough to be off my guard. I must give myself time to think of how to move things on from here. It never does to rush at things.

It has taken me a while to settle. Immediately after I received the insulting letter, I had the urge to go downstairs and trash their flat. But I smothered the impulse. It would have felt fine, but I am practiced at keeping cool.

I have decided to give it a month, no visits to their flat, no pacing or radio to bother them, no action whatsoever. They will calm down, get their precious sleep, and relax. They will think they have won. Their foolishness at thinking me so easily put off will work in my favor. I will bide my time.

A few days of this, and I find myself bored. So I have taken again to staying out at night, to driving around in my car. I've missed my nighttime vigils at the riverbank, missed being out in the dark. The city won't be as dark or as silent as Cold-Upton, but it will serve the habit, at least.

Three or four times a week, at around eleven o'clock I start getting ready. I fill my flask with gin, put it into a carrier bag with my cigarettes and a thermos of strong coffee, and place it conveniently on the front passenger seat on top of the cashmere throw I took from under the assistant's nose in Harrods. The throw was the last and the biggest thing I bagged. I simply threw it over my shoulder like a pashmina and walked away. I cut off the security tab in the lavatory and dropped it behind the toilet before leaving the store. The cutting left a hole, repaired now. It is hardly noticeable. Five hundred pounds' worth of the finest cashmere. A good swan song, and no thief caught.

I drive as myself rather than Mayfair Lady, face scrubbed, dressed down in the padded jacket with a fur-lined hood that I bought especially for my night drives.

Once out of Mayfair, I head over to Kensington. People watching is more interesting here; the high street is teeming until late at night. I stay parked at the far end of the street for a bit, just long enough not to draw attention, before driving the less obvious route through the tree-lined streets to Notting Hill. On Westbourne Grove, I check out the designer shop windows and look into the restaurants, which heave with claques of bumptious bankers, who vie for tables with the media crowd. Art and finance, a testing mix of people, who no doubt despise each other. It's fun to watch their polite sparring for tables.

An hour or so before driving home, when the restaurants have closed, and there are not so many people about, I park on one of Ladbroke Grove's residential streets and with the sound low, listen to the radio or to one of my books on disc; I'm halfway through *Ripley's Game* at present. I drink my gin and smoke. Sitting in my dark coat with the hood up, I enjoy being the watcher of the night's events. Cats slink about, a rat once popped up from a drain, and I have even seen an urban fox, sitting untroubled in the middle of the road, eating from a discarded pizza carton.

Lovers pass by with their arms around each other. I saw a man hitting a woman once; the slap I could tell was so big and hard that she staggered before he pushed her ahead of him. He looked back and caught sight of me, put up one finger in that vulgar way, and gave the woman another shove as though to say to hell with being seen by me. She was his burden; he would do as he liked.

Drunks weave their way along the streets, tripping over curbs, managing somehow to stay upright. I sometimes wish that I could get as intoxicated as them, be out of my head for a while. But no matter how much I drink, my mind is always perfectly clear.

I find it strange that I am not noticed more often. Perhaps people don't care to look into the shadows. I duck down when the odd car comes by, occasionally a police car, although it annoys me that I have to take such a necessary precaution. I hardly think that being in one's own car is a crime, whatever time of day. I don't wish to be questioned, though.

Over the months I have learned the best roads to park on, the quiet end of Bassett, with its huge trees shading the pavement, and the poshed-up St. Helens Gardens, where I squeeze in between the Porsches and Range Rovers. Occasionally I have seen a handover, drugs, most likely, and once a woman hanging around the corner of Lancaster Road, wearing white high heels and a short skirt, was picked up at two in the morning by a man on a Harley-Davidson. West ten, where the wealthy live alongside their more straitened neighbors, is both trendy and edgy.

When the weather is bad, or my mood so gloomy that my thoughts bring me down and sap my energy, I cannot be bothered to go far. On those nights I sit in my car in the apartment's private parking area, where I can keep in sight Wifey and Hubby's windows. The flickering light from their television goes off around eleven fifteen, followed by the light going on in their bathroom. They spend longer in there than it generally takes for two people to wash their faces and brush their teeth, two heads silhouetted behind the white blind as they move about. If I had to guess, I would say they shower together. Then to the bedroom, where a soft light illuminates their striped curtains for a moment before it's switched off. When they are at home in the evening, they are rarely up past midnight. And their sleep? Untroubled, I imagine.

To lessen the chance of being seen, I have smashed the four yellow bulbs set behind metal grills in the wall facing the parking lot. It will be a while before they are fixed.

My own sleep is more a series of naps than a proper uninterrupted night's rest. The dreams that come now are worse than the white empty ones of the past. I suffer visions of Pipits. Sometimes I am walking its halls even as it burns; in others, it appears as it used to be, its soft rose brick lit by evening sunlight, the leaves of the copper beech restored to their former beauty, winking in the breeze. To wake and know that it is lost is heartbreaking.

What will satisfy me now? Only owning the Stash land and ridding myself of Henry. In my head I picture achieving those two things. I imagine walking Pipits' meadows in sunlight, seeing the mound of earth under the trees in the shade of the woods, where Henry will lay, finally broken. I picture

Gloria in widow's weeds, the color drained from her face, hugging Noah to her, her luck changed forever. Nothing will truly comfort me until that vision becomes reality.

I wonder how long I can keep up this unsettled London life. I cannot claim anywhere as home anymore. Gloria has robbed me of that luxury. For now, though, I must finish the job of dispensing with my irksome neighbors. Tick them off my list of things to be dealt with.

The thrill went out of my special shopping trips even before I finally stopped them. It wasn't as though I was pitting myself against equals; the game had become too easily won to sustain the excitement. Anyway, most of my bounty has gone to the charity shop that deals with the aged. Best to get rid of the evidence, I think.

Dressed as Mayfair Lady, I take bags of my shoplifting spoils to donate and am made to feel like some kindly upper-class woman doing her best to help out.

"Downsizing," I explain. "One cannot keep everything."

I have even been asked if I would consider donating some time to work in the shop. A couple of hours a week would help, they say. It is easy to tell that they find me charming, a cut above their usual customers.

I guess it is the sort of thing a lonely Mayfair Lady might do, so I'm thinking about it, although I am not sure if I could bear the fusty smell of the place.

24

GLORIA IS DELIGHTED THAT I am coming to visit.

"Hard to believe," she says, "that it's more than two years since you were last here. It's been difficult for you, I know; so many reminders. And now having to cope with this terrible news about your neighbors."

"Yes, just dreadful," I say. I infuse my voice with the sympathy she expects.

I guess apart from this latest drama, she believes that I am finally healed from the shock of the fire that almost killed me. That I am ready at last to come and admire all that she and Henry have achieved while I have been away.

I'm feeling the tiniest bit jumpy about what happened in the apartment's parking area around two in the morning a little over a week ago. The incident solved overnight the problem of my difficult neighbors, but because it wasn't planned, it's all a bit of a hodgepodge, and I have to be careful not to say anything that might connect me to the event. Usually I work better when I have a strategy, but hey-ho, I cannot help feeling pleased with myself for my quick thinking without one. Straight off the cuff, as they say.

I'm confident the police don't suspect that I had anything to do with it. I cannot be sure, though, that I was not seen by some worthy citizen spying from his window. I was in my darkened car, I had my hood up, and there was nothing of my daytime disguise to identify me, but there are people in the area who have seen both personas, so I can't be certain that I wasn't recognized. I confess that it is a niggle, a small concern; although, surely if there had been witnesses, they would have turned up before now? Another week or so, and if no one comes forward, I can relax.

It was a bonus that there was no lighting to illuminate the area. Not that I had planned the occurrence, when I broke the bulbs. I am entirely innocent of premeditation.

I'm not on the run, but I do feel the need to get out of London for a bit. I could do with a break from the questions the police keep coming up with. They have gone over my statement with me three times now. Do they know something and hope to catch me out? They have my car still, will have it for some time, they say. It only took a few hours to find it, and apparently it was not where I had dumped it.

"So upsetting for you," the young policewoman said. "Your car was definitely the one."

I think I managed the appropriate look of quiet horror when she told me that.

"Are you absolutely sure?" I gasped, with feeling.

"Yes, absolutely. There was a positive blood match, and flakes of paint that match the trash bin were found on the back fender."

"Oh, how horrible."

I was surprised they had spotted the car so far from where I had left it.

"A council estate in Islington," she said. "A bad area for petty crime."

It couldn't have been better; a stranger's fingerprints on

the wheel, those of some small-time yob no doubt, his DNA all over the interior.

The fingerprints they can't account for are not, they are surprised to discover, on police records. The car is being stripped down to its bones, every little crevice searched for evidence.

My mind is working overtime, a worm of caution wriggling in me, keeping me alert. It's a good thing; it would be all too easy to slip up and subtly change my alibi the more I am asked to repeat it. Since the incident, I have thought of several little details that I could have added to give my story the ring of truth. What I was listening to on the radio, for instance; how, when making a late cup of tea, I heard a car accelerating, that sort of thing. Now that those ideas are in my head it would be easy to forget that they were not in my original statement. And revealing them might bring doubt on myself, when really my report of being at home alone, being asleep, hearing nothing, is simple and quite good enough. I've never been the type to arouse suspicion.

I have wiped clean the keys I had to the downstairs apartment and dropped them in the Thames. The water gulped them down in an instant. Gone for good, like so many other secrets held in its chilly depths.

So I have finally accepted Gloria's invitation to spend the weekend with her and Henry at Alice's house. My property, of course, so I hardly need an invitation, but I will never think of that limited place as anything other than Alice's house.

The rental car smells of new leather and an ersatz sort of floral polish. I threw out the cardboard deodorizer in the shape of a miniature Christmas tree that hung from the interior mirror. Its bobbing about annoyed me. Such useless things.

I thank heaven the points have been removed from my driver's license. The police cannot get me on that, at least. They asked about them, though, so they must have looked me up.

"A difficult time," I said. "I don't usually drink, but my husband had just left me for another woman. It is no excuse, I know, and I bitterly regret it."

I left a long pause, swallowed hard, then said in a shaky voice, as though attempting to recover myself, "It cost me a fortune in taxis at the time. My husband would have been ashamed of me." I let my voice hesitate a little over "my husband," and gave them a weak smile.

They echoed my smile with pitying ones of their own. I could see what they were thinking; they had that concerned look in their eyes. Where would a woman like me find another man to take the errant husband's place? The female officer even gave my shoulder an encouraging pat as I saw them out.

They have been dusting the couple's flat for fingerprints and will find mine there, I suppose. Well, that's not so odd after all, neighbors visiting each other. I will tell them I was a frequent visitor, invited for drinks, and dinners, for coffee with Wifey. Who is there to deny it now?

I CAN STILL HARDLY believe what happened that night. Under different circumstances, I would take some of the responsibility for it, but really I was pushed to the brink by them. I cannot be blamed for hitting back.

Everything that took place in the lead-up to it came about after my month of lying low. I had been watching them, of course, had even passed them in the street once or twice and given them a chastened nod of my head in greeting. I felt sure they were taken in by my new quiet demeanor.

It occurred to me they might connect the absence of mishaps in their apartment with my having been seen off. Not much I could do about that. But they couldn't know for sure, and little mishaps happen to us all every day, don't they?

I had yet to set the details of my final plan. Minor accidents hadn't worked. I strained to think of what would. I wanted them gone. So, I had to do something that would make them leave, and leave quickly. I thought of gas leaks, booby-trapping the electricity, but I couldn't be sure that those kinds of faults wouldn't start a fire that might put my own flat at risk. I have had enough of fires; they are unreliable.

It occurred to me that I might fill their bath, let it overflow, flood their apartment and the one below it. They might have to move out while the place dried out, and they would have to pay for the damage, but it would hardly see them off for good. Experience has taught me that half-hearted strategies rarely get the job done. Perhaps a visit to their apartment would stimulate some ideas.

That morning when I entered their hall I was in good spirits. I wanted to try on Wifey's new coat, which I had seen her wear on the previous weekend. I fancied that it would suit me better than her. My visit, though, was to be mostly a reconnaissance, a catch-up to reassure myself that nothing much had changed. I would read their email, get up to speed on their lives. I was looking forward to making myself a coffee, reacquainting myself with the place.

Two steps in and the noise came, unbelievably loud, a piercing squeal that deafened me and set my heart racing. I froze, unable to move for a second or two until I realized what the squealing was. They had installed an alarm.

I stumbled out of their apartment, leaving their door open, and took the stairs to mine in such a panic that I tripped and banged my knee hard on the sharp edge of the top step. I felt sick with the pain of it, but I didn't slow down, not for a second.

Later I would be disgusted with myself for losing it, for fleeing as though I were already being pursued. It was weak of me. I should have been better prepared. But I hadn't seen anyone install the alarm, hadn't heard any test runs.

Safely back in my own flat with my door double locked, I took a few deep breaths and began to gather myself. The alarm was still rattling on, the hateful sound muffled now by my distance from it. It was not as distressing as it had been, but I wanted it to stop. I needed a bit of silence to think.

A bruise was already blooming on my knee, and there was blood, globules of it on the surface of a big nasty-looking graze. I felt humiliated. I had allowed them to make a fool of me.

By the time I had changed into a pair of Mayfair Lady slacks to cover the bandage on my knee, and reasoned myself back to near calm, I saw a police car pull up outside, and on its tail, Hubby, in his flashy four-by-four.

Shortly after that, the alarm abruptly stopped. I heard

nothing for the next half hour or so, and then my doorbell rang.

"Yes, of course I heard the alarm," I told the police officers. "No, I didn't see anything. Alarms are always going off in this neighborhood. You get into the habit of ignoring them."

"The door was open," one of the policemen said. "But no sign of damage to it or the lock."

"Oh dear," I said, "how worrying."

I wondered, as I answered the police's questions, whether Hubby had said bad things about me. That didn't seem to be the case, though. My questioners were charming, kind even. They advised me to be careful, to keep an eye out for anything suspicious, suggested I get an alarm installed myself. I told them that I would.

It occurred to me that I should have closed Short and Tall's door as I fled, but I hadn't been thinking straight. With the door shut, it could simply have been taken for a faulty alarm, as I had told the police, a common enough occurrence around here. But the open door, with no signs of a forced entry, posed a question. It was a bit of a worry to me, although the police said with nothing stolen, it wasn't a high-priority crime. Hubby had told them he was sure he had pulled the door shut when leaving that morning, but he couldn't swear to it. So it would go on record as an attempted breaking and entering. They asked me to be alert, and to keep my eyes open for any strangers lurking about.

"I will, of course," I said. "We must all play our part in upholding the law."

I was still too shaken to go far on the nights following the alarm fiasco. I sat in my car in its private space, sipping my gin and going over in my head just how sneaky they had been, and how they must be so pleased with themselves for outwitting their intruder, laughing about how they had most probably scared the life out of him, out of them, out of me. I believed they would have me in the picture as a possibility at the very least.

I confess to hating them. I have never liked their type, cocky and full of ego. But I am angry with myself for letting their alarm fill my head with fright. It's an embarrassment to me that I ran away without thinking to close their door.

THERE WAS A HALO around a soapy moon on the night of the incident, and the shadows were thick, the air humid. As I settled myself in my car, I knew that there would be rain later. The sky is hard to read in the city, too much sodium light messing things up, but country girls know about halos; we know what it foretells when the stars are misty, and what it means when there are hundreds of them, or none at all, in the sky.

The lights were out in their apartment, and their car was gone, so I knew that they were off somewhere. With friends, most likely, or dining in one of the upscale restaurants they were always recommending on their Facebook pages.

I was maddened that my actions appeared not to have had an effect on them. They were getting on with their lives as though I didn't exist. My knee, bruised black and swollen from the fall on the stairs, was hot to my touch and throbbing a little. A cold anger sat in me like a lump of ice.

I heard the growl of their car's engine before I saw it, before its lights slid along the parking lot wall, and it rolled into their space two over from mine. Ducking my body down, I made myself small, so as not to be seen.

Hubby made a big deal of getting out of the car, tumbling unsteadily from the passenger seat as Wifey killed the lights. Couldn't hold his drink, I suppose. There was giggling, and I raised my head a little and saw him push her against the car and kiss her, a long, swaying, drunken sort of kiss. Then he opened the trunk, and she took out a couple of plastic bags and handed one to him. I heard the clink of bottles, the rustle of what sounded like potato chip packets. They had probably had a picnic somewhere along the line, although I'd seen him eating in the car before. The cause of his tubbiness, I expect.

With their free arms around each other, they walked unsteadily toward the trash bins, which were directly behind my car. As they lifted the heavy metal flap of the middle bin, I heard them laughing, and my anger, under control mere moments before, turned to rage. They were laughing at me, confirming to each other how insignificant I was, how easily they had seen me off. Other Beloveds, untouchable Beloveds, standing there in my space. The lucky bastards, laughing their winners' laugh.

It was obvious what I had to do. I don't remember even thinking about it. I was driven by blind instinct. When I saw in my rearview mirror that they had their backs to me, my hand reached out and released the hand brake. Then I took hold of the steering wheel and pointed the vehicle in a straight line toward them.

The car rolled smoothly down the slope, and in the moment before it hit them, they turned, and I saw their shocked faces gleaming like pearls in the moonlight, and then came a thudding sound and a strangled cry, hers I think. I watched them fold into each other as though they were made of cardboard. As I turned to get a better view, the hood of my coat slipped down, and I knew with a blast of exhilaration that in the brief second before blacking out, Hubby had recognized me.

I sat quietly in my car looking around the empty parking lot and up at the darkened windows of the houses that over-looked it. Nothing. No lights flicking on, no calling out from anywhere. Things seemed to be going my way for once.

I started the engine, and with my foot shaking a little, but light on the accelerator, I drove forward, getting the car into just the right position, and then I reversed over them again, repeating the motion three times. I think that it was three times. Well, certainly no more than four.

Then I cut the engine, opened my window, and listened for signs of life. It wouldn't have surprised me to hear moaning, to hear them calling for help, but they were mute. In my wing mirror I glimpsed their bodies pleated into each other like a big, half open fan. I turned the car to face the entrance and drew alongside them; the entwined lovers lay still, her arm at the oddest angle, his head pushed into hers, blood seeping, no movement, not even the softest whimper.

I thought about getting out of the car and checking them, feeling for a pulse, perhaps, making absolutely sure that they were lifeless. But there was blood. I might step in it, place myself at the scene. I told myself not to panic, although I was in no danger of that. My mind, which had been working on pure instinct, suddenly clicked into clear thinking. Of course they were dead; no one can survive being run over four times.

I congratulated myself on already having a plan. Exiting the parking lot, I headed toward Bayswater.

A rougher district would have been a better spot to abandon my vehicle, but concealed in my dark hood and walking at a good pace, I could leave Bayswater and be home in under half an hour. The shorter the walk, the less chance of being noticed, surely.

I would report the car stolen after the couple was discovered. It would be too risky for me to be the one to find them. I wondered briefly who would. A neighbor? The postman?

The police would think that whoever stole my car had run over my neighbors in a panic when they were caught out in its theft. They might even indulge the idea that it was the same person who had attempted to burgle the couple's apartment, returned to create more mischief.

I chose a road I had cruised before, lined with tall white houses. Some of the houses had wrought iron balconies, and I saw a nursery school for the children of the rich: bright red door, the little darlings' artwork stuck on the windows. There were a few lights on here and there, I guessed more for security than that the residents were up and about behind the expensive drapes. I double-parked a good way down from the street lamp, beside a bulky silver Volvo.

Farther up toward the main road I heard the tinny sound of a car door slamming. I kept calm and waited until whoever it was had time to get to where they were going. I took my keys out of the ignition and dropped them into my bag. It was a stroke of luck that my car was old, old enough to be "hot-wired," an easy stealer. I doubled up some tissues and wiped the steering wheel and door handles clean of prints, the sort of thing a common thief might do. I didn't want my prints to be the only ones on the car, better that there would be none. Then I got out and left the driver's door open, as though the car had been abandoned in a hurry. Even in the dim light I could see a dark smearing of blood on the back bumper, and splatters of it on the paintwork. I think that I must have imagined that I could smell it, too.

As I hurried away, the rain came on, a flurry of droplets that had slowed to a drizzle by the time I crossed the road alongside Hyde Park. My knee was still hurting, not as badly as earlier, just a dull sort of ache. I would put ice on it when I got back.

It was late, but there were still cars and a few people about. So as not to draw attention to myself, I kept my head down and my pace steady. It was important to get this part right. If I were noticed anywhere near where I had left my car, I would be a suspect, perhaps the only suspect.

It was quieter in my part of Mayfair. The restaurants were closed, their discreet clientele long since departed. On Green Street, a taxi sped by with its for hire light off, and behind the taxi a dark gray car crawled along the curb beside me for a bit, its driver asking through his opened window whether I fancied some company. I didn't answer at first, didn't look at him, but when he persisted I told him to fuck off or I would call the police.

"Bloody women," he shouted as he pulled away. "Fucking whores, the lot of you."

Safely back in my flat, I realized how tired I was. It was the kind of tired that empties you out, makes you tremble a little. I went to my window and opened the curtains, keeping my eyes raised. And there, outside, as ever, the black night, the world still turning, a giant poker wheel dispensing good fortune on the Beloveds. Not the downstairs Beloveds anymore, though. I had pitted my will against their luck, and won.

If I were ever going to run, to get away from the scene, it should be now. But what would be the point? Even if someone had seen me earlier, what had he seen? A person, hood up, in a dim unlit area, stealing my car. If he had seen the couple being run over, then where were the police? I knew to trust my instincts. Everything around me was normal, as it should be: no commotion, no one banging on my door, the house silent. Perfectly, beautifully silent.

I lowered my eyes to the scene of the incident. The couple had not been discovered. I could see in the shadows the outline of what looked like a discarded sack or two by the bins and knew that it was them.

And suddenly, cutting through the night hush, came the violent whoop of a siren. I held my breath as the shriek faded into the distance. An ambulance perhaps, or the police on their way to some city ruckus. Nothing for me to worry about. I closed my curtains, made an ice pack for my knee, and poured myself a drink.

25

S HE WAS DEAD ON arrival, her head crushed beyond repair. He will be next, and soon. At least the police say that they don't hold out much hope for him. If he ever wakes from his coma, it is likely he will be brain damaged.

"It's murder," the male detective says. "The bastard wanted them dead."

"I don't think I want to live here anymore," I say to the policewoman in uniform, in my best Mayfair Lady voice.

I notice some sort of coded look between her and the detective. I wonder if they have their suspicions, but I don't think they do. It is probably more about sympathy for me than anything else.

"I understand," she says. "I wouldn't want to myself. Do you have someone you can call on to stay with you?"

"Not really," I say. "But I will be all right. It is shocking, the kind of people that are out there, isn't it?"

She gives a nod and shrugs. "What a world, eh?"

"Poor things. Who found them?" I ask.

"An electrician," she says. "He was pretty shaken up. Kept saying he only came to fix the parking lot lights."

"Oh yes," I say. "I noticed they had been vandalized."

She stays for a while after the detective has left. "Shall I put the kettle on?" she asks, as though she is used to making herself at home, used to dealing with damaged people. She has a habit of sucking air through her teeth, which I find rather unpleasant.

"Oh, yes of course, how kind," I say. "It is me who should be offering you."

I have succeeded in charming her. I can tell she likes me, but I don't trust her. She sneaks questions into her conversation in a dogged sort of way that tells me she is not one to accept things at face value.

What do I know about the American upstairs? she asks. When is he returning? Would I go over my memories of the night it happened again? Perhaps I remember some little detail that would help. Did I ever argue with the poor young couple?

I will not be caught out by her. I tell her that we were not always on good terms, and that they were quite a noisy young couple, but that we had settled our disagreements and become rather friendly of late.

"I'm often asked downstairs for coffee, the odd meal," I say. "Oh, I mean, w-was often asked," I stutter.

I say I liked her, young Angela, for that is her name, that she and her husband, Tom, were a charming pair when you got to know them, and that it felt good to have such people in the building. It was the first time I had said their names out loud. I hoped that I had managed to infuse the sound of them with familiarity. Angela and Tom. Poor Angela and Tom. Dear Angela and Tom.

"Before they moved in," I tell her, "it was often just me alone in the building."

"A bit scary," she says.

"Yes." I swallow hard, take a deep breath as though I am about to cry. "And now look what has happened."

She is ready with the tissues. Suggests counseling: the fallback for every disaster, it seems. She can arrange it if I want. What faith people put in other people. It makes no sense at all.

"Not an easy thing to get over," she says sympathetically. "A terrible, terrible thing."

AND NOW HERE SHE is at my door again. Hubby has gone, left this life. I can tell that she has been crying. Strange, since she didn't know him. Very unprofessional.

"He never regained consciousness," she says. She raises her shoulders, opens her hands, her distress thick in the air. Her lips are quivering a little. She is unfathomable to me.

"Inquiries go on, but so few leads. We are hopeful, but—" Her jaw is drawn tight, her big brown eyes widened as though in surprise. She can't stop moving, distributing her weight from one foot to the other, as though she is steadying herself. It makes me feel a little queasy. I have trouble holding her gaze.

I mimic her concerned face, reach for a tissue, would re-create her tears if I could. I picture the burned-up remains of Pipits and manage to moisten my eyes.

"It is obviously a lad from the big estate where the car was found," she tells me. "Nobody's giving anything away, though. Snitches end up crippled or dead there."

"The big estate?" I ask.

"Islington," she says. "Sounds posh, I know, but it's

rough in parts. If it wasn't for the murder, I would have said boy racer, although they usually go for something smarter. Sorry, but they do."

"Oh, that's fine," I say. "I've had that car for years. Seemed daft to change it when it was so reliable."

"Well, I expect that you will get it back soon."

"Not sure that I want it anymore."

I can hardly believe it. Some idiot actually did steal my car. Some creep up to no good in Bayswater saw the opportunity of an easy ride home and took it. I feel so lucky. An oasis of pleasure, water welling in what was previously a dry desert.

The police are sticking with their original idea that some small-time criminal, slinking around Mayfair, wanted to get home in a hurry but was caught out by my law-abiding neighbors in his attempt to steal my car. Fearing discovery, he heartlessly did them in. Hah!

Wrong area, wrong theory, but whoever he is, the little crook has done me a favor.

"It's odd that his fingerprints are not on record," the policewoman says. "You would have thought someone who could murder like that would be on record for something. It's strange that yours are not on the wheel, though. We think he must have cleaned it off once, and then gone back for some reason and neglected to wipe his off again. Maybe he left something in the car."

"I have no words, Officer," I say, and head toward the bathroom. "Excuse me for a moment."

"My name's Anita," she says. "Call me Anita."

I lock the door behind me and hug the knowledge to myself. I give a little skipping dance around the bathroom.

My body feels light; I am almost happy. I hadn't realized how worried I had been. Hubby might have proved to be a medical miracle, sat up with mind intact and pointed his finger. Now he has been dismissed, rubbed out of the picture. And my car actually was stolen. I could hardly have hoped for more.

My disagreeable passage through my life is over. It is the aftermath and I am free. I feel like throwing everything off, Mayfair Lady, life in this testing city I have tired of. I think about selling the apartment, selling Alice's house, and starting out fresh.

I hold the dear little leather box close to my chest and tell my plans to House. We agree that it is time to make Henry disappear, to claim our land. I have been thinking I might let Pipits' earth sleep fallow, let the weeds reign. With the Bygones dismissed, it could lay undisturbed. As to their pretentious house, that creature will be allowed to decay, to be eaten up by Stash earth.

Then, after, what? I wonder if I could live abroad. The South of France, perhaps, some warm little town with not too many tourists. I might marry again. Not someone old like Bert; I couldn't bear all that sloppiness again. Old men are soft; they cry too easily. Someone nearer my own age would be better. Anything is possible now. It is the end. It is the beginning.

26

Y OU MUST COME TO us," Gloria said on the phone. "You
shouldn't be alone after such a terrible event."

It has surprised me that the so-called murder has been in
the papers and on the television news, as though it is of na-
tional interest. News these days is absurd, not news at all:
endless pictures of talentless girls preening in their naked
selfies, celebrities on the red carpet telling us who designed
their outfits, stories of welfare cheats and bigamous marriages. Everything must be reported, even accidents in private parking areas, it seems.

"I'll come soon," I reassured Gloria. "No need for you to
worry. I'm fine, just a bit upset, of course."

"Shall I come to you?" she offered.

"You could, I suppose. Maybe bring Noah," I said, before
I remembered that if Anita called, she would expect Mayfair
Lady, the alter ego my sister has never met.

"Oh, you wouldn't like that," she laughed. "Honestly,
Betty, Noah can wreck a room in seconds. The thought of
him in your lovely flat gives me nightmares."

"Well, I'll come to you, then, after all," I said quickly, and
then changed the subject. "So Henry is doing well?"

"Ever expanding," she crowed. Of course she was referring to his business, not his waistline.

And she wasn't just boasting, or playing the role of supportive wife. I saw one of Henry's pieces in Liberty's some months ago, a shallow translucent bowl in an enchanting shade of blue with streams of cream rippled through it. It was perfection—overpriced but really stunning. Something has happened to Henry's talent; it has turned from minor to major. I think that I can take a bit of the credit for that. Henry needed to suffer a little, to dig deeper to discover what he is capable of doing.

I'm not looking forward to seeing him, but I need to get out of the city for a bit, so needs must. I've noticed that a couple, married from the look of them, dressed in a budget version of country—tweeds, waxed jackets—have been to the dead couple's former flat. I'd say they were Hubby's relatives: the woman had the look of him, short and solid. I saw them enter and watched them leave a couple of hours later, with some suitcases. Shortly afterward, a moving van arrived and took away the furniture. There has been no sign of the landlord. Anita says he is out of the country, but they have been in touch. He is devastated, apparently.

I have placed a bouquet outside Hubby and Wifey's door. A card with it reads *rest in peace, dear neighbors*. I chose the flowers carefully, pure white blooms, roses and Madonna lilies, a buttery satin ribbon tied in a generous bow around crisp snowy tissue. Bert would have approved.

Anita was inspired by my gesture to do the same. A bunch of mixed flowers with that plastic ribbon they use to decorate wedding cars. Hers rather spoiled the pristine charm of mine.

———

I HAVE INFORMED THE police, through Anita, that I will be away for a week or so. They seemed indifferent to my announcement. I am neither witness nor suspect, so no need to report to them anything of my comings and goings.

"I'll let you know if anything new crops up," Anita says. "You go and enjoy yourself. Try to forget it for a bit. Nice for you to be with family." I can tell she is surprised that I have any.

I drive the rental car, with my little leather box strapped in the seat beside me, along the slower, prettier route, on the old road to Cold-Upton. Motorways are hideously boring, with mindless people flooring their cars and oldies causing accidents by going too slow. In any case, I want to see the last of the cherry blossom giving way to the laden boughs of hawthorn that is often referred to as May blossom. I've always felt it is the blossomiest of all the blossoms.

The weather is warm, hotter than I have ever known it at this time of year. And I have timed it just right; the May blossom is out in the hedgerows, white snow, pink candyfloss. I remember once as a child picking swags of it for Mother. It was a dazzling present that I thought would impress her. I was excited to have thought of the gift and knew something like it would never have occurred to Gloria. But Mother was appalled at my offering. She wrinkled her nose, shook her head, and said that she couldn't have it in the house.

"Silly girl," she scolded. "Don't you know that it is unlucky to bring May inside?"

Mother was full of such foolish notions: a hat on the bed brings bad luck, a bird in the house is a sign of death, an acorn on the window ledge keeps lightning out. I have no truck with such dippy superstitions myself. I was surprised that Mother, who, despite her failings, was smart, had put faith in them. Gloria is no better. I have seen her nod and say, "Morning, Captain" to a magpie, seen her caution Henry for walking under a ladder.

My long-ago gift to my mother of the May branches, so pretty when first picked, were left to wither on the compost heap. I watched them shrivel, turn from rose pink to brown, and then to slime, before they were made into maggot food along with the potato peelings and the yellowing cabbage stumps.

Mother had no idea the pain her refusal of my gift inflicted. I wondered at the time if she would have made an exception if Gloria had picked the blossom instead, if the branches would have been arranged in her favorite vase, displayed in pride of place on the hall table.

I shake away the memory of it. Time does not heal childhood wounds. Revisited, their pain is hardly diminished. They are dredged up by sneaky little triggers: the seasons, music, tastes and smells, every damn thing. They leap from their shallow hiding place to cut you up.

I know that visiting my sister's near-completed house on the site where Pipits once stood will stir pain, but it must be done. Their new build trespasses on Stash earth, after all, earth I feel the need to crumble through my fingers, to touch base with. And I should visit the spot where Mother's ashes are buried, that is only right. Will they have thought to prune the buddleia that guards the plot? Will they have started on restoring the garden?

Gloria tells me everything is going to plan and that if the good weather continues, the building will finish on time.

"Unheard of for builders to be on time," she says, gloating a little. "And honestly, Betty, we love it already. Just wait till you see it."

"I can't," I trill. "So exciting."

I will steel myself for the sight of it. It won't matter if I wobble a bit. They will assume that my emotions are still raw from the old house having burned, which, despite that it is almost two years since that blow, is no more than the truth. Let Gloria and Henry think that I am grieving for my young neighbors, too. Of course they will be curious about that, but I will tell them I do not want to talk about it. It will be obvious how deeply it has affected me when I inform them that I am going to sell up in London and move away from the city.

The truth is, I do not want to think about it anymore. It is not as if I wanted to harm the couple. It was a matter of chance, them being in the wrong place at the wrong time. I feel sort of sorry for them now, of course I do, but what happened was their own fault. It was they who intruded on my life, they who moved into my space, they who tried to take over.

My stomach drops a bit as I turn into Cold-Upton. Force of habit sends me in the wrong direction, toward the gates that still open onto Pipits' drive. I turn the car around and park up by the churchyard. I need time for my breathing to slow, for the mixed-up feelings churning in me to settle.

A mob of argumentative swifts are dive-bombing the church spire, picking off the midges that circle the warm roof. It is a familiar sight in the parish at this time of year. I relax into the thought that the world moves on but nothing much changes in my village. Despite the fire, despite my having to put up with Gloria and Henry, I am home.

I think of my spot by the river, those boys gone, perhaps. I would like to be there now, watching, thinking things out.

I stop at the shop in the village to buy Gloria some chocolates and Henry a bottle of their best wine, which isn't saying much. Good manners are important, even with family. The woman Agneta is there as ever, the same innocent smile on her face. She smiles at both good and bad news—a nervous habit, I suppose.

"Ah, there you are," she says as though she has been expecting me. "Heard you were coming."

———————

THERE ARE BIRD DROPPINGS all over Alice's path. They are on Gloria's car, too, big white and green splodges of them. The windows of the house could do with a good clean, and the paint is peeling on the front door. Henry and Gloria are living rent-free; the least they could do is to keep the place up, to leave it in good enough order for me to sell when they move out.

A run of annoyance overtakes me. Such bad behavior is ungrateful, to say the least. I should know by now, though, that my sister hardly notices such things. She is a messy person with a messy mind.

"Oh, goody, you're here," she gushes, standing in the open doorway. "I thought that you would never arrive."

Noah is at her side, straining to get past the barrier of her legs. "He's always trying to escape," she says, picking him up. "Proper little bolter, aren't you, Noah? Have to watch him twenty-four seven."

I notice tiny changes in Gloria's looks since I last saw her in London. There are shallow lines on her forehead and around her mouth, a slight wariness in her eyes. I wonder what has put these early signs of aging on the face of the pampered child, the indulged wife. What possible demons could my beautiful sister be battling?

I summon a smile and put my arms out to take Noah. As though he remembers me, he comes to me without a murmur. He is toddler-heavy now, a baby seal, all muscle. He presses his cheek against mine. It is damp, and his hand clutches a bunch of my hair and pulls it toward his mouth.

"He is fascinated with hair," Gloria says, laughing. "Don't let him yank it; it hurts like the devil."

The feeling of Noah in my arms is not unpleasant. I am reminded of how it was between us when he was a baby. He knew then that I did not coddle. Does he remember that he must be a good boy for me? Noah is the only relation for whom I feel the slightest connection. Strange that he should be Gloria's child.

27

I DAWDLE THROUGH THE WATER-HOLE field on my way to the garden, skirting the nettle patch that Gloria, in a rare show of temper, pushed me into once in our childhood days. I cannot remember what we were arguing about that made her do it, but I do recall her being the one to get in trouble . . . for once. Mother, aghast at the sight of the stinging red patches on my face and arms, made Gloria apologize to me. Her sobs and lisping penitence made the blister rash worth the pain. She was sent to pick dock leaves to ease my discomfort, while Mother fussed around me. She didn't cuddle me as she would have done Gloria, but she gave me lemonade and a ginger biscuit, food in place of love, and it was good enough. On the rare occasions she was moved to hug me, I never did like the feeling of being smothered.

Pipits' woods are dark and cool. I think of the mushroom spores truffled into the earth between copse and meadow, waiting to show themselves in the autumn. The unfortunate miscarriage of that episode, the aftermath, and Henry's revival come to mind. I deserve recompense.

I am not ready yet to see the new house full-on. I told Gloria that once I have wandered the garden, I'll meet her for coffee at Henry's studio. I'll walk slowly along the path to it, letting their palace impinge on my peripheral vision inch by inch so that it is not so much of a shock.

In the orchard the apple blossom is already confetti beneath the trees. Tiny, barely visible acorns of apple bud spot the branches, and only the smallest amount of frostbite taints the leaves. A breeze runs through the wide border of pampas grass at the orchard's wall, which is high and dry, and smells of the sun. It's unseasonably warm, and everything is racing into summer before its time.

The "Foundling Rose" is in sprout on the wall, long stems of thorns waiting for the flowers to bloom. We christened it that because even Mother never knew its ancestry. It didn't quite fit any description we looked up. I like that it set itself there, that it is nameless; the mystery of it is sweet somehow. Should I ever see it elsewhere I would recognize its single madder-red flower in an instant; half dog rose, half anonymous, a lovely feral thing.

The garden is unkempt, neither in ruins nor at its best. I can tell that some feeble attempt has been made to bring order to it. The buddleia, despite the instructions I left, hasn't been pruned. And there are weeds on Mother's little grave plot, greener than anything else around. The earth there has settled so that if not for the buddleia, one would hardly know where she rests.

The summerhouse door is open, and the cushions on the wicker sofa, which clearly have been allowed to overwinter there, have a run of mold along their seams. Apart from a stubborn patch of blue, they were bleached of their color by the sun years ago. There is a tabby cat, brown stripes and quite young, I think, curled up on one of them. I wonder who it belongs to. It watches me from a half-open eye, pretending to be asleep. I think of the stalker dog, the way it hounded me, and wonder again if it was eaten by the fire: if it met the end I had planned for myself.

I cannot place what my feelings are concerning the survival of the summerhouse and Henry's studio, along with the old outbuildings scattered around the grounds. It's as though the arms and legs of a loved one have survived the trunk. So odd!

A poor attempt has been made at clearing the beds, which despite the lack of care, are full of promise for June, one of the best months for flowers, roses and lilies and agapanthus, and the grand lacelike hydrangea, showing off their colors. Already there are bees feasting on the allium, which is only half-open.

But the soil has not been turned, and the weeds have been cut down, not pulled out. They will be back before you know it. I hear Mother's voice in my head. *Cut before June, back too soon.* The garden is both joy and anguish to me now. It would have pleased me more to see an allotment of weeds, not a flower or shrub surviving, no hope of resurrection.

A part of me wants to run. Another part wants to get a spade and start digging. The old ache begins to fill me up. This should be my garden, my orchard. The fields should be mine, the woods, too. I want this land, Stash land, all of it. Why should it be Henry's? Before he turned up here, who had ever heard the name Bygone in this village?

Outside Henry's studio they have laid a flagged terrace. The windows are closed, the slatted blinds raised. I can see through into the interior, glimpse dust motes in flight and shelves of powdery pottery lined up waiting for decoration. As I pause at its open door, hot air hits my body. I smell the cindery odor of the kiln at full blast.

I try to stop myself from looking toward the new house, but despite the effort, I am aware of it at the corner of my eye. Its presence tells me that something solid has filled the space where Pipits once stood. The sun is glinting off it, daggers of dazzling prisms splitting the light.

Henry and Fi are sitting on the new terrace at a green ironwork table, drinking coffee. There is a bowl with cat food in it placed near to the studio door, and a cat flap has been set low in its bottom panel. So the creature is theirs.

Fi has bright blue stripes in her hair and painted wooden bangles clacking around her wrist. She has lost weight but still looks as if she could do with a good scrub.

"Hi there," she calls in a mock American accent.

"Nice life for some," I say.

Henry stands and offers me a coffee. I take the seat that will have my back to the house.

"Gloria is on her way," he says. "We want to show you the house together."

Oh, God, can I bear it? "Lovely," I say. "I am looking forward to it."

Everything in and around the studio has been tidied up. The paintwork is fresh, and the brickwork has mellowed a little since I last saw it. They have planted a Russian vine at the corner where the smoke damage blots the bricks. A bad choice. I know the variety; it will have taken over the whole building by this time next year.

Big terra-cotta pots have been perched at each corner of the new terrace, empty of plants but filled with dark, freshly tumbled earth. If they can do this, why can't they keep up the garden, take care of Alice's house?

"We plan to fill them with geraniums." Henry nods toward the pots. "'Lord Bute,' I think, those lovely dark red, almost black ones."

"My idea," Fi says.

Just as I am about to say that the flowers of "Lord Bute" will hardly go with the green table, Gloria calls out "Hello," so that we hear her before she appears, pushing Noah's stroller in front of her like a recalcitrant lawn mower, bumping it over the humps in the grass.

"Oh good, coffee," she says, plonking a freshly made Victoria sponge on the table. "He is asleep at last. If he doesn't get his morning hour, he's a horror for the rest of the day. He likes the bouncing, our little man."

"Does he really still need a daytime sleep?" I ask.

"Yes, and you would, too, if you were hurtling around at five a.m. every morning."

"Wish I could have one," Henry says.

"Have you met Eddie, our studio cat?" Gloria asks. "The sweetest little serial killer you will ever come across. God knows how many mice he's done in."

She says that Noah will sleep for an hour at least, more if we're lucky. Henry peers into the buggy, smiles indulgently at the sleeping Noah, and kisses Gloria, a brief welcoming peck on the lips. Fi pours Gloria a mug of coffee and adds a generous splash of milk.

"How lovely, thank you," Gloria says, and gives Fi's arm a little squeeze.

And suddenly there is less oxygen to breathe, and I feel a tightness in my chest. We are Gloria's audience, there to admire her, to appreciate her cleverness at producing Noah, her skill at baking such a plumped-up yummy sponge, her beauty, her perfect wifeliness.

"You look lovely," Henry compliments her.

I wonder what he sees that I don't. Gloria's jeans could do with a wash, the same for the white T-shirt that her bra-less breasts are straining against. Henry obviously sees something gorgeous; I see a big contented hausfrau, spreading what I find to be her dubious charms while absorbing all the available light.

The four of us sit together at the ironwork table on the newly flagged terrace, the three of them smiling as though all is right with the world. The cake is cut, the coffee replenished. We make a pretty picture, I should think. A happy family picture, like one of those overly sweet Victorian paintings: Father, Mother, sleeping child, domestic bliss.

AT FIRST ALL I see is a huge cathedral of glass, the sky and the garden reflected in its silvery acres of window. We are mirrored there, too, a trio of minimalized people, as though we are viewing our altered selves in the hall of mirrors at a funfair. We might be three dwarfs standing in front of a mountain; the scale is hardly human.

"It is so much bigger than I imagined," I say, as though I am impressed.

"I know, wonderful isn't it?" Henry exclaims.

"We'll be in by the end of August," Gloria says. "Such heaven!"

It isn't how I imagined it would be; the usual glass cube, a template of what passes for contemporary and has done for the past three decades. It is something else entirely, the likes of which I have never seen before. It is a schooner of white sails and crystal walls, a light-as-air ocean liner about to set sail. I feel nervous about going inside, as though by crossing the threshold I am betraying Pipits.

I have never seen a house without a front door before. There are locks on the big sliding windows and number pads with codes to gain access through them.

"Open sesame," Henry says, and hits A1234 on the pad, and I hear the clunk of an unlocking mechanism.

"Easy to remember," I say.

"When you think about it," Henry says, as though he has. "We don't need front doors. This way you can let yourself into the house from multiple entrances."

"What about callers?" I ask. "I don't see a bell anywhere."

"We're sorting that out," Henry says.

He flattens his hand against the huge pane of glass in front of us, and it takes off, rolling on its runners until it opens wide enough for the three of us to enter together, stepping abreast.

Inside, the light is pure and clean, hardly changed from that of the outside. Polished cement floors roll through the huge rooms in a seamless cream-colored carpet. There are brushed steel skirting boards and butler's sinks, solid marble worktops, fields of tiny halogen lights set in white ceilings, cupboards with no handles that open at the slightest pressure, and those light switches that Gloria raved about, only requiring a hand waved in front of them to work.

"And look at those stairs," Henry says. "Aren't they just the most beautiful stairs you have ever seen?"

He pauses beneath them as though he's in a trance. I can see what he means, actually: see why the soaring structure has affected him so. The glass staircase—can it possibly be glass?—floats in the air with no obvious support, like something Cinderella might glide down in a Disney movie. It is the color of sea glass, a soft ethereal green. A curving, burnished steel handrail that feels like satin flows the length of the staircase, finishing in a finial flourish. I run my hand along it, and some primal feeling that has been secretly camping within me is brought to life for a moment. The exhilarating sensation is almost immediately replaced by remorse, as though I have been worshipping at some false altar.

"Is it safe?" I ask.

"Of course," Henry answers, a touch tart. "Up you go."

I can tell that he wants me to gush, to ooh and aah over every little thing. But I do not feel like playing his game. I feel instead like crying, getting as far away from the place as possible.

But the bedrooms must be seen, the bathrooms, with their limestone tiles from Israel, crooned over, the wide hallways with pale pink plaster, like some ancient Italian ruin, breathlessly admired.

"We thought," Henry says, "that we would leave the natural plaster as it is. It's the perfect background for hanging art."

"It must have cost a fortune," I say.

"Well, probably not as much as you think," Gloria says.

"Although, despite the insurance money, I wouldn't like you to see the size of our mortgage," Henry adds.

I cannot visualize Gloria and Henry living here. My sister doesn't understand the principle of putting things away; the concept of a place for everything is alien to her; her way of living will ruin the look of this homage to minimalism. The gleaming concrete floors will be stained, the bins will overflow, there will be clutter everywhere, and the faint trace of Noah's overnight training pants that he has progressed to wearing, not quickly enough disposed of, will taint the air.

How ridiculous that Henry has built this house for his careless mate. It makes one wonder if he knows his wife at all.

28

I N THE UNCOMFORTABLE BED in Alice's guest room, I
dream of the glass house. I see myself on the floating
staircase. I am not gliding down it as though in a fairy tale,
and the staircase is not the same as it is in real life. In my
dream, its steps are so deep that I have to jump from one
to the next, the possibility of falling more likely with every
leap.

I run through the big rooms and hear the heels of my
shoes clicking on the cement floors: little hammers knocking
in nails. There are immense canvases hung along the hallways, all of the same painting: streaks of red and white,
blood and bandages.

A huge tree grows up through the center of the house,
breaking through the landings, of which, in the dream, there
are many. It has split open the roof on its race to the sky.
Through its leaves I can see the stars tangled across the
heavens.

When I wake, it seems that I have been crying. My
cheeks and my pillow are wet. Night sweats have soaked my
nightdress, and drenched the sheets.

I am quite surprised. I hardly ever cry. Perhaps in my desire to obliterate the pictures in my mind of Pipits' successor,

I drank a little too much gin last night. I feel sick and have to dash to the bathroom, where I heave up some disgusting yellow bile.

It is not yet dawn, the bats are still out, but I know I won't be able to sleep again. I dress quickly and let myself out of the house as soundlessly as I can, so as not to wake Noah.

Forgetting for a moment that the smart rental car is mine, I look around in the gloom for my old one. Strange how habits are so hard to break.

It is quite lovely by the river. The water is liquid pewter, a dull silver with green wispy weed performing a slow waltz just below the surface. The relentless engine that drives its depths is dancing to a faster rhythm, though. Clutches of ducks are going with the flow, allowing themselves to be taken downstream. I wonder, as I have often wondered, if water has memory, if it knows me, recalls my deeds. I open the car door, hear the swoosh of the river's deep swell. Overhead a wedge of geese fly in their v formation, and then, warning his prey, the petulant cry of a buzzard tracing circles in the sky, the early-morning hunter.

I should be at peace, but I can't settle. It is the dream, perhaps, or whatever inspired it. I take a swig of gin and wait until I get the hit of heat through my chest.

I get out of the car and walk to the center of the bridge. Images swirl in my head of cats in sacks and tools sinking to the river's depths. It makes me sad to think about what I have had to do to keep my own head above water. I think of Mother, and of Pipits, and of my childhood years, which, if not for Gloria, would have been perfect. If not for Gloria.

When I left London just yesterday, France seemed appealing. This morning, not so. It is useless trying to find my way to a different home. I am indelibly marked by my birthplace. Cold-Upton is my home. But where should I be, now that Pipits is gone? What is to be done?

29

I TAKE MY LEAVE OF Gloria and Noah in Alice's kitchen. Gloria is still in her nightdress, the one she bought for her honeymoon.

Bridal white then, yellowing now.

Noah is tottering around the kitchen floor, throwing his wooden bricks about, pleased with the clatter they make. He is talking now, and calls me Bettel, which Gloria thinks is sweet. Before you know it they'll all be calling me Bettel. How they love nicknames.

The porridge Noah had for breakfast is stuck hard around his lips, little specks of it on his chin. Not for the first time, it strikes me how like Henry he is. The shy expression, those sandy lashes, his wonky smile.

"Come back soon," Gloria says. "Come and help us move in."

"I'll try," I say. "But I can't promise."

I am dreading going back to London, to the apartment that holds no charm for me now, but I don't want to stay, not with Gloria, anyway.

"I have to put Alice's house on the market," I inform her. "You will clean it up before you leave, won't you?"

"Of course," she says. I can tell that she is offended.

"I'll call at the studio to say goodbye to Henry," I say. "I'd like a last stroll in the garden."

"We are getting someone in to do it," Gloria says. "On a regular basis, you know. We want to get it back to something like it was in Mother's day."

In my day, too, I want to snap at her. But best to leave on a good note. I have already upset her with the cleaning jibe.

I throw Noah a smile. He smells of sour milk and the honey he had on his porridge.

"Be good, sweet boy," I say. I was going to kiss him, but the sour smell puts me off.

Gloria picks him up and escorts me to the door. I turn on the path to see that she has grabbed his hand and is making it wave to me.

"Oh no," she exclaims. "There is bird shit on your car."

HENRY, WEARING WHAT LOOK like oven gloves, is in the middle of taking a batch of thin shallow bowls out of the kiln. I glimpse Fi with her head down as she sets up paints and brushes on the long table.

"Just saying goodbye," I call through the door. "Don't stop."

"Oh, okay," Henry says. "Have a good journey."

I know that, if it weren't for Gloria, he wouldn't keep our friendship up. Some cord between us was frayed when he chose my sister over me, and now that it has snapped, he would like to pretend it was never there.

Henry doesn't care to look back. Like a lot of artists, he makes up his past to suit his present. Leave what you don't like behind, weave a story around yourself of the artist's difficult start, of the passion and integrity it took to get to where you are now, and pretty soon you will believe it yourself. If it takes integrity to dump one sister and take up with the other, then I'd say that Henry has plenty of it.

As I walk away, Fi comes to the door. "We'll miss you," she says proprietorially. "Have a good journey."

"Mmm," I say, disliking the way that she has found herself a legitimate reason to be around all the time now, and that she makes herself so at home.

I know that I must go, but something in me is hesitating. I will take my leave of the garden and then motor slowly back to London. The thought is not cheering. I am reluctant to settle back into the apartment, and I do not want to see Anita, the police officer who seemingly has befriended me. How long is she planning for us to stay in touch? Perhaps she thinks that we are buddies now. My heart sinks at the thought of transforming myself once again into Mayfair Lady. I do not wish to do it ever again.

I pass the belle etoile, man-high already, and just in bud. I think of it as it was in full flower in that last summer before the fire. I think of Gloria, commenting, as she sailed past it, "Mmm, nice pong." To Gloria, that heady, enchanting perfume was merely, a "nice pong."

I bury my head in its leaves and can already smell its faint odor. By the middle of June its flowers will be extravagant creamy cups of clove-like fragrance. In full bloom it lends something of vanilla, and the decadent tuber rose, to the air around it.

I find myself itching to get to work on the beds, but it

would take weeks to sort them out, and even if I gave it a start today, they would be grown over in no time.

I doubt it will do much good, but I will write to Gloria and list what needs to be done. I will stress that I found it hard to bear seeing all my hard work count for nothing. I cannot believe that whoever she employs to look after the garden will have a good enough eye, or sufficient knowledge of our special plants. And Gloria, who has no eye at all, will be too easily satisfied.

To soothe the itch, I fetch a spade from the back of the summerhouse, and throw myself into dividing the big clump of iris I warned them would need doing months ago. The cat comes to have a look at what I am up to. Cats, such nosy creatures. I shoo it away with the shovel.

I wash my hands in the summerhouse sink, scrape the earth off the soles of my shoes, and settle myself on the wicker sofa. What am I rushing back to, after all? A city that I have fallen out of love with, a life that has utterly failed to please me.

———————

A1234, AND I AM in. Somewhere upstairs a workman is whistling, painting, I think. I block the sound from my mind and wait in the airy space of the hall for my heartbeat to stop racing. I wonder why I feel the way I do. It is not as if Henry or Gloria would mind me looking around again before I leave.

I suppose it could be the dream that has brought me here. I hadn't intended to return to the house, after all. But I was drawn back to it through the garden by some unseen, compelling force.

I stand beneath the floating staircase, just as Henry did

the other day, and this time I give myself over to the marvel of it. This time I feel like oohing and aahing.

It is a strong house, crafted in glass and steel, fashioned to resist storms, and the occasional earth tremors that we are subject to here: a house to inspire confidence. There is no give in it, no dark places to slip into, no pigeonholes to hide trinkets in, yet still it is seductive somehow.

I make an effort to recall how Pipits had stood on this plot: a gentler, softer version of a home. But along with the emotions attached to it, the image of it is dwindling, too. It is natural for old loves to fade, I suppose.

The workman comes down, says he heard me, thought that I might be Henry.

"I am Gloria's sister," I say. "Just having a last look."

"Take your time, I'm off for a tea break if that's okay," he says as though he has to answer to me.

Through the big windows I watch him walk to his van, wonder why he would rather take his tea in its limited interior, when he could take it in this amazing house.

Alone now, I am free to wander. I let my leg brush against the silky steel skirting, let my hands linger on the cool marble worktops. In the main bedroom I look down the drive to the gates, and the distant view is the same as always. If the copper beech hadn't fallen I might be looking out through its branches from the window of my old bedroom.

The workman has left grimy footprints on the floor; his dust sheet is so filthy that it is more likely to mark the floor than protect it. A tide of irritation floods through me. There is no need for such slackness.

I picture in my mind the sort of paintings I would hang in these generous halls, a new collection, so as to begin at the

beginning: big canvases, simple, unframed, nothing too or-
nate, inkblots for callers to interpret how they will.

I feel the need to indulge myself in the modern, in everything vernal, avant-garde. That's the curse of a creative
nature. The need for change, the letting go of what was.
Things that once seemed beautiful to me now seem stuffy,
overdone, old hat.

If I were mistress here, it would never be untidy. Everything would be in its place, clean and shining and ordered.
Living here, I would feel clean and ordered, too, a counter-
part to my beautiful, messy sister.

Back in what Gloria calls the reception area, I tap the
switch that automatically rolls the blinds down, and they slither
to the floor, throwing the room into shadow. Stasis overtakes
me, so that I feel as if the ground is holding on to me.

I am attached to these acres by blood, to these ancient
ley lines, to the land I was born to own, to this magical place
that has been stolen from me.

As I pause, breathing in the scent of the house, I hear a
faint ringing, a soft beelike hum, making its way through the
rooms, along the halls, down through the atrium of the house.
I go to the kitchen, and the hum follows me. It is there, too, in
the long room that is to be the study. I feel it vibrating
through the floors, making my feet tingle. I feel it through my
hands when I place them on the walls. It sings down the staircase, hovers playfully around me. I put my lips to the stair's
handrail, and I feel it pulsating, the soft thudding of a heartbeat. The house is filling up with sound and movement.

And then, faint, as though it is whispering from the top of
the soaring staircase, I hear it speak.

"Elizabeth. Elizabeth."

The Beloveds

MAUREEN LINDLEY

This readers group guide for *The Beloveds* includes an introduction, discussion questions, and ideas for enhancing your book club. The suggested questions are intended to help your reading group find new and interesting angles and topics for your discussion. We hope that these ideas will enrich your conversation and increase your enjoyment of the book.

Introduction

As sinister as Daphne du Maurier's classic *Rebecca*, *The Beloveds* plumbs the depths of sibling rivalry with wit and menace.

Betty Stash is not a Beloved—but her little sister, the delightful Gloria, is. She's the one with the golden curls and sunny smile, the one whose best friend used to be Betty's, the one whose husband *should* have been Betty's. And then, to everyone's surprise, Gloria inherits the family estate—a vast, gorgeous pile of ancient stone, imposing timbers, and lush gardens—that was never meant to be hers.

For Betty, this is the final indignity. As she single-mindedly pursues her plan to see the estate returned to her in all its glory, her determined and increasingly unhinged behavior escalates to the point of no return. *The Beloveds* will have you wondering if there's a length to which an envious sister won't go.

Topics and Questions for Discussion

1. How are Betty and Gloria different? What does their behavior tell us about the two sisters?

2. Describe Betty's connection with Pipits. What draws her to the family home?

3. "No matter how my sister and her kind show off their sweetness, their so-called goodness, they are made of more than honey; we are all only half-known" (p. 13). Would you agree with this statement? Is being "half-known" a good or bad thing? What parts of people are often shared? What do people usually keep to themselves?

4. Discuss Betty's earlier relationship with Henry. Why did she like him in the first place? Why did Betty believe Henry had feelings for her, and therefore had betrayed her?

5. Betty seems to view the world in terms of "me vs. them." Who are Betty's enemies and why?

6. Shortly after the reading of Mother's will, what does Betty discover about her husband's relationship and how does she react? Were you surprised?

7. Why does Betty smash the bowl of pudding and poisonous berries? What does this change indicate in Betty's character?

8. How does she feel about Alice's death? How does her former best friend's absence influence the atmosphere at Pipits?

9. Revisit Betty's reaction when Henry starts packing away Mother's old possessions. Why does she disagree with her brother-in-law?

10. Betty says Helen is "nothing but a common thief" (p. 107). Why does Betty describe Helen this way? How would you describe their conversation? What incites the attack?

11. "All people really want is for someone to stand by their side so that they are not alone. The thought of being alone terrifies them" (p. 118). Do you agree with Betty's thinking? When she denies this statement applies to her, how did you react? Do you believe her?

12. In the letter that Betty's father wrote to her mother, he says, "We rarely regret the things we do. Only the things we do not. Marry me, and we will see the world

together" (p. 132). How do his words affect Betty? What happens to her original plan?

13. What sparks her final plan to burn down Pipits while also sacrificing herself?

14. Betty takes on the identity of a Mayfair Lady. When in disguise, how does everyone see her? How does Betty view herself? How does this differ from her normal self?

15. Describe how Betty's relationship with Gloria, Henry, Fi, and Noah has changed throughout the novel. What's her state of mind as she leaves the new grounds?

Enhance Your Book Club

1. Compare how the sisters treat the house throughout the book. What do their actions toward Pipits say about each character's psychology and beliefs?

2. The conversation between Betty and Gloria on p. 228 alludes to Charlotte Perkins Gilman's *The Yellow Wallpaper*. What other parts of the novel remind you of this influential story?

3. "And then, faint, as though it is whispering from the top of the soaring staircase, I hear it speak" (p. 311). Imagine how the story might continue after the novel's last lines. What happens to Betty?

4. If you were in Betty's shoes, how would you have reacted to losing your best friend, lover, and home to your younger sister? How do you think Betty's life would have unfolded if there were no Gloria or any Beloved? Now imagine your reaction as a Beloved.